Desert Cupcake

Cake Life Series, Book 2

KB Raphael

"A great quote by Albert Einstein states: "The field is the sole governing agency of the particle." Einstein is saying that the invisible forces (the field) are responsible for shaping the material world (the particle). To understand the character of a person's body or health, one must consider the role of the invisible energetic field as a primary influence."
-Bruce Lipton

"If people vibrated at the frequency of love, they would perceive themselves from a higher mind, meaning that they would define themselves as love. They would judge less and enjoy a lot more."
-KB Raphael

Part 1

1

What Awaits

As they do every day all over the world, spirits and ghosts walked all around her house that night. Not that this is a ghost story. Peppermint, a blue Russian cat, was no special breed, just a rescue, who sat warning the darker spirit that kept circling his pet. As a cat, Peppermint did possess the ability to see spirits and to be able to psychically ward them off. But this isn't a story about the cat, either.

It is actually the story of an older, half-crazed lady named Isadora. At 5'8" her height alone was enough to make her presence distinguished, but her mane of hair and the look on her face, regardless of her expression, were enough to quiet anyone before her, even a ghost.

Still, tonight as Isadora slept she was vulnerable, open and susceptible to the suggestion of darker energies from the entities on her property and she would have easily had all sorts of nightmares, if it weren't for Peppermint's own energy. As he loyally slept by her side, his spirit played hockey, knocking every puck of energy that launched at Isadora, not allowing even one to hit its goal.

Isadora slept soundly, dreaming instead of a new stranger. A tall, gorgeous younger man, a stranger who, as Isadora's luck would have it, would be perfect for her- if only he weren't gay.

2

Meet Sebastian Blazul, A Free Spirit About to Take a Road Trip

When you live in New York, you don't have a car. This means that Sebastian thought he'd like to have one to drive away from there. He sat at a table almost falling asleep as he watched his best friend, Dr. Samantha Jaspar – or Sam – who had just re-connected with the love of her life, Nick Andrews – or Kole. Long story. Anyway, Sam and Nick had met in St. Martin about half a year ago. Unbeknown to Sam, it had been love at first sight. However, love doesn't do well when it is interrupted. In St. Martin Nick had had to suddenly return home for work. They had both assumed their time together had been a fling and they'd lost touch. Until Sebastian reunited them. He thought he was a superhero for having done so.

A bored superhero; Sam and Nick were disgusting now! Sebastian went from thinking that they were two of his favorite people in the world to thinking that they were two of his favorite people- who he didn't want to see. He figured that once they'd had a couple good fights and weren't swooning over one another he'd want to see them again. In the meantime, even though Sam was like family to Sebastian he was mildly annoyed. It's the worst when your best friend is in love and you are alone.

"Hon?"

OK, Sebastian might have given you the wrong impression. That was his date or boyfriend, William – who doesn't go by Bill. Sebastian was a handsome man; he had dirty blond hair, getting dirtier every year, and a handsome body, which was getting softer every year. Still turning heads, he thought of himself as a young 38 year old (he's gotten touchy about his age, make sure to say that 40 is the new 28 if you talk to him).

Sebastian had no siblings, at least none that he knew of. His homophobic father had often been cruel to his mother, so you never know. Sebastian's British mother, Rose, was delicate and exquisite like the flower. At times she had been thorny and *cheeky*, always protective of Sebastian, but mostly she was everything to him. His American home served tea, scones and her British wit. She had been his hero until she died, many years ago, leaving Sebastian alone in the world and hungry for people he could belong to.

Having grown up American, he had attended college where he studied design and fashion before going to work for Elle Magazine in New York. He thought fashion would be his life, but after years in the industry, the end of that career and the betrayal by his boyfriend were a sore subject as well…

Back to William, yes, he was grand. Smart, rugged, friendly and down to earth. William had a way with the world, they just seemed to get along fabulously. Perhaps that's why he was a screen writer. Orchestrating life or words and characters was pleasing to him. This was a part of what he and Sebastian had in common. Life seemed to like them and treat them well.

"Sorry, what, hon?" Sebastian asked William. They had spent the last couple of weeks traveling through the Florida Keys and southern Florida with Sam and Nick. William had been great. Fantastic. Sebastian liked that William was a few inches taller than Sebastian; he liked that William was slender, had dark, short hair and wore glasses. He looked like a younger, more handsome version of Tom Hanks with sassy glasses, Sebastian thought.

Yes, he's brilliant, loving, compassionate; he's a screenwriter. I like that he's creative. Sebastian was both bored and lost in his own thoughts.

"We were talking about driving up through Orlando next. Disney or Universal?"

"I want to go to Magic Kingdom." Sam said, turning on the sad puppy eyes and looking at Nick.

"Babe, you'd love the rides at Universal. Don't you want to visit the Harry Potter attractions?" he countered.

"No, you want those rides." Sam snarled as love oozed out of her eyes at Nick.

"And I want to go to the Animal Kingdom Park, looks like your vote will decide, hon," William repeated to Sebastian.

"William, what do you want to do with your life?" Of course, Sebastian's question confused William.

"Is that like, a trick question?" William asked, looking at everyone for a clue.

"No." Sebastian answered flatly. Everyone was quiet for a minute, waiting to see what was up with him.

"Nick, William, would you consider walking around the mall to give Sam and I a few minutes to talk alone over dessert?"

"Uh, yeah, of course, buddy." Nick and Sebastian had met in New York when Nick had been using the name he grew up with, Kole. This nickname had come from a cousin who couldn't pronounce 'Nick-Kole-lass', so he'd called him 'Kole' and it had stuck. When Nick had traveled to St. Martin, he'd been trying to go by 'Nick', which he'd used with Sam. So now he had two first names.

Sebastian and Kole had hit it off, both having been in the marketing and fashion industry. They had talked about creating a new business together, which seemed unlikely now. Once Sebastian had figured out that Kole was Nick, he'd asked him fly down to Key West where he and Sam were on vacation. Sebastian surprised them both by bringing them back together, having thought that this would be great. Nick and Sam would be together and he and Kole would be business partners. However, Nick's mind had been replaced with a monkey-mind, which often happened to men in love. Similar to a one-track mind, Nick thought only about Sam and, like a monkey, he was very grabby so that his hands were always on her. It wasn't that Sebastian was jealous, it's just that Sebastian had been close to Sam and now instead of being his BF (best friend), she was more like Nick's other half.

"Sure, hon, that'll give me a chance to get to know Nick better." William agreed. He and Nick stood up. Nick leaned over to kiss Sam goodbye, "We'll be back in 20? Sound good?" he asked Sebastian.

"Perfect. Thanks."

Sebastian waited for them to walk away. "Love, I need to talk."

Dr. Samantha Jaspar was a psychologist, a great one, and she'd only gotten better when she consulted with Sebastian. Her new virtual partner, Dr. Cindy Rosenthal, had been introduced to Sebastian; Cindi had also learned to appreciate his simple and powerful insights into their clients. Sebastian wasn't trained in psychology, but Cindy and Sam had initiated him by their own right, swearing him to the professional secrecy of a colleague, since colleagues were encouraged to work together.

"What's up, Sebastian?" Sam asked as she tried shifting into her therapist mode.

"Would you like to see a dessert menu?" asked the waitress. "It's The Cheesecake Factory, after all."

"No, I'm wonderfully full. Thanks, the pasta was divine," Sam answered, dismissing the waitress who began to turn away.

"Yes! Slice of cheesecake," Sebastian demanded almost at the same time. Sam was shocked. They had cooked and dined together extensively and she couldn't remember Sebastian ordering dessert but once or twice, since he was always watching his "girlish figure."

"What kind? Classic cheesecake?"

"Yes."

"Whipped cream?"

"Yes."

Now the waitress left and Sam turned to Sebastian, a serious look on her face – the most serious look she'd had in weeks. Dessert and whipped cream? Something was amiss!

"What is going on, Sebastian?" There was no more need to try to slip into her therapist mode, it was there, it was serious and it was honed in on Sebastian.

"Love, I'm not happy. And I'm not going to Disney or any other happy place in Orlando."

"Oh, cupcake, did something happen with William?"

"No. Are you kidding? That man's a saint, he's perfect!" The unhappy look on his face confused Sam. "Love, I've had enough dessert. Now I want something for me."

As if on cue, a runner brought Sebastian's cheesecake with two forks and set these on the table.

"Ah. I see," Sam said as the visual clue of the cheesecake arrived. "Something changed. You want to *eat* your sweets now, not *date* them."

Sebastian nodded as he stuffed a huge mouthful of cheesecake in his mouth. Sam recognized that gesture- cramming sweets in your mouth to try to make yourself feel better.

"Mmmmm. You should have some," he said, some crammed cheesecake falling from his mouth.

"You don't make it look so good," she toyed. She pointed to his napkin, "You'll need that."

She took a bite of his cheesecake tasting the incredible, rich flavor. "Okay, this is fantastic!" Then she turned to the topic at hand, "So, what is it? Did something happen with William?"

"No, that's not it. I'm telling you, he's everything, the full package."

Sam wanted to make a joke, a sexual innuendo about William's "full package", but decided this wasn't the best time.

"It's just not what I want, Love. I don't want to settle down- I'm not there. Nick and I were supposed to go into business together- don't, don't say you're sorry. It's okay. You two are there, you're in love, you'll get married and live happily ever after. It's just not what I want. I want to – well, I don't know. Maybe I want to go to Napa and learn more about wine. Maybe I want to open a restaurant, like you'd said." Sebastian took another huge bite of cheesecake.

"I'm sorry, Sebastian. You've always been there for me- You brought Nick back into my life. You want something more, I get it." Sam looked at his cheesecake. It was a huge slice which would have been many bites for her to eat and which he'd almost finished in just two forks-fulls. "I'm sorry I stole your business partner," she smiled gently. "But you do have me, Sebastian. I'm your family."

"Thanks, Love, you know that means everything to me." He took the rest of the cheesecake on his fork, raised it to his mouth and then put it back down.

"I used to think I had it all and that I'd work in the fashion world forever. That's not me. That's just not me anymore," he said, looking up to meet her eyes. "It's time for me to go and find what I'm after.

I'm feeling a bit empty, I want to fill my life. You know, create something for me."

"Fill your life," Sam said, looking at the cheesecake. Sebastian followed her eyes to his dessert. He couldn't believe it was practically gone, and now his stomach started to feel funny, saturated with sweetness. Too much sweetness.

"So, are you thinking of going to California?"

"Yes. I'm going to buy a convertible and drive out. I just decided." He truly had just decided. He made the best split-second decisions when he heard that little voice in his head, like he just had.

"What about William?" Sam winced, "He is great. Will you invite him to go?"

"No. I need to go alone. Besides, I'm going on a diet, effective immediately because my stomach feels awful. No more sweets. Tequila is easier on my stomach than the cheesecake. I hope I don't throw up."

"You never drink tequila as fast as you just ate that cheesecake. I think that was a record."

"Yeah, get the check. I'm going to a dealership next."

"So, no more dessert, cupcake?" Cupcake was Sam's pet name for him, which she was uncomfortable using most of the time. "What about candy?" And 'candy' was what Sebastian called the men he found attractive, because they were 'eye candy' pleasing to see and taste all over.

"Nope, no more sweets of any kind," he said insistently.

And that is how Sebastian came to his cake-free diet. No more *cake* for this man – which was really a euphemism for sex or candy. This cupcake was on a mission to find something more.

3

The Road West

Staring at the white convertible, William blinked, then lied, "I get it." He didn't get it at all. Twenty minutes ago his new boyfriend, another couple and he were dining at The Cheesecake Factory in West Palm Beach. They were enjoying the good life, traveling together and William was enjoying a new adventure. He'd stepped out for a few minutes with Nick and, next thing he knew, Sebastian had bought a car and had declared that he was heading west. Alone.

William realized he better sweet talk a ride, fast. "You're not looking for a long-term thing. I can handle that, just friends. But if you let me come along, as a friend, we can keep each other company. You'd have someone to talk to at lunch; you'd have someone to take over driving when you are tired. It could be great for us both. I'll keep you company until I'm called to fly out to LA."

Sebastian hesitated a little, but agreed. "Sure, hop in." At this point, Sebastian was on a mission and he thought that William understood: they had had fun, but Sebastian wasn't looking for romance. Falling prey to William's slick words, Sebastian felt having William come along would be mutually beneficial. William loaded his suitcase in the trunk, a smile on his face.

Sebastian gave Sam a big hug saying, "Love, I'm a phone call away."

He turned to Kole, "The open road is calling me, my future is calling me."

"I understand. I'm not complaining about having Sam all to myself," Kole nodded. "I'll take care of her. Go, man, go west, go to wine country and then maybe we'll build our business."

Hugs were exchanged. Sebastian and William got into the almost-brand new convertible to speed up the freeway.

Sitting behind the wheel and sliding into the plush, white leather seat, Sebastian purred. What a car! He couldn't believe what he'd done. He'd bought a new car and changed his travels over cheesecake. Still, it felt right. He had the sense that that slice of cheesecake might have been the best cheesecake of his life.

He looked to William in the passenger seat. "Traditionally west is the direction for exploring more, right?"

"Yeah, I guess so." William was waiting on a deal out in Hollywood for one of his projects, so he figured that since Sebastian was going that way... "Your road trip is like a modern western screenplay I haven't written," he remarked, still trying to digest what had occurred in the last 5 hours. Not that it was complicated, mind you, and William was brilliant to say the least, it's just that it often takes people a while to adjust to a change. The plan had been to travel with Sam and Nick heading north. Sebastian had told William that he guessed that Sam and Nick would head back to Boston where Cindi, Sam's business partner lived. Now all of that was being left behind as they sped up I-95.

Being gregarious and always up for something new, William figured he'd go along for the ride and inspiration, since any creative writer wishes for such unexpected and potentially wonderful new experiences.

And this had been *unexpected*. William had stepped away at lunch and Sebastian had shifted gears. He'd bought himself a used 2014 white Mercedes SL and announced that he was heading west to Napa Valley. He transferred some money on his phone and paid cash for his new car. Surprise, surprise, surprise. Sure, William was a little hurt, but he focused on the wonderful, whirlwind experiences he'd had since meeting Sebastian. Besides, William was nobody's fool. He didn't expect a life partner out of this, he had wanted to enjoy himself. He was.

♥

"Can we stop in New Orleans?" asked William. They had taken the top down on the Mercedes, so it was almost impossible to talk. The wind was so loud that even the specialized speakers were hard to hear. The drive had been only white noise so far.

"What?" Sebastian asked. "Do you have to go to the bathroom?"

"What? No!" William brushed his hand saying, "forget it."

It was like they were playing charades. They'd quickly chosen some sign language, or maybe they invented some signs. Grabbing their own pants meant "bathroom time"; pointing at their mouth open meant either "I'm hungry" or "thirsty". Nodding their head to the side with their eyes closed meant that they were tired.

A half hour later they stopped to have dinner in the town of Stuart. William had read some good reviews of an Italian restaurant in a house that was reported to be expensive, but worth it. Finding the house was a little challenging, but finding parking was like a small miracle.

Twenty minutes later, Sebastian sat, sipping his Napa Pinot Noir. They had ordered the chef's seafood pasta special and Sebastian already felt as though he were facing a new, brighter future. He had altered the course of his life. Sure, it had only been a couple hours on the road, but still. He'd made the change. All his life, things had improved when he'd made changes for himself. A part of him already missed Sam, but Sam had a new life with Nick. It was time for Sebastian to focus on filling his wine glass with the most exquisite wines in the US. Napa, here I come, he kept telling himself.

"This is one of my favorite wines," he was delighted.

"Hon, that's what you say about every wine you try!" William drank from his glass, "But it is good, I'll give you that."

"So, what did you ask me in the car?"

"I'd asked if we could stop in New Orleans. I love the city and the beignets there."

"I've never been- it's always sounded so interesting, crazy. I love good food, do you like the food there?"

William hesitated before answering, "Well, you have to like spicy and a certain flavor. Creole spice. If you haven't been, we should go! It's like nowhere else."

"Sure, I want to explore!" Getting into the spirit of things and feeling better overall, Sebastian was feeling enthusiastic now. "I'm putting myself on a wine trip. Everywhere we go I'll see what the wine is like!"

"Can we also go by Santa Fe too? I've never been and I've heard the galleries are world-class! They say there are more galleries on one street there than there are almost anywhere else in the world."

"Really? I didn't know that. Let's look at the map."

By the end of dinner, they had established a few things. William finally received the email he had been waiting on, he was due in LA in a week. This meant that they would have to choose between the 10 hours it would take to drive to New Orleans or the 27 hours to Santa Fe. Then they would have 3 or 4 days to be in New Orleans or Santa Fe before William flew out on the 6th day. He deferred to Sebastian, who would be driving the rest of the way by himself. Sebastian looked at the map and saw that New Orleans meant taking the 10 freeway whereas Santa Fe meant the 40. The 40 went through Dallas, the 10 followed the gulf. Well, he'd had plenty of water and ocean at this point, so Santa Fe it was! They decided to spend the night in Stuart and then head out as early as possible for two 13 ½ hour driving days to get to Santa Fe.

4

The Land of Enchantment

Looking back, Sebastian was glad that William had asked to come along on the trip. Sebastian could spend time on his own just fine, but William was knowledgeable and had been better company than Sebastian would have guessed. As they got closer to New Mexico, and that they were increasing in altitude, William mentioned that historic Route 66 went through the state. He told Sebastian about Roswell and the story that an alien space ship had supposedly crashed in Roswell, had been covered up by the government and then taken to Area 51. This gave birth to alien conspiracy theories. Being from the west coast and knowing some of these stories, William a great guide since this kind of information didn't spread in the fashion world.

They had just zipped across the state border where a sign welcomed them to New Mexico, "The Land of Enchantment."

For some time now they had been driving with the top up on the convertible, the novelty having worn off. They had both had enough white noise, bugs and charades. They had agreed that air-conditioning and conversation were not as glamorous as having the top down, but far more accommodating.

"So, what does that mean?" Sebastian asked. "Land of Enchantment?"

"Oh, hon, it's probably just a marketing gimmick."

Changing subjects, Sebastian looked to William, taking his eyes off the road, "I'm glad you came with me. It's made the trip more fun."

"I thought it would. Sorry I won't make it further, but spending a few days together in Santa Fe will be fan-tas-tic!" he sang.

"Listen, I've been meaning to talk to you. You are awesome. I told Sam that you are wonderful, perfect. I'm sorry if you were looking for something more."

"Oh Sebastian, please! Hon, I'm a grown man. I get it, you want something for you in your life first. That's important for a man. That's good. Look, you're great. If we don't stay good friends, that'll hurt."

"Thanks." He genuinely appreciated the compliment, valuing William's friendship. "You are a dear. And, you are tons of fun. Fashion is no longer my world," his voice became deeper, "I need to fill my life again. Time to find what the hell is next for me. Time to try something different. I don't know, maybe Santa Fe will be a great place to start."

"I'll drink to that!" William joked. "Hey, Santa Fe is also known for being spiritual. Maybe you could find a good fortune teller and ask him or her about the wine thing!"

Sebastian looked at William to see if he was joking or serious, "You think? I've never done something like that before." Was he really considering such a ridiculous notion? "I don't know."

"You're kidding! You never have? Oh, this is the place, hon! Now you simply have to! Tomorrow we'll have to look for such a person."

Sebastian wasn't sold on the idea, but what could it hurt? "Well, maybe. I also hear they have great food. Let's start there."

"I'm already looking on my phone, hon! I'll look for a good breakfast place for tomorrow morning. – Oh, listen to this, you'll like it as a marketer! It says here that in the early 1900's Santa Fe was bypassed by the railroad, decreasing it's popularity. Artists, writers and retirees came for the cultural richness, landscapes and the climate. The city then worked to position itself as a tourist attraction, which is when they adopted their unique architecture. Buildings downtown were restored or erected in traditional styles, called the Spanish Pueblo Revival, reminiscent of the initial village adobe homes. It says these homes were characterized by their mud walls, which are made with stucco now, their canales, which are like rain gutters, and vigas, or wooden support beams that protrude through the exterior walls. Buildings are always 'earth tone' colors and, although Santa Fe county doesn't require the Spanish Pueblo style, the market greatly prefers them."

William took a breath. "Hon, I'm beside myself! I feel like I'm walking onto a movie set-"

Sebastian looked over to see William exit this world and enter the world of his imagination. *I'll give him a moment*, Sebastian thought to himself, reading the pleasure on William's face.

Ten minutes later William's attention came back to where he was, in the car, heading for Santa Fe. "I'll look around for a classic hotel!" Now he swiped and read his phone's screen for a while. "La Fonda! Says here this hotel is one of the oldest in Santa Fe. The hotel has a little authentic French bakery. They say you have to go early or everything is gone!"

"Yummy!" Sebastian responded. "Sounds promising. That I can commit to."

"Yes, a French breakfast and then we'll find a fortune teller!" William said, making sure that Sebastian knew that this was happening. Sebastian nodded neutrally. They'd been driving for hours and hours, now they were close to the city. It was dark and they just barely made it into town. They checked into their La Posada, their hotel downtown, and then turned in, looking forward to a good night's sleep and pastries for breakfast.

❤

The next morning they found that they weren't too far from the French bakery that William had found the day before on his phone. They quickly realized that parking was going to be difficult on the narrow streets of Santa Fe, attributed to it being one of the oldest cities in the US. So, they walked.

Santa Fe was mesmerizing. William was inspired. He was enthralled with the idea that Santa Fe was a high desert and, online, it said that a high desert meant that they had cold, snowy winters even though it was arid and droughts were an on-going problem.

"It's like a riddle," William thought aloud. "It's dry, it snows and most of the state is brown with little to no foliage. I guess we're close to the mountain, so there are trees in town here. It's awesome here! It's like a living oxymoron!"

"Who's a moron?" Sebastian laughed, giving himself a point as William shoved him.

"Hon! I'm gathering ideas for my writing! I'm exhilarated! My writer's soul is being fed all sorts of ideas!"

"Contain yourself and don't spill," Sebastian taunted. "We're here."

They entered the hotel and asked for directions to the bakery, just a small door. They walked in to a fair sized, crowded bakery. It was a tight fit between the rustic tables, chairs and benches all painted chocolate brown. It smelled wonderful and the baker's display cases were filled with crepes, different quiches, cakes and various danishes and croissants. They made their way to the counter to order, squeezing by people.

"I'm getting intimate with strangers here, it's like paradise!" William sang.

They started with spinach crepes and lattes. The crepes were fantastic, so they each got a chocolate croissant for later. The lattes not so much, so they checked their phones for a Starbucks and headed deeper into downtown to satisfy their espresso fix.

Next they walked by the oldest house and the oldest church in the US.

"I didn't realize how much history is here," William remarked, staring at the old adobe building. "It's not what I would have expected."

"What did you expect, hon?"

"I dunno know. A little house on a prairie maybe?"

Sebastian laughed, "Is it possible you watched too much television growing up?"

"No, it's my field." He informed. "Besides," his eyes mischievous, "who says I've grown up? Ha! Point for me on your scoreboard."

"Alright hon. Let's go ask about the 'Oldest buildings." They crossed the alley to go into the oldest house, now a museum.

"How is it possible? The east coast is older." Sebastian asked the lady at the counter in the oldest house. This was more of what William expected. The house, now museum, was small, tiny. It was a square room, no more than 20 by 20 feet. This was all a gift shop. There were two small doors. The short, four-foot door was marked "Museum." The other, normal door, was marked "Private."

"This part of the country was established by Spaniards first, even though we joined the union later," answered the New Mexican woman. William couldn't tell if she was white, Mexican, both, neither… He felt like a male version of Alice in New Mexican-land because he was discovering so many new wonder-filled things to expand his writer's mind.

"If you want to pay $5 you can go in our museum," she said, pointing to a room with a small door. Alice would have to duck if she were to walk through, so William debated asking if the woman would offer a potion labeled "Drink Me" so that he and Sebastian wouldn't have to crawl through the door. "The museum is all about the story of DeVargas and the 3 witches."

Sebastian bit his lip, "Hon, I think I'm good. Sounds like a great story though-" The look on William's face made it clear that he agreed.

He turned to the woman, "Well, you are so colorful, sweetheart," William complimented, "but sounds like we'll pass. Can you tell me where we can find a good card reader?" William could feel Sebastian's face turning pink. "I would love a good Santa Fe reading," he said, trying to raise Sebastian's enthusiasm.

"Head to Rainbows & Magic for that shit," said the woman whose sweet voice suddenly became very cranky.

"Oh," William's eyes widened. "Well, thank you. We'll be on our way. Rainbows & Magic," he said incredulously, "Far out!"

5

New Friends at the Tune-up Café

Growing up Sebastian's two favorite pastimes were reading and watching TV- well, what used to be television before cable, Netflix, Hulu, Amazon, YouTube…

Among his favorites were "The Munsters" because, like himself, they didn't fit into any mold. The show also helped explain his monster of a father. Reading distracted him. As a latch-key-kid, his mother had to work, since his deadbeat, homophobic father wasn't much of a provider. When his father was home, Sebastian avoided him, his abusive behaviors, and the constant yelling.

Having grown up on the east coast and in London for a year, Sebastian was accustomed to the fast-paced life of big cities. He learned how to get ahead in life and the big city, his most valuable lesson from "The Munsters:" do not to expect people to understand how or why you are different; be easy going.

This is likely why he'd gone into fashion and design: he had also learned at an early age that you can't judge a book by its cover, and yet the best dressed and presentable people were accepted, respected and had the best experiences. Marketing, image and presentation were everything.

Sebastian always looked his best. Even when driving in circles.

Realizing that the book store that had been recommended to them was too far to walk, Sebastian and William had gotten the car and driven around in circles for 20 minutes on the narrow and rounding downtown Santa Fe streets.

"Aha! Finally! There it is." William hadn't been sure how much longer he could push Sebastian to keep looking for the place that the crass shopkeeper had named. He was relieved that they'd found the shop. He was surprised at how un-kept things were here, like the dirt driveway. He shrugged it off because it was obviously an old, converted house. It was unique.

Sebastian parked the Mercedes, turned the engine off and gave William a look as he shook his head "no."

"Come on, we made it. Besides, I'm hungry. Let's go in, look around. If nothing else, we can ask for a local place to eat. Let's go in," he enticed.

Sebastian opened the car door. "OK, OK. But only because I am hungry. And hot. It is so dry here. I think my mouth is cracking." He stepped onto the uneven, loose, rock-covered dirt driveway and walked towards the entrance.

Sebastian read the sign above the gate, "Rainbows & Magic," and the byline underneath, "May The Magic In Your Life Be Colorful."

"I'm not getting a good feeling," he turned to William. "What the hell does that mean?"

William smiled awkwardly and walked ahead opening the front door before Sebastian backed out.

Stepping inside was like stepping into another world. The scent of sandalwood and sage greeted them at the door, incense sticks burning. They were surrounded by merchandise. On their left, above their heads and on their right there were wind chimes, hanging crystals and fairy figurines. At the entrance they were meant to set a mood and probably sprinkling invisible pixie dust onto them. Sebastian shook for a second as a chill ran through him. He took a couple steps past the entrance. To his left was a hippie behind the counter. The store had rooms further down past the hippie, straight ahead and to the right. Everywhere he looked Sebastian saw *stuff*. It seemed the store sold everything: books, pipes, crystals, jewelry, candles, decorations, deities, clothes and far more. Sebastian didn't even know where to look because there were at least 100 items on any given shelf or rack. *Complete visual overload*, he observed. No marketing at play here, said his inner expert.

William looked around. *Boy, this place was like a goldmine of craziness!* He could draw upon this later when writing. He saw surprise on Sebastian's face and figured he better act fast.

"Hi there, we were told you have tarot card readers here?" he asked the man at the counter.

"No one is in today but you can find cards and fliers that way," he said pointing. "All the way in the back."

"Thanks."

William lead the way through a small maze of rooms, tables and more junk. Just when he could see a room with fliers, a voice could be heard speaking. He then caught sight of a sign at the door to this room, which he read:

"Is Silent Knowledge Filling Your Life? Presented by Isadora," he read aloud.

They stopped to listen. "-people live their lives with fear, they live with emptiness walking by their side.

"When you go deeper, when you connect with Silent Knowledge, my angels, your life is no longer silent. You will no longer feel empty. You will be full of love, joy, health... Sooner or later everyone will come to fill themselves from that depth, from that unseen force; everyone will come to hear that Silent Knowledge. How soon will you come to hear?

"I was like you, and you and you," she said, pointing at people in her audience, "I see you. I know you are longing, looking for answers. I see you," she said as she turned to look at the second person she had pointed at, "I see you, I know you are lonely and sad. I was there, but look at me now. Can you see me, angels? Can you see the love that is in my eyes? Can you see the joy that flows through my soul? Can you see how filled I am?

"I am no longer alone, ever. It doesn't matter whether there are people with me or not.

"I never wonder what is next, what is the meaning of life or who I am – I have great meaning."

Sebastian stood straighter, as though she were speaking to him. His eyes and ears opened wider to absorb her words. To William's surprise, Sebastian walked in the room and took an empty seat. William followed right behind him.

As they entered the room, Isadora stopped speaking and looked straight at Sebastian, ignoring William.

"Welcome, my angel. I've been waiting for you to arrive." Then, as if this made any sense, she turned back and continued speaking to the room. Sebastian sat, not knowing what to think.

"My angels, come learn to connect to that Silent Knowledge. Our workshop is in two weeks at "Iza Ranch" located down highway 14. The sign-up sheet is going around – space is limited – oh, Mary just informed me that we only have 5 spaces left. Thank you for being here today, my angels," she positioned her hands into the prayer position. "Blessing to you all and may you all find that inner God and Goddess."

This ended the lecture so everyone began to get up and speak. The small, rectangular room had two windows behind where Isadora stood. The rest of the room was lined with bookshelves, save a small wall with a large cork board entitled "Community Services Offered." This board had far too many fliers and business cards to see or read, since they were stacked on top of each other.

Sebastian and William looked at each other. William raised an eyebrow, surprised.

"Wow, I wasn't expecting that. How wild, do you know her?"

"No, never seen her before in my life!"

William put his hand on Sebastian's leg to calm him.

"Hello," Isadora said, standing before them. "You entered just as I was speaking of needing Silent Knowledge in your life, how interesting." She spoke as if she knew him.

"Yes, that was *interesting*, to say the least. I'm William, this is Sebastian. You must be Isadora."

She nodded in agreement but mostly kept her eyes on Sebastian.

"May I ask, Isadora, what is Silent Knowledge?"

Now she turned to William as if he had just shown up and spoken for the first time.

"Oh, angel, there's no short answer." She then turned back to Sebastian, "Pardon, it's just that I dreamt you'd come. And here you are." Her eyes were checking to see that yes, he was, in fact, the man in her dream. She reached out, placing her hand on his shoulder. "It's nice to meet you." She removed her hand and turned to William.

"I'm starving. Why don't you join Mary and me at lunch at the 'Tune-up Café' and I'll begin to tell you about Silent Knowledge."

William smiled. He saw that Isadora wanted to spend time with Sebastian. He figured that this was pretty much what he had been after in a card-reading, but better.

"I don't think you posed the invitation as a question. I think we're meant to go," he responded looking straight at her.

"So true, angel. Do you need directions?"

"Sebastian, lunch? Do you want to follow her over?"

"OK, hon."

What the hell is going on, Sebastian asked himself. He thought back. *They entered a hippie store- there! That was probably the problem.* New York had places like these, but they were places that might as well have not existed because they didn't exist in Sebastian's fashion, high-end world.

He followed William out and gave him the key to the Mercedes, "You drive."

"Hell yeah!" Sebastian had done most of the driving on this trip, so William took any chance to drive the Mercedes that he could.

Following Isadora and Mary was a much faster way to get around. The restaurant had only been a couple blocks away but William now knew how confusing the Santa Fe streets could be. Again they turned off an asphalt street and onto a rock-covered dirt parking lot. How retro!

They met in the parking lot where Isadora told them to call her Iza, as her friends did, and she introduced Mary.

The Tune-up Café was wild, which seemed to be the theme of this 'Land of Enchantment'. They walked past the outdoor seating with umbrellas and Tibet prayer flags to go in the front entrance. It was one o'clock and the place was packed. Inside there were tables made of doors – not what Sebastian would have thought to make tables out of, but it worked. There were booths, a bar with high stools and a lot of decorations. Lanterns hung everywhere; blown up photographs of nature were framed and placed on several walls and a Buddha statue blessed one corner table. Sebastian mused at the smell of frying onions, soup and his eyes hungered at the glass display with scones by the hostess stand.

"Iza! Welcome! I'll have a table for you in a minute," the slender hostess with long, grey hair said, hugging her.

"Thank you, angel. How are you?" Isadora held her elbow and looked deeply at the hostess.

As the waitress answered, she saw that Iza's table was ready and took them back to the corner booth with the Buddha.

"Enjoy!" she said, handing them their menus.

Sebastian, now feeling more like himself, looked the menu over, "What do you recommend, Isadora?"

"Angel, you're not from around here."

"No, east coast."

"Ah, that explains a lot," she smiled. "We have New Mexican food here. That's what we are famous for; foodies come from everywhere to try our Christmas burritos."

"Oh?"

"Start with the drinks, angels. You'll want to consider the chocolate, the 'agua fresca' or 'prickly pear' iced-tea."

"Chocolate? What are you talking about, honey?" Sebastian asked. Whatever had spooked him had passed. His usual friendly and loving self was now shining through.

"It is Mexican chocolate, for drinking. Ancient drink, angel."

"You had me at chocolate!"

"I'll try the 'agua fresca'!" William looked to Mary, "Is it like juice?"

"Yes, but it's made fresh with real fruit. Try the watermelon."

"Hi folks," welcomed the waitress. "I'm Sage, I'll be your waitress. What can I get you folks?"

"Chocolate and a burrito!" Sebastian said enthusiastically. He loved cooking and was excited about new foods and flavors.

"Red, green or Christmas?" she asked, jotting his order down.

Sebastian took a second trying to figure out what the hell she was asking. Then he remembered that Isadora had said Christmas.

"Christmas? Christmas. What is that, sweetie? Do you put snow on it?" he chuckled and looked at William, who smiled and then looked to Sage for the answer.

"Salsa. Red salsa, green salsa or Christmas, both." Sage now looked irritated like she'd had to explain this many times before and as though she always got smart remarks from guests.

"Oh, then I'll stick with Christmas." Sebastian smiled. "Is it spicy?"

"Yes," she huffed. "It's salsa."

"I'll nut up to it!" Sebastian was referring to a show he and William had watched. "Nutting up" meant getting your man-parts in place and being tough before a challenge.

"Yes, you will! I will too! Do you recommend the same or something else for me, Mary?" William asked.

"Try the pupusa, just pick your filling. That way you can share and try them both."

"Great!"

They ordered and then settled in to talk.

"So, tell me your story, Isadora," Sebastian prompted. Then his phone rang.

"Iza, angel."

"Iza, yes."

"I'll give you a short version, angel, and tell you about Silent Knowledge too. Actually, you should come to my meditation group tonight."

"Really?" William asked, still hungry for these new, radical experiences. His writing was going to get so much richer and colorful.

A song chimed on Sebastian's phone. "Hi Love!" he answered. "Hold on," he looked up at William, "It's Sam. I'll be right back." William nodded.

Iza, who wasn't accustomed to people taking phone calls when she spoke, was bothered for a second. Then, realizing who had called, she said, "Is it his girlfriend?"

"No," William laughed. "We're gay. But I can see why you might think that. He's very different with Sam. She's the only one he calls 'Love.' They are best friends, family really."

"Oh, I see." Sure enough, she seemed to understand more than William thought he'd said. She thought for a moment. "Tell me a little about you two. How did you come to Santa Fe?"

"We met in Key West. I'm a screen writer and I had some time before going to LA to negotiate my latest work. Sebastian was heading out to Napa Valley, so I came along for the trip, until I fly out in two days."

"Oh, you are both traveling, just passing through. Or so you think."

"Yes, and I always wanted to see Santa Fe. So, here we are! Wait, what do you mean?"

"In my world, nothing occurs by accident, angel. Have you been up to Taos? Or have you been to Ten Thousand Waves?" William shook his head no. "Chimayó? Madrid?" She had pronounced Madrid as Mah-drid.

"Mah-drid? You mean Madrid, Spain?"

"No, angel, it's a town just south of my ranch."

"No, we just got into town yesterday. Last night. So, why do you think we are here if not because it was on the way?" William was intrigued. There was more going on that he could have planned for, but what was going on?

"Well, let me put it this way. You didn't just spend the night. How long are you staying, angel?"

"We planned to be here a couple of days. I'm flying out soon. You can ask Sebastian how long he'll stay before he goes," he said pointing to Sebastian.

"That's what I mean, angel. It's no coincidence that you planned to stay here longer. There's a deeper purpose to the trip."

Before William could ask more questions, Sebastian came back and sat at the booth again.

"Sorry everyone, I hadn't talked with Sam yet."

"How is she, hon?"

"Good. She and Nick are around DC now. What'd I miss?"

"William here was telling me that you two planned to stay here for a bit on your way to Napa. How long will you stay in Santa Fe, angel?"

"It depends, I don't really have plans."

"Yes, I imagine you'll stay for a little while, as I told William. You are here for more than sight-seeing. As a matter of fact, you should come see my ranch tonight and consider renting from me. I have a little apartment that goes for $880 per month. I'm guessing that's 4 nights in town."

Sebastian looked up at Izaa, "Really? Yes, it is only about 4 nights. That may be a great idea." He turned to William, "What'd you think, hon?" Sebastian calculated quickly. A month's stay without costing an arm and a leg, a new car which had put a dent in the cache, still plenty left but no need to waste it… great!

"Why don't we check out of our hotel, go see Isadora's ranch and decide. We can always check in again, if we want to."

"Here you go folks," Sage announced as she served the typical New Mexican dishes.

Everyone enjoyed lunch, although it was a bit spicy for Sebastian and William. But the flavors were rich and full, the chocolate was thick, delicious and certainly a drink made for the Gods.

"Mmmm," Sebastian thought the chocolate would be worth coming back for. "What a great recommendation, this is divine."

"I can make you some at the ranch, even spice it up a bit, if you like angel."

"Yes, please." Gratitude and pleasure were all over Sebastian's face. "I think I like it here!"

"Just wait, it'll get better. Now, I haven't told you about myself or Silent Knowledge yet, but it's getting late. Silent Knowledge has brought you to Santa Fe and to meet me, angels. I'll tell you more when you come out to the ranch. Say around 7?"

"Yes," responded Sebastian and that little voice inside him. He had no idea who Iza was, nor what Silent Knowledge was, but he knew she spoke truth. It resonated in him. This was why he was traveling, to discover some new things. So he felt comfortable jumping in feet first.

6

Isadora's Story

After dinner Sebastian and William went back to their hotel. The front desk informed them that it was too late to check out and not pay the night. They had an hour before it would be time to head to Iza's, so they walked around getting to know where some of the shops and museums were and then walked up to the beginning of Canyon Road. William was beside himself to see the street with all the art galleries on it.

The architecture of this old town was unique; most of the galleries were adobe homes that had been converted into galleries. While William admired the pricey and exquisite art, Sebastian admired the stucco walls, the canales that protruded from the roofs and were used for drainage. It was as if time had stood still in this town, though he could think of no past that held this architecture. Like Sebastian, it was beautiful, original and in a class unlike any other. He admired the colors of the adobe buildings too: peach, tan, white, brown… looking though his professional design eyes, he thought this was wonderful. No wonder Santa Fe attracted so many tourists. Life felt simply wonderful here. No mad rush, like New York. No putting business before people. Everywhere he looked he saw people, trees, art. It was clear that quality and living from the heart were more important than profit and business.

♥

A couple hours later they were back in their hotel room and Sebastian packed his bags.

"I think I'll be renting one of Iza's places. I don't think I'll stay here tonight even though it's paid for. What do you say, William?"

"No problem, hon. I think that's a great idea. Iza has me intrigued, I'd love to stay there tonight. I hate that I'm flying out tomorrow." He smiled warmly at Sebastian, "I think you're going to have a great time here. If you don't mind, maybe once I'm done in LA I'll come back. If you're still here – or maybe even if you're not."

"Yeah, I know what you mean. It feels like Iza knows something that you want to know, something about yourself. I guess you did better than a card-reader, hon. You got a witch of some sort!"

"A good witch!" William turned to his things and began packing.

"What do you think she meant when she said that stuff about Silent Knowledge bringing us here?"

"Us? I think she meant you, hon. She couldn't take her eyes off of you." He laughed, "I don't know what's in store for you, but I'd sure like to stick around and find out. This is an AOAL; I think you are in for an 'Adventure Of A Lifetime!'"

"I hope so." Sebastian turned to his suitcase. "The hotel is first-class, but I won't miss it." He zipped his suitcase closed. "Let's head to the ranch!"

♥

Iza's ranch was several acres. The driveway was a long dirt road which was bumpy and worrisome in his new car. He took it slowly, minimizing the threats of a dirt road to a low car with shock-absorbers built for the Audubon. It was the longest driveway he'd ever seen, about half a mile. He was relieved to reach a parking area and to find shade under a tree.

The parking area was in the far corner of her land and opposite to the highway, which was why the driveway had been so long.

"First let me say that I already like you both. I'm so glad you came, angels. I have class in a few minutes. Would you like to come to the meditation class or would you like to talk afterwards? You can always walk around the ranch and get to know it, get settled in, if you like."

"Settling in sounds good, but I want to stay, Iza. Can I write you a check?" Sebastian asked.

"I rarely say no to money, so that would be great. Write it out to this name," she pointed to her name written out on her desk. "Here's your key. Do you need a second room?"

"No," William answered. "I leave tomorrow anyway."

"Come, I'll show you your casita."

"I like the sound of that, 'Casita.' Little house, right?" William asked.

"Yes, yours is right this way," she said, walking out her door. "Oh, hello Peppermint. This is my cat, I also have a dog, I'll introduce you when I see her."

"'Casita', I like that! I have a good feeling about this," Sebastian commented as he appreciated the landscaped grounds.

The center of the property had a beautiful fountain and a couple of benches around it. Flowers and several small gardens grew between curving paver pathways which led to four little casitas; a fifth, wider path, lead to Iza's house. Garden beds and taller shrubs and trees served to beautify and create a little privacy between the casitas. Iza's house had a large front porch where, Iza said, she liked having dinner parties. They walked down her path, next to the fountain and then turned up a smaller path to the "Blue Moon" casita.

The casita had a small porch with a table and two chairs out front. The door was deep blue with a golden moon and a few stars painted on it. Iza opened the front door. Inside the one bedroom casita there was a small kitchen with the usual appliances, a low counter and two barstools. Over the sink was a window, where Sebastian could imagine the morning sun shine streaming in. The living room was perfect for his part-time satellite work for the magazine: on one side of the room was a couch and a comfy chair facing a window which showed off the garden, and on the other side there was a desk against the wall. Sebastian looked at William, excitement written all over his face. Iza smiled and nodded.

"I'll see you after class, which is in the last casita with the yellow door. It's called 'Hawaiian Sunset."

"Thanks Iza!" they both sang. She stepped out and closed the door.

"Honey, I love this! Look at the nice big desk and the burgundy chaise! I love the end table next to it! I can totally see myself working here!" Next Sebastian looked up to the French doors leading to the patio, large wild flowers lining one edge of it. "I love it!"

"It is adorable, hon. I can see you on cloud nine here. Let's look at the bedroom!" William was just as excited. He thought this could be the perfect place for him to come and write his next screen play.

They entered the small bedroom and were instantly taken by the room. One wall was all rock, as this part of the casita had been built up against a cliff. A beautiful photograph of the Santa Fe skies in the evening hung on this wall. The bed was up against the next wall and a large window was on the wall across from the rock wall.

Sebastian sat on the bed, "Oh, it's like a cloud! It has wonderful padding," he hummed as he lay back on the bed. "And it's blue!" The Blue Moon casita's theme colors were a deep blue and gold. The comforter, similar to the front door, was a dark blue with scattered gold stars. Big, fluffy gold pillows, save one deep blue pillow with a golden moon, added a luxurious feel to the bed.

"The bathroom is dreamy too! The shower curtain is similar and the tile in the tub is fantastic!" William admired. The bathroom tiles all looked unique, special. Everything was custom made, colorful. "It's relaxing just being here! Like a B&B, only better!" William stepped out of the bathroom. "You're going to love being here!"

"I bet you wish you were staying, hon!"

"Yeah- actually, I just might come back when I'm done in LA. We'll see. For now, I'll take the couch tonight. Should we have a glass of wine on your porch or should we walk around?"

"Wine! I'm celebrating. I think my time here is going to be everything I wanted!"

"Enchanted, like the state motto?" William smiled.

"I think so," Sebastian nodded.

They sat on the porch and poured themselves a glass of wine. They saw Peppermint walk by, who meowed at them.

"Hello there, fellow. Sorry, no wine for you." William leaned down to pet him instead.

"What a friendly cat." Sebastian sipped his wine. "This is one of the best glasses of wine I've ever tasted!"

"Hon, you say that about every glass!"

"Yes, but now I'm purring, like the cat!"

They both laughed and delighted in the late summer's warm evening air, the cozy setting and, of course, the wine.

♥

An hour later Iza called to them.

"There is a lot more to life than meets the eye," she began. After class she invited Sebastian and William to her porch to tell them more about herself. They'd brought wine. William and Sebastian lay in the two hammocks that hung between the beams that supported the roof to the porch. She sat in the rattan rocking chair. Sure, Sebastian and William couldn't reach their wine glasses, but they started to hear crickets singing, Peppermint meowing as he chased invisible things and they felt the cool night welcoming them to the ranch. Every now and then they sat up to drink.

"Once upon a time I was unhappily married. My husband and I had married young and I didn't realize that 'give and take' doesn't mean sacrifice myself. He had affairs, I had alcohol... it was ugly.

"Ten years later I began seeking change in my life. I began meditating and going on retreats and I went on a fantastic one with a girlfriend. The man leading the retreat was magnificent. I saw in him the ability to change and improve my life; I saw that life really could be lived a completely different way and that I was meant to spread my wings and fly.

My marriage was a shambles anyway, so I got divorced and began working intensely under this man's mythidology."

"Mythidology?" interrupted William, suspicious of a word he didn't think existed.

"Yes, angel. Myth and method. My word," she said, warning him to let it go. "See, when you get deeper into Silent Knowledge and into understanding life, you realize that you don't understand. You become keenly aware that all of life is based on perception, how you see things; myths. That means that no one is truly right or wrong, they all have their own myth about how life works. The difference is in the person. When things are right for you, when things in your life feel as though your life is supporting you and when you feel that you can be yourself and have what your heart needs, then your methods, your way, is the right way."

"For you, you mean your way is the right way for you?" Sebastian asked, his interest peaking.

"Well, yes, but likely for someone else. Let me give you an example. No matter who you are or what you believe, there are basics in life. We all thrive on love; everyone must feel empowerment over their own lives otherwise their relationship with power becomes perverted; everyone needs to feel good about themselves or they impose themselves on others. Everyone needs love, acceptance and approval. There is nothing right or wrong about this, it is just required for our human survival, the way food is."

Sebastian thought about this and something didn't quite make sense to him.

"Iza, I am not a spiritual man, but I can see that you have a flair about you." He turned to William, "You see it, don't you?" William nodded in agreement. "I believe you, you have something. You aren't overtly happy, but you are deeply happy. I want that."

"Yes, I know, angel."

"But, you can't chase love from others. I'd be miserable if I'd done that."

"Absolutely. These are often misunderstood. Love, acceptance and approval must come from within and be given to yourself. Then your cup will runneth over and you will generously share these with others. So, these spiritual foods are what you must feed yourself."

Sebastian nodded in agreement and smiled at her explanation.

"You see, darling angels, there are universal truths, if you like, that have nothing to do with right or wrong; they have nothing to do with religion or lifestyle. They are universal. They come from somewhere… silent. When you learn to go deeper within, you find that you are connected to that silence, that Silent Knowledge.

"I spent many years relearning everything I thought I knew; a lot of time unraveling who I thought I was to find who I truly am. I took time to learn to love, accept and approve of myself. Because of this I am far more authentic and I can connect more deeply within myself than most anyone I know. I can tap into Silent Knowledge, which is how I knew you were coming, Sebastian."

"What?" Sebastian's eyes widened and William thought that he lost a little color in his face.

"I knew you were coming, Sebastian. I knew you would be handsome and a great person." She hesitated a minute, "What I didn't know is that you'd be gay. I'm sorry sweetheart, but that's disappointing."

Iza was at least ten if not twenty years older than Sebastian, and even if she hadn't been, he really was gay. This wasn't the first time a woman had expressed disappointment at his being gay. He had learned to take it as a compliment. He smiled at her.

"The other thing I don't know is why Silent Knowledge has brought you into my life.

"Well, boys, that's it for story time. I'm turning in. If you have any questions let me know. I'll explain anything else you need to know about the property in the morning. Welcome, I'm thrilled you are both here."

"Iza could I come back after LA? Do you have another casita for rent?"

"Of course you can, angel. Let's work the detail out in the morning because I need to look on my computer to confirm that I have a free casita. Oh, one more thing, Peppermint sometimes finds guests he likes to go and stay with-- don't be surprised if he comes knocking on your door."

"We'd love the company! Good night."

♥

7

Iza's Charmed Land

The next couple of days flew by. On the drive down to the airport, William reminded Sebastian that he might be picking him up at the airport again soon.

Sebastian said he would like to sit in on a couple of Iza's meditation classes, which she said she'd include for Sebastian since he was staying on the property. She added that he could always opt for a private session with her if he wanted to go more deeply into any topics.

Iza had also invited him to have breakfast one morning, thus finding out that Sebastian liked cooking and making breakfast. She then decided that this could be a regular thing-- she appreciated having the help and his omelets were fantastic.

Sebastian quickly got into a routine. He generally made his way out to explore Santa Fe to see a tourist attraction that Iza had recommended during the days. He spent a couple hours working virtually for the magazine in the afternoon and then spent some time on his porch, or Iza's, watching the vast, fluffy Santa Fe skies floating by. It suited him. In New York he had been a successful yuppie; during his time in St. Martin he had relaxed and tapped into an Island-Sebastian. The ranch offered him yet another version, one which combined the City Sebastian and the Island Sebastian. He called this version Sky Sebastian because this version offered him the best of both worlds and held the promise to find his purpose. Like the vast skies, Sky Sebastian was large and, for the first time in his life, he felt like all opportunities were opening to him. Right now, life was perfect.

There was a knock on Sebastian's door.

"It's Iza," she said.

"Come on in, honey," he called out and then met her at the door.

"I just wanted to let you know that we are going to have a storm tonight. Expect lightning, a lot of wind and possible internet outages. I hope you aren't planning on going out tonight."

"No, I'm going to call a friend. Thanks for letting me know, Iza."

"Sure, angel." Iza then spotted Peppermint at Sebastian's door. She leaned over and picked him up. "I better take you in. You don't want to be out in this weather."

"Meow!"

"He's been coming and keeping me company the last few nights. I guess he knew William had gone."

"He probably did. I'll take him, unless you want me to leave him?"

"No, go ahead. Good night."

"Good night, and don't forget, it'll be a storm but all is well!" Iza said as she walked back toward her house.

Every day Sebastian texted Sam to see how she and Nick were doing and to see where their travels were taking them. It had only been a few days since he'd talked with Sam on the phone, and a few more since he'd talked with Cindi, but it was time to call them both. He texted Sam and Cindi and asked if they wanted to do a group call.

"Hello, dear," Cindi answered her phone.

"Hi honey, how are you and Arthur doing?" Sebastian asked.

"Hi Cindi, hi Sebastian!" Sam chimed in.

"It's been a while since we all talked. I'll go first," Cindi began. "Arthur and I are doing great. He's doing well at the university and Sam and I are doing well with our practice. Oh, that reminds me, Sam dear, I have a new client for you. His name is Rogart and he has self-image and self-confidence issues. He's young, so I think you'd do well with him."

"Oh, great. Send me his information. We are in the DC area. We're going to stay here for a week or so but I think I have someone to refer you to as well. I'll let you know when I'm certain." Sam responded.

36

"I'm going to have to require that you ladies only talk shop without me, I want to hear how you are doing!" Sebastian complained.

"What are you talking about, dear? You are part of the shop! Alright, how are you and where are you? My two colleagues and I don't even know where you two are!" Cindi said playfully.

"I'm in Santa Fe and it's breath-taking here. I checked out of my hotel and rented a casita just a few miles south of town. I love it, it's so quaint and cozy. I'll text you both pictures of the sunset today."

"Wow, Sebastian, you hadn't told me," Sam said surprised. "How is William? And, are you staying for a while if you are renting a-what did you call it?"

"A casita, a little house. It is on a ranch, Ranch Isadora. There are a few other little houses too. She rents them out and she gives classes in spirituality. William loved it, but he already left for LA. I suspect he'll come back and rent his own casita."

"Wow! I'd love to come visit you, Red!" Sam said enthusiastically.

"That sounds fascinating, dear. Now, why is she calling you Red?"

"He's not a cupcake anymore, Cindy. He's given up candy!"

"What's this?" Cindy's personality had changed since she'd met Sebastian and become business partners with Sam. After living a routine life for many years as a therapist in New York, she decided that she wanted a change. That was when she'd met Arthur. Since then Sam had commented to Sebastian that Cindi had become very colorful in her dress, her speech and her character. She now joked and played with life.

Sebastian had only met Cindi earlier in the year through Sam, but he and Cindi had hit it off from the start. Sebastian now wondered if the changes that Cindi had made in her life had been her giving herself more love or approval, like Iza had talked about.

"Yeah, hon. I was thinking of talking with you about it, I'm on a diet. No more candy."

"Did things not work out with William?" Cindi asked.

"No, nothing like that. The man's perfect! It's me, I left the fashion world and now I don't have a career. I need to find out what my life's about. I want more than a part-time gig for my old magazine. Does that make sense?"

"It makes perfect sense to me, Sebastian," Sam answered. "I wish you were here, but I'm glad you are chasing your wine interest."

"You know, Love," Sebastian's pet name for Sam, "My interest in food and cooking is at the forefront right now. I suppose it is a good combination, wine and food. I think I'm going to cook a dinner for Iza tomorrow."

"Catch me up, aren't you working for the magazine?" asked Cindi.

"As a consultant only, and it's part-time. I need to find what's next, so I'm looking out here."

"I must admit, dear, this all sounds fantastic." Cindi was an excellent psychologist who wasn't easily impressed and yet Sebastian always seemed to do just that. "You and Sam know how to chase your dreams. Sounds like you really enjoy Santa Fe. Will you stay out there?"

"Do you mean move? No, I don't think so. I'd like to be closer to family," by which he meant Sam. "And my new colleagues," he added lovingly. "I do like it out here though. I feel like I might discover my true calling here."

"I want to hear all about it as you go, dear. I think the process could be a great study for my clients. I sometimes get clients looking to find their purpose, but I don't send them on road trips. Don't you think his technique could be fascinating, Sam?"

"Yes, I was thinking the same, Cindi. Nick just texted me, we got tickets to a play at the Kennedy Center. I have to run."

"Ok, Love."

"That's fantastic, I hope they are good seats, dear. Have a great time."

"Thanks, love to you both. Talk soon!" Sam hung up the phone.

"Keep me updated, dear. I want to hear about this Iza. I don't think I'll be able to come see you, but I wish I could. Probably not the best way to start a marriage," she chuckled.

"No, I don't think Arthur would like his new bride taking her first trip without him. It's just as well, I'm in a one bedroom casita."

"How did you find the ranch?"

"I was in town. William was convinced that it would be fun to find a card reader but we found Iza giving a talk in a bookstore. We talked with her and before I knew it, everything worked itself out for me to stay here. The grounds are lovely, Cin. And she gives delightful meditation classes. I'll have to send you pictures."

"Please do. Let's talk again soon, dear. It's getting late here. Take care of yourself."

"Here too and we have a storm coming. Give my best to Arthur."

He hung up and headed to the bathroom to take a nice, hot bath before bed. Tired, he was looking forward to bed, not realizing that Iza wasn't kidding. The storm was so loud it woke him up a couple times.

8

Learning To Ride A Bike

Sebastian got himself ready and headed out. When he left his place he ran into a friend as he walked by her open door. She was talking with her friend and laughing like she and Sebastian never had. She told Sebastian something about class or some other detail before turning her attention right back to her new friend. She and Sebastian hadn't been the greatest of friends, but still, Sebastian had been replaced. Turning his attention toward his day, he headed downstairs and onto the street.

He came out the building and turned the corner. Right away he saw two tall, blond men standing around and talking. They looked like twins. It was like he was in college again because across the way in a café everyone was talking to their friend, everyone was young and had backpacks and books; it just had that college vibe.

Sebastian walked down the street and stopped at a bicycle that was chained to a drinking fountain. He tried to lean in and drink water, but the bike was in the way. It was awkward and his bag on his back was falling forward. He did manage to drink a sip before giving up.

He stood up and straightened his bag. This triggered a memory which flooded in- he remembered being in public with a tall, dark-skinned man that he was attracted to. He recalled the feeling that the man was attracted to him too, but something stood in the way. Sebastian couldn't recall what and didn't care. The two of them were on the ground- had they fallen? – and Sebastian was close to the man, very close. He felt that pull of attraction toward the man, the interest, the draw; feelings the man clearly reciprocated. That was their last, intimate moment. What had made him think of this?

A commotion pulled Sebastian out of his day-dreaming and back onto the street. Behind him in the coffee shop everyone stood at once to watch the excitement. Through the wall of windows, Sebastian saw two police officers amongst the coffee-goers. The officers faced the street, their guns drawn, aiming at the two blonds, the twins, out on the street. Sebastian followed the direction the guns pointed towards to see that the twins had their guns drawn too. Now Sebastian stood right by the twins and wondered what direction he should go in to get away as a flood of bullets raged out of their guns.

"Uh!" Sebastian gulped for air as he sat straight up in bed. The sun was shining through the window illuminating the realization that it had all been a dream.

"Meow!" He heard Peppermint outside his place. Sebastian got out of bed and headed to the front door to let Peppermint in. Looking outside he saw Iza pulling weeds near the fountain.

"Good morning," she called. "We had quite a storm last night. How did you do with it?"

Sebastian, still waking up, rubbed his eyes and then waved hello. "Morning Iza, honey. Actually, the weather was fine, but I had quite the dream."

"Well, come on over, angel. Have some scrambled eggs and sausage and you can tell Katriana all about the dream. She's a dream expert."

"I'd love to! Be there in 15."

9

Meet Katriana, Master of Dreams

Sebastian headed over to Iza's house.

"Knock, knock! Other than the dream, it is like waking up on the edge of paradise here!" he greeted. "I love sitting outside in the fresh morning air and just listening to nothing. You've carved out a piece of heaven here, honey. Can I help with breakfast?"

"I thought you'd never ask. Yes, angel, that is why I live here. Heaven is the idea. Here, you get the eggs going, I've started on the sausage. Katriana should be over any minute."

"Does she live here?"

"Yes, in the casita with the red door, the Red Hibiscus. Oh, here she is. Good morning angel!" Iza stepped away from the kitchen to greet Katriana with a big hug.

Katriana was something else. Sebastian was taken back by her presence: although she was slender, it felt as though the presence of a sumo wrestler had entered the room. Katriana was a bit too thin so that her cheeks were tight against her bones making her face look like a skull more than a head. Her clothes were simple, but she was loud.

"Gud morning, Iza!" Her greeting resonated throughout Iza's whole house. Sebastian didn't mind strong women, and Katriana's arms were so thin that she looked weak, but he could tell that this woman had undeniable emotional strength, despite her looks. At the same time, Sebastian could already tell that this was a woman of power. Just as he thought this, she looked up to spot him.

"This must be the dreamer! I heard you came from dream and now you had dream too!"

"Yes, well, I thought I came from the east coast. I'm Sebastian. It is nice to meet you Katriana. You have such presence. You must turn heads everywhere you go."

Katriana leaned back, pulled out a cigarette and stared at him. *Ah, that explains the low, raspy voice*, he thought. She was so small, where did the boisterous voice come from?

"An you are perceptive. Come out! I can't wait to talk to you."

"Yes, I think you are going to surprise me. Let me dish you up, breakfast is ready. OJ?"

"You cook too?" she asked, turning to look at Iza. "You weren't kidding. He the full package."

"Yes angel, but he says he really is gay." Iza turned to look at Sebastian, a hungry look on her face. "We need to have a conversation about that." Then she turned back to Katriana, "You'd be surprised, he is more tuned in than he knows or you may have guessed. Why are all the good ones taken or gay in my life?"

Katriana laughed, "I don know, but if you have dream bout it I might be able to splain to you!"

Katriana stepped outside as Sebastian and Iza dished up the eggs, sausage and juice.

"I hope you don't mind turkey sausage, angel," Iza said to Sebastian, "Katriana doesn't eat red meat."

"Maybe she should, that woman is the only underweight person I've met in twenty years!"

Iza laughed, "Angel, I didn't think you were that old!"

They stepped out where Katriana sat at a glass table, a large dog by her side. Sebastian set dishes on the table, noting that the dog weighed more than she did. The dog sat by her side, guarding her no doubt. He was another manifestation of her power.

He and Iza sat down too. The morning was crisp, a black bird went flying by-- or could it be a raven or a crow? Sebastian took a deep breath of the fresh morning air. It felt great to be some where so open. The skies were endless here, which meant that the opportunities in life were too. *This is just what I needed*, Sebastian thought, referring to the open feel of a life of opportunities. New

York sometimes squeezed him, allowing little room for doubt or change. Santa Fe felt like it gave him the time, space and opportunities to explore and re-define his life; re-define himself.

He turned to focus on Katriana. "You are like a superhero character. You are so thin, honey, and you have a dog that is twice your size!"

"He not my dog, *Sebastián*. He Iza's. But I been told that more often than you may think." Sebastian smiled, agreeing. *No, I'm sure you've been told that plenty*, he thought to himself.

"He's an Akita and his name is Kia, but I think he has adopted Katriana. He never leaves her side," huffed Iza.

"Is possible that if I left, I have to adopt him," she said laughing, her native language coming through. "Ok, tell me bout dream."

"Meow! Roaw!" Peppermint cried, announcing his arrival.

"You don't say, Angel?" Iza replied. Then she looked up at Sebastian. "Peppermint here tells me that your dreams weren't all your own last night."

"Excuse me?"

"Oh, don't worry. It just means you have unseen help around. The question," Iza pondered as she turned to Peppermint for a clue, "Is whether it is good help or bad."

"What?"

"*Espera*," Katriana jumped in.

"Spanish? You don't look Spanish."

"She's not, she's European. But she grew up in Spain." Iza explained.

"You confusing!"

"You can always tell when she's thinking deeply because her English gets worse." Iza explained and then turned to Katriana. "I'm confusing?"

"Him! Him you confuse!" Katriana threw her hands up in the air, annoyed because Iza was just being troublesome. "You love this! Ah!" She turned to look at Sebastian with a calm smile. Her frustration was gone. *Sebastián*, she mean here are spirit and she think they give nightmare." She took a deep breath, slowing herself down, re-grouping herself. "She is wrong." Clearly, her English was better when she slowed down. "Dream are dream and I am the

Energy Master, no?" she asked Iza, her finger up in the air with great authority. Iza bowed her head. "Ok. Dream are only you energy. They can pick up other energy, we can talk 'bout that. But they are you."

"*Ahora*," Katriana's face now became serious. Where she was soft and welcoming with Sebastian, she was being stern and authoritative with Iza. "You! You want know why you no have boyfriend? Here is! You being too forceful! *Siempre*- always you are like that!"

Iza raised a brow, sizing up Katriana's words. "Angel, you know I can't help it. I'm a strong woman."

"No!" Katriana said with more Spanish in her tone than English. "You are not being *femenina*. You will never catch man when you manly! I know, I married!"

"Your husband is on the other side of the world!"

A screechy exchange of high-pitch sounds followed. *Am I glad I'm gay*, Sebastian thought. He'd seen cat fights and women bitching at each other, but this was different, strange and eerie. Iza and Katriana almost seemed to be speaking a different language, though they weren't. Was it the tone? Maybe, or maybe it was a whole different frequency. Could Sebastian understand their words? Yes. No. Should he eat his eggs or say something? He looked at Katriana's dog, Kia, who he could have sworn, was looking at him, just as confused.

"Ladies, are you friends? Are you fighting? What is going on?" he finally asked.

"Don't fret, angel. Katriana and I have these debates sometimes. It's a part of what makes us work so well together."

"What the hell are you talking about? You were just screaming at each other!"

"No, we not." Katriana informed.

"In a heated argument."

"Not entirely, angel."

"Ok, what do you call it?" Sebastian asked smugly.

"Talking. Sort-of. A bit of an energy match," Iza said, as if nothing.

"Energy match?" Sebastian repeated to see if this rang any sort of bell in him. No, it sounded like BS. He looked at Iza hesitantly. "Energy?"

45

"Angel, we tend to deal on a different level. It's like we are talking, but we are really racing through and looking at our energy."

Sebastian waited to see if she would add to this, or if this would start to make sense. Nope. He looked at her again.

"She's suggesting that I'm in conditioned energies, not a pure energy of my essence. I'm disagreeing," to which the dog growled, finishing her thought. Iza stopped to look at Kia. "You don't think so either?"

Kia's tongue hung out of his mouth. He tilted his head to the side.

"He knows." Katriana said, meeting Sebastian's eyes. *"Vamos,* see Iza problem-"

"My problem?"

"Well, one of them," Katriana acknowledged. "Her problem, she not open all the way. Too masculine. *Demasiado.*"

"Hormones?" asked a confused Sebastian. Breakfast was starting to taste funny.

"No, no. Energy." Katriana paused for a minute to see if this meant anything to Sebastian. "Ok, he no know about gender," she concluded, looking to Iza.

"No, angel. He no know." Iza made fun. She turned to Sebastian, "Why aren't you having breakfast? Isn't it good?"

Sebastian, smooth, suave-Sebastian always had an answer in life. He knew how to handle any situation and, boy, had he run into some situations in New York. Smart, smooth-tongued Sebastian always had something clever to say.

He bit his lip, speechless. *What the hell? Are these women crazy?*

"Iza," he began, looking for one of his pocket suave sayings or a smart compliment. Befuddled by these crazy ladies, nothing came to him. Instead, those were the words that came out - "Crazy ladies."

"No!" Katriana cried.

"No, no," Iza corrected. "Not crazy. Misunderstood, no doubt. Honey-angel, you are being introduced to another way of life. We just live by energy so everything in our lives looks different than what you are accustomed to."

Realizing what he'd said out loud, Sebastian felt a touch of the heat from embarrassment rise to his cheeks. "Did I say that? I'm sorry-"

"No, you should not be." Katriana said with authority. How that small, bony frame exuded such authority still baffled Sebastian. "You meant it, you just don-know the difference of 'crazy' and 'centered'. *Mira*, crazy es 'loco'. People crazy. They do crazy thin, they don know themsef, how they are, how feel. They do thing - many thing - that hurt them, but they don-know. If they know, they would see that it is crazy to do.

"We not crazy. We do for us." Katriana ended there, leaving room for Iza to fill in any grammatical blanks. Kai, like Sebastian, now felt a bit more calm, assured. So, he lay back down. Back to his hard work of sleeping.

"There are different key components to living a spiritual life," Iza picked up where Katriana had left off. Iza's voice was back to that of the lecturer the day they'd met. "Gender is one; who or what you live your life by is another and that is what Katriana is talking about. See, angel, when you live your life by what others say you should do, by what society or your family define as success, then you are living an impoverished life. I say 'impoverished' because this is a life that has nothing feeding it.

"Katriana and I tap into other realms, we tap into energy. Energy essences." Iza suddenly stopped and looked to Katriana. "Oh, look. We've done it, we've overwhelmed him. And the day is getting on, we have to get going."

"No, please, go on. I'm fascinated. I turned away from what my father said, he was homophobic. If I'd listed to anything he'd said, I'd probably have jumped off the Brooklyn bridge twenty years ago."

"So what did you listen to? What did you live by?"

"My mother, though she died when I was young. Then there was no one."

"So you listened to you. That's what makes you special, unique, angel.

"Gender flow is another topic that we'll have to talk about some time. At it's simplest, I'll say that there are two flows. We each have a flow, masculine or feminine, which generally coincides with our bodies; we utilize each flow, though many are unaware. To master life, you must master the flows."

"Go on, I want to know more. I also want to have you explain energy. You use it so much, the word, I mean."

"Sure. Tapping into energy requires you to tap into you, into your divine energy. Since we do, we may look crazy, but we are furthest from that. We are the opposite end, though we are more than just sane. We are truly connected to our divinity. It provides a door to that Silent Knowledge; it provides us things you'd never guess: knowledge, wisdom, guidance and more."

Sebastian looked surprised, "Like magic? You are saying you tap into magic?"

"No, but you can certainly think of it that way."

"You do look a bit witchy."

"You're not the first to say that."

Katriana laughed. "You won't be last either!"

"She likes being called a witch," Iza explained. "I guess I don't mind either. It distinguishes us as reaching into those energy realms and it is far more true than our being crazy."

"*Sí, sí.*"

"My God, I know two witches!"

Iza smiled. "Angel, come to class tonight. You sound like you are ready for something more in life. You should also consider my 'Dancing with the Moon Personalized Day' offering. It gives you a full day to go into the issues that are keeping you in the dark about your life or about what you want in life."

"An I go, I be there for you too, *Sebastián.*" Katriana's pronunciation of Sebastian's name was spoken in Spanish and it had a wonderful ring to it.

"I'll do both," he quickly agreed.

"The Mood Day is expensive. You are welcome to invite William back or whomever you choose."

"OK, I will. I'll write you a check, hon. I'm going to check with my best friend and my psychologist friend too. Can I pick a day after I've talked with them?"

"Of course. Now I have to get online. I'm still trying to get more people to sign up for my workshop. Otherwise, I'm going to have to consider canceling."

"I was a marketer, hon. Can I help?" Sebastian offered.

"Yes, stick around, won't you?"

"I need to get to *cosas* also." Katriana said.

"It has been captivating meeting you Katriana."

"Oh, we no get to your dream! Well, we talk tonight, here on patio. After dinner. No?"

"I'll be here! OK, Iza, let's look at your marketing.

After suggesting a few ideas to improve her website, he headed back home. He was captivated and taken with her, well, with them both. They seemed tapped into and aware of things which governed life, and yet, which no one knew about. They seemed more like wise sorceress, but 'witches' would do. He couldn't wait to call Cindy, Sam and William. William would get an absolute kick out of all of this; Cindy and Sam might re-invent their profession. At his casita he picked up his keys to head to town. He'd call his friends from his car on his way into work.

10

Come Meet My Witches!

Sebastian had found that life worked better for him when he had a routine. That way, he made sure to get to everything that was important to him. This morning he'd already partaken in his push-ups and his morning walk. Breakfast with Iza had become part of his routine and now, he was heading into work. He sought out coffee shops that he liked, making them conducive to his work. Just as he was heading to his car with his laptop, he remembered that someone in town had told him that Madrid had coffee shops and plenty of gay men.

Working in Madrid today! Let's see what that's all about!

Sebastian drove slowly, as always, on the dirt driveway, leaving Iza's ranch. He headed south on the picturesque highway that curved up and down the mountains. It didn't seem like he was up over seven thousand feet. Where one might expect pine trees and forest in the southernmost range of the Rocky Mountains, there was little foliage was even two feet tall. Most of the dry landscape was shrubby when it rained, which wasn't often. Junipers were the only mystery plant that seemed to grow well in this otherwise barren landscape.

On his way to Madrid he called Cindi.

"You have to come here, honey. My new friends, I call them my witches, they will knock your socks off." Sebastian paused, thinking, "First, I get a point for calling them *my witches*."

"Oh, why is that, dear?" Cindi asked curiously.

"You'll see when you come. Honey, I am changing my stance. Tell Arthur that you have to fly out for work. Next week! I promise, it will change the way you see humans. It will redefine psychology for you."

"Oh?"

"I'm scheduling a 'Moon Day' with her and I want you and Sam to come. I might even invite my boyfriend back."

"Boyfriend? Sam told me that William was good looking and a great guy and that she didn't know why you two cut if off, and he went to L.A. What's the story? "

"Well, yes. True. I told Sam that I'm on a diet." Sebastian's voice now flared. "No manly sweets, hon. No beefcake or cupcakes for me. I'm alone in the desert!"

Cindy chuckled her usual laugh; her laugh was sophisticated, but almost painful to hear.

"I'm focusing, hon! You of all people should understand that!"

"Yes, of course I do, dear. You know I just like having a little fun with you, Sebastian. Not many handsome, young gay men for me to let loose around, you know." Sebastian laughed to himself. Cindy's definition of letting loose was like cleaning the house on a Friday night - for fun.

"Honey, you - must - come!" he emphasized. "My witches are deep, they know everything and they claim to work in energy. Besides," he deepened his voice, "you could write a book on the psychology of these two."

Sebastian could feel Cindy leaning into the phone to hear him. "Really? Go on, because my editor is on me for a new book."

"Well, I promise, honey. I *promise* - you could probably write three! The way they interact with one another, the way they fight-"

"Fight? Are they lesbians?"

"No! And, they corrected me. They said they weren't fighting, that they were doing something screechy in energy." Sebastian gave Cindy a nice, dramatic sigh. "Honestly, honey, you have to see it to believe it. Come! Next week! Tuesday?"

"You are making tall promises, Sebastian. If you were anyone else, I'd disregard this conversation the minute I'm off the phone, but it is you, so-" Cindi paused to make sure she wanted to say this, "so, I will tell my new husband I'm going away. These witches of yours better be good, dear."

"You won't be disappointed, honey. Just being here is like nothing I've experienced on the east coast." He paused dramatically one more time because, even though Dr. Cindy Rosenthal was a refined and top-rated psychologist, when it came to talking with Sam and Sebastian, she loved a little drama. "You know me, hon. I don't make promises I can't keep. I'm also inviting Sam. Still, if it helps, I'll ask Iza to make it official. You need professional development, right?"

"Actually, yes, that would help. Then it would be easy to come. Do you think she can issue a certificate of participation- for a workshop? With a psychological name?"

"I'll ask Iza, but I'm sure she can."

"Alright, you, I'll book a flight to come out asap and coordinate with Sam. Where do you recommend I stay?"

"Iza runs workshops, so I'm sure she can accommodate you. I'll email you to get you in contact with her."

"Wonderful, dear. We'll see you soon!"

Sebastian had ended the call just in time. As he got closer to the town of Madrid, he noticed his cell phone reception bars rapidly dropping. He adhered to the speed limit signs, having been warned about the generously distributed speeding tickets along the highway.

"Cute town!"

The town was only a couple miles long, so he drove through once and chose a coffee shop to visit. "CowArt. Really? Ok, I have to try that!" he told no one at all. There were a couple choices, but only one that was in, or was part of, a gallery.

He parked and walked into the gallery.

"Welcome!" Inside the gallery a man was walking towards him, arms wide open. He was tall, slender, had bleached-blond hair: handsome, great eye candy. *A little diet cheating is OK*, Sebastian thought, grinning.

"Hello," Sebastian began, shifting modes. It was obvious that they were both gay. To his disappointment though, Sebastian saw a wedding band on the man. Sometimes you just have a sugar craving and just a little fix would do. *Oh well*, he thought, *cake diet. No sweets. No fun.*

"Welcome to 'Gallery CowArt & Coffee!'"

Nope, Sebastian thought. *There is nothing like this in New York. Oh my!*

"Oh my!" he repeated his thought, having liked the way it sounded.

"Yeah, I know," smiled the man, nodding his head. "CowArt' is a name no one ever forgets! I'm Sean, how can I help you?"

"Sean, nice name." Sebastian wasn't referring to Sean's name, but was delivering a subtle compliment. So what if Sean was taken? There were 'plenty' of gay men in Madrid, he'd been told. If they were like Sean, Sebastian could enjoy some great eye candy. Maybe make a few friends, with benefits.

"Well, Sean, I'm Sebastian. I'm staying at Iza's ranch for a while and I came on her recommendation looking for a coffee shop to work in. Do you have Internet in your café?"

"Oh, sweet pea, we don't!" grimaced Sean. "Madrid is made of three factions of people," he waved his hand, lifting his index finger. "Old, burned out hippies," now a second finger went up, "off-the-gridders and, well," he squeaked, raising a third finger, "us!" He bit his lip and sighed. "Most of those folk like 'the simple life,' so they voted the free Google cell tower down! We hardly have cell phones." He rolled his eyes dramatically. "Only one place in town offers interned and they are expensive as hell." Now he put his hand on his hip, "Bad for business."

"So much for working here. OK," Sebastian said, re-focusing on candy. "Uh, I also heard there was a great pool here!" By this, Sean knew that Sebastian meant a great pool of men to fish for, but Sean knew that Sebastian probably wouldn't like it here.

"Yes, well, sweet pea, you are one handsome devil! Don't let Dave, my honey, hear me!" He flung his arm up in the air, waving off his words, so that Dave couldn't hear them, as though Sean had cleared the air. "Where are you from?"

"I'm an east coaster, I spent a lot of time in New York. I used to work there."

"Oh!" Sean raised both his eye brows. "That's quite the scene. I've been, you know, back when I was single." He gave Sebastian a knowing smirk. "Don't get me wrong, I'm happy! Dave and I got married a year ago and opened our dream gallery!" Sean held his hand out, showing off the gallery.

"Still, sweet pea, I don't think this is going to be your cup of tea. A gay hippie? Don't take my word for it, but you look to clean-cut, too nice. Walk your cute little self down to the bar at the end of the road. You'll see what the pickin's are like." Sean's voice no longer flared or held enthusiasm. "Dave and I are imports. Good thing too, or I'd still be single."

Now Sean looked around to make sure no one was listening - not that anyone else was in the gallery. "Sweet pea, you are the cutest thing I've seen in this town - next to Dave, of course. Here," he said, walking to his desk. He picked up a business card and wrote down his number. "If you want a married couple for friends, call us because you seem great. Otherwise, New York swank doesn't usually find much to swagger in this town. Unless you like dirty teeth and bad manners, to say the best about most of 'my people' here."

Sebastian turned around to see someone walk into the gallery.

"Good morning, Sean. How were the weekend sales?" The man that walked in was ragged. Clothes, facial hair and just the way he stood were all ragged. Being a man of class and style, above all, Sebastian thought twice about this town. He suddenly remembered the people he'd seen walking around town when he'd driven in. He prided himself for being non-judgmental, lest he be judged as a gay man. However, he also prided himself for taking care of himself. Sometimes he wondered if people cared about themselves at all.

"It was a pleasure to meet you, Sean. I appreciate all the advice. I'll call you, bye." Sebastian said, ducking out of CowArt.

"Shite." Disappointed, for sure. He looked to his left and to his right down the main street here. A sign caught his attention, "The Mad Hatter Restaurant."

"Mad Hatter?" The name sparked his curiosity and he was hungry.

Like almost every other building, the restaurant was a converted house. He saw a couple of tables outside under the porch, quaint.

"Hello, grab any table. I'll bring you a menu right over." Greeted an older woman.

This was a 'typical' small town restaurant in the sense that everything was simple. Simple cement floor, basic wooden table, chairs and benches. *Odd, some of these* (the tables and chairs, he meant) *seem small or short.* Perhaps he too, like Alice, had grown bigger, except he didn't remember doing so.

His grey-haired waitress came over. She looked like she was in her 50's or 60's; she was pear-shaped, but acted like she was much younger as she juggled several tasks here. She smiled. There were only a couple other patrons, but she still seemed rushed.

"Can I get you something to drink, sweetie?"

"Iced-tea, please."

"We don't refill them. Water. Plain or sweetened?"

Just then a younger man came in, maybe in his 30's.

"Sorry, Gam, go."

She frowned. "'Bout time. Iced-tea for him, ask what kind." She turned to Sebastian, "Our waiter, Trent, will take care of you now. I'm going back to the kitchen." She handed Trent the notepad and pen and disappeared to the back.

"Was that plain or sweetened iced-tea?" Trent had a wad in his mouth. Not something you really see in New York. Sebastian didn't think that people still chewed. Thought it was just a movie, old western thing.

"Unsweetened, please."

Trent smiled, revealing the chew stains. "Let me know when you're ready to order."

"Wait, where's the restroom? I need to wash up."

Trent nodded, knowingly. *Tourists!* "Nah, man, no plumbing. You have to go out and around the building, to the right. Go all the way behind the building down the alley. Port-a-potty there. Should be soap." He turned and walked into the kitchen.

Suddenly Sebastian lost his appetite. Stunned, he thought for a second. *No plumbing? How do they cook? How will he wash his hands to serve my food? How-*

Trent walked back out of the kitchen with Sebastian's iced-tea.

"Uh," Sebastian said, backing away from the tea. "Why don't you refill?"

"Water. No water in Madrid. Coal ruined it. We have to have it delivered from the jail."

"Bullocks." Sebastian calmly pulled out his wallet, handing the waiter a $10. "Got a text, gotta run."

Heading out, he looked around, his eyes more open now. The town was fine, but maybe not his mecca.

Sebastian walked around town just to see what was here, what the people were like and to see who would be in a bar this early in the day. Once he had a feel for the town, he laughed, because Sean hadn't exaggerated about the people. Clearly not Sebastian's kind of cupcakes. Oh well, he'd call Sam and William on his way back. Suddenly, Sebastian recalled William as being more handsome than he'd previously thought.

11

Dreaming Up Dinner

Shortly after she saw Sebastian's car leave, Katriana went to Iza's.

"Iza," she said, letting herself in. "You were right, there something about him."

"Do you know what?"

"I have idea, no certain yet. A gift for you, *si*. A gift."

"That sounds wonderful to me. Dinner tonight? He's cooking."

"*¿Si?* Many gifts!" A large smile came over her, now that someone was cooking for her. Kia, ever faithfully by her side, raised his nose into her hand, agreeing that he'd like to be cooked for as well. "*Si*, I come. Now I go smoke."

"Yes," Iza said from her purple, velvet couch where she sat working. "Take your cancer sticks outside!"

Sebastian came over in the evening to prepare dinner. He knew he had a great set-up at Iza's. His expenses were low and she offered company when he wanted it and an equipped kitchen in which he could be creative. In no time at all he'd put a salmon salad together with almond slices and a creamy yogurt dressing.

Katriana, Iza and Sebastian sat outside for dinner. Katriana smiled knowingly at Sebastian, which made him uncomfortable. As an adult, he rarely felt awkward. He shifted in his seat.

"You will like it here. Many gifts you will receive." She said. She put her plate down, after only having had a couple of bites, and swung herself in a hammock, smoking.

"That's not food, angel."

Sebastian said nothing. He figured that this was why Katriana was skeletal.

Ignoring Iza, she turned to Sebastian, "You were brought here by Silent Knowledge." Iza nodded in agreement. Sebastian still didn't grok this, so he changed the subject.

"Katriana, Kia. Why is he always by your side? What is he protecting you from?"

"Not protecting. Grounding." She didn't let him question this, "What your dream?"

Sebastian recounted last night's dream.

"You are good dreamer. OK, you must know energy to know what dream is communicating." She closed her eyes. "In dream, you go out and find difficulty to drink water. That energy of a block. You see? Difficulty is block, it is keep your experience not smooth. Yes?"

"Sure, I get that."

"Your friend is now friend with another. Loss energy, *si*? It feel like something taken, is energy sensation of loss. *Si?*"

He nodded.

"Then you in a gun fire. You threatened. That energy more obvious, no?"

"So, what does it all say?" Was she making sense? The dream still seemed like it made no sense. Night-time gibberish.

"You feel you lost something, someone. You feel you are threatened. That why you came to Santa Fe."

Katriana didn't ask, she didn't doubt her own take of his dream. Sebastian, on the other hand, was trying to make sense of this.

"Angel, most people don't acknowledge how they feel, especially when they feel things that they'd prefer not to feel. The first causality is *know thyself*. This means that we are all meant to know ourselves, our passions, our weaknesses; our loves, but certainly our feelings, thoughts. That is why so many people have nightmares and can't sleep. They are avoiding how they feel. When they don't consciously acknowledge it during the day, it tries to come through subconsciously at night.

"You lost your best friend, she got engaged. You feel threatened. That's why you are looking for more meaning in your life."

"Holy shite!" Now he understood. He was amazed. A crazy dream with twins and guns, a water fountain. Now that Iza had spelled it out for him, it made sense. "You are right, so right." He stared, transfixed trying to soak it all in.

"Is normal dream."

Normal? Wait, "Katriana, why twins?"

"You feel split, no?"

"Oh. Right on." He thought for a moment, "No, wait. I thought I that made sense, but now I don't."

"You have conflict feelings. Split. Happy for your friend, unhappy for loss. Split."

He exhaled, letting the confusion go. "Yeah, right." Now he looked at Katriana, swinging in her hammock, smoking in the settling sun. "You're amazing! How you tap into the energy in *my* dream. Wow!"

"You good too. You have good awareness. That very good."

"So, angel, how was your day?"

"Huh, funny you should ask, iza. I went down to Madrid. It's a bit of a crazy town," he said, trying to be delicate so as not to insult anyone unknowingly.

"A bit."

"They don't refill iced-tea?"

"Madrid has quite the history. They say Walt Disney went once at Christmas time and saw the town lit up with strung lights, horse-carriage rides, hot chocolate for sale on the road and several other sweet things. He was inspired and got the idea to create 'a magic kingdom."

"Impressive, I was in the town that inspired Disneyland?"

"The very one, or so they say. It also has a haunted past. Coal town, but after the war they found that the coal that the war had been demanding from them, was then deemed 'bad' coal. The war ended and the town's coal economy came to a painful end. The worst part was that the coal mining affected the underground aquifers and polluted the water."

"That's terrible." He felt sorry for the town. "No wonder, the restaurant didn't even have bathrooms."

"The Chitty. No, poor Ma'Beatty. She works hard and her son is showing no interest in helping."

Sebastian assumed she meant his waiter, but he wanted to change the subject. This just wasn't uplifting and he was already dealing with his subconscious telling him he felt abandoned, threatened.

"What do I do about my dream? What do I do with the message?"

"See, he aware. He show promise, Iza." Katriana smiled, impressed with herself.

"You check to see what you need, angel. You check whether you need to give yourself love, acceptance or approval."

He thought about this. He figured he needed to feel like he had his family, his BF back. Not that he didn't want her to be happy with Nick, or Kole; not that he didn't want her to marry and live happily ever after. He just wanted her to also be there for him. He knew she would be at some point, once the relationship wasn't so new and exciting. So, what did that translate to? Love? Acceptance- nope, it was the first. *I don't feel loved.*

"You two are witches. You work magic. I'll take the plates in and I'm going to retire, work on this need."

"You do that, angel. Leave the dishes. You made dinner, we'll take care of these."

"Thanks. Good night, my lovely witches."

"Oh, Sebastian, one last thing," Iza's tone now taunting. "Are you still going with being gay?"

"Yes Iza," he spoke as he walked away without turning around. "I'm still gay." Truth was it was cute and sweet to be told he was handsome in this way.

"Alright, if you insist." That meant, 'good night.'

"Buenas noches."

He waved and went home to figure out how to deal with this need to love himself.

♥

The next few days Sebastian worked to get ahead of schedule, since Sam and Cindy would be coming to his 'Moon Day' soon. He was looking forward to seeing them. He felt close with them both and he missed the less frequent consulting sessions due to new relationships and Sebastian's new adventure.

12

Dreaming With The Moon

Iza and Katriana walked into the Hawaiian casita with the orange door, to find Sebastian on the couch, his arm around Sam. Sebastian's other friend, Cindi, sat in a chair talking with them.

The Hawaiian building was grand; it looked larger on the inside than it did from the outside. The front door was special. Old and heavy, made of real wood, the intricate carvings made it look to be from a castle or a gate taken from an exotic land, perhaps from Indonesia or Bali. Upon entering, there were four or five wooden chairs along the wall to the left or right of the door. The middle of the room felt vast, like a spoken word would cause an echo. The only furniture here were a love seat, Iza's chair and another plush chair, that Katriana sat in. One smaller chair accommodated Cindy. These seats were arranged in the middle of the room forming a circle. Light entered the room from the two side walls where large, picture windows showed off the scenery. The wall opposite the front door had a small stage and an altar on either side of it. The deep green carpet relaxed guests; the walls, colored with the slightest hint of yellow, warmed the space. Large photographs of Hawaiian landscapes hung next to the stage. It looked as though thirty people could comfortably sit in here and it was evident that the space was set up to be flexible. Flexible, the couch and chairs were on sliders. Thirty people could sit here comfortably. Iza's plush chair was the crown jewel. The fabric was a deep red-color; a high back gave it a royal look. It looked like it had been custom made for the Queen, the perfect piece by a fireplace.

"Hello angels." Iza greeted as she entered. She saw Sebastian snuggled up to Sam on the couch. Then she turned to Katirana and her dog, "Well, he isn't gay after all. Clearly this is his girlfriend and he was just making sure to save himself by saying he's gay."

Katriana smiled and turned towards the visitors.

"Cindi, Sam, these are my *brujas*, that's Spanish for witch," Sebastian introduced. "Let me go around the room: Dr. Samantha Jasper, or Sam, Dr. Cindi Rosenthal, or Cindi, Isadora Augustine, Keeper of Silent Knowledge, or Iza, and Katriana Montecello, Curandera, or shamanic healer."

"Hello ladies, Sebastian has spoken quite highly of you," Cindi greeted. "And, you are right, Iza, they act like a couple."

"Well, I can see that you and I see eye to eye," Iza responded. "He is adorable, right?"

"And yummy, but only Sam would know." Cindi smirked.

"Yes," Katriana joined in, "Iza is not convinced that he is gay."

"I'm gay-" Sebastian said flatly.

"But that is because Iza likes young, *guapo* and unavailable." Katriana said, sitting in a chair with a high back, her dog laying right by her.

Cindi looked to Iza, who was not denying this at all, and then she looked back to Katriana. "How keen of you, dear. Have you known Iza for long?"

"Yes, a couple of years."

Sebastian tried to use this opportunity to shift the focus off of himself. "Katriana is from Europe, her husband is still there; she's been living in the US for many years."

Cindi ignored his words. "I don't often meet people who understand human behavior the way you ladies seem to. Sebastian was impressed, which is meaningful to me. I'm feeling like I'm in good company."

"You have no idea, angel. So, he is calling us his witches?" Iza turned towards Katriana. "Then shall we work a little magic?"

"You are going to love this, Dr. R." Kat said.

"Call me Cindi, dear. All of my witchy friends do!" All three ladies laughed. Sebastian and Sam looked at each other. They both felt like sitting ducks.

The three witches turned to stare at Sebastian.

"Angel, what are you usually like with your lovers? Are you dominating or dominated?"

"Are you receptive or ravaged?" Katriana added.

"Oh, do you mean am I masculine or feminine?" Sebastian asked, thinking that he knew where the witches were leading him.

"Close." Iza answered, keeping her eyes on him like a hawk. He could tell that she was watching his every move; his energy too. A couple days ago she'd said she could see and read a person's energy. Iza's weren't the only eyes fixated on him.

"It depends, honey." Sebastian said coolly. One of his strengths in life was being able to handle any situation with humor or swank. "Domination is a strong word. I'm not into S and M, but sometimes I'm on top and sometimes on the bottom. I like to mix it up."

"Who was your greatest love?" Iza continued, leaning forward.

Sebastian rolled his eyes recalling his past lovers. "I'd say it was Roby. I was in love, and I liked receiving him!"

"Iza, he is gay," Katriana stated.

"No angel, look at the way his energy has opened and shifted since Sam arrived." Iza looked at Sam now, "Welcome to The Ranch, angel."

"Thank you," Sam smiled meekly. "It's nice to meet you both."

"I know, his energy is different with her, but he's gay." Katriana insisted.

"Yes," Cindi assured, "he could have had Sam all to himself- well, and maybe he did. However, he also reunited Sam and her boyfriend. They are madly in love."

Iza and Katriana both turned to look at Sam, searching her with their eyes.

Sam squirmed in her seat, *I thought this was about Sebastian.*

"Well how do you explain that? She is attached to him, but has another lover?" Iza asked Katriana. "An open relationship?"

"No, I'm gay!" Sebastian was now losing his cool. He and Sam were under attack.

"Let me see," Katriana said, her accent growing thicker as she concentrated on Sebastian's energy and not her pronunciation. She was staring at him, no, through him. "I think I see a past life." She now turned to Iza, "That is why they are so connected."

"Soulmates?" Sebastian asked, feeling a bit better. "I told Sam that we were soulmates from the day we met."

"Yes, there is the confirmation," Katriana said to Iza, talking as if Sebastian weren't even there.

"I am fascinated, ladies." Cindi's intrigue was thick. "I don't know if I believe in such things, but it would explain these two. Sam said that Sebastian was very gay when they were in Key West and he's been with William, who confirmed his preference."

"That's true!" Sam chimed in.

"Still, there is something about these two. And, it would also explain their night together." Cindi added.

"What? I want a night, too!" Iza stomped her foot.

"I'm gay!" He gritted his teeth, looking at Cindi. "So much for confidentiality."

Cindi looked to Iza, "Dear, you sound like a child demanding a cookie!" Then she turned to Sebastian, "Sebastian, dear, you said I was at a psychology conference. Among colleagues we share to improve."

Sam looked at Sebastian.

"You two slept together?" Katriana asked.

Ugh, "Maybe. We aren't sure." Sam had been quiet and had been feeling cornered, but now *I'll defend Sebastian,* she thought. It was really meant to keep the focus off her. She turned to Sebastian.

"What is going on? Who are you? You aren't acting like the Sebastian that I know at all."

He squinted his eyes, perhaps looking for himself, but didn't respond.

"Where's the scoreboard? Where's the smart ass?" she continued.

Still no response. Now all eyes were on him.

"As I live and breathe! I can't believe it. I've never seen you speechless and I've never seen you lose your cool, Sebastian."

"Love, I'm on an adventure searching for my soul, so I'm not my usual self," he defended.

"Oh, and he calls her 'Love'," Iza said to Katriana. "I want a night," she said, as if Katriana would be the one to grant it.

"I think you've got him, wait." Katriana said, raising a hand to Iza.

"Got me? I'm gay!"

"That's not what I mean." Katriana's dog now sat up, as if he too were interested in the conversation. Just then Peppermint came meowing at the door, so Iza let him in.

"Hello, come on in and join the party." She said.

"Sam thought she was pregnant-"

"You got her pregnant?" Iza and Katriana shrieked.

"That's what I thought too," Cindi responded calmly. "But no, Nick, who she is madly in love with, he was the father." Cindi clarified.

"Can I speak?" Sebastian huffed. No one seemed to hear him.

"Three witches and now I don't like any of you!" The three ladies looked at each other and smiled.

"Sam thought she was pregnant – by Nick – and we went to a party. We had this lethal drink, she came to me for comforting, so we kissed, cuddled, but that's all either of us remember." Sebastian couldn't remember when he'd last had to explain himself. Frustrated, he felt like he was tripping over this own words and thoughts.

"We woke up naked next to each other, but it's not likely…" Sam's defense of Sebastian was weak, so she didn't continue.

Katriana raised her eye brows, "Yes, there is huge karma between these two. Even if all they did was kiss."

"I'm g-!"began shouting a defensive and angry Sebastian. "Karma?" *What the?* He looked to Iza and then turned to Katriana, "What Karma?"

"Alright, angel. We just needed to bring you to this energetic place within yourself." Iza said, her demeanor and tone completely changing.

"Oh, I almost see it." Cindi jumped, "Continue!"

"It's not whether you are gay or not, angel. We were looking at how open, how vulnerable you are and are willing to be.

"Let me back up so that when we talk about your intimacy issues, they will make more sense." Iza said.

"Yes! He does have intimacy issues; we spoke about it one night over tequila!" Cindi was practically jumping out of her seat. "This is so exciting!"

"Angel, this is what I live for. If it wasn't exciting, I would learn to knit like an old granny." Iza rarely met people like Cindi who understood the deep soul work that this work entailed.

"You know," she said, turning to Katriana, "I think we should break for lunch first. Give him a breather, don't you think?"

"Yez," she nodded. As if Kia understood, he sat up and looked to her. She stood and pet him, "Yes, it's time for lunch." She looked at everyone, "Sebastian, why don't you and Sam go to lunch. Us ladies will go on our own. We'll meet back here in two hours."

He nodded and the three witches exited their magical casita, leaving a void behind.

Sebastian sighed at the thought that he'd invited Cindi here and that she was more excited than he'd ever seen her, all at his expense. He removed his arm from Sam's shoulder and leaned his head back. It was still early in the morning, but he thought of Dali's painting of warped clocks which demonstrated elongated time. That was what he was experiencing now. Warped his body, because he was feeling stiff and tight; this was so not him! The New York city version of Sebastian was a mover and shaker; he was on the ball and he was a deal maker! In St. Martin, he had relaxed his zippy and business-shark ways and he'd tapped into Island-Sebastian, a man of heart, feeling and joy. What he wasn't – ever – was a stressed or stiff man. Life didn't faze Sebastian, Sebastian was fascinated by life.

Today was a fluke, he reassured himself. Little did he know, that tomorrow would be too. He sighed and braced himself for the longest day of his life.

Then he turned toward Sam, "You ready to go in the Mercedes again? I named her Agnes, after my speedy grandmother."

Sam stood and faced him, extending her hand to help him up. "Agnes? Speedy grandmother? Who are you?"

On his feet he hugged her, relieved to just be with her, back to the world of Sam and Sebastian.

"I'll take you to my favorite restaurant in town – and we'll speed all the way there."

13

La Posada

The new Mercedes was like a masseur. Sam sat back, closed her eyes and let Carlos the exotic masseur take over.

"Ohhhh!" She groaned.

"Nice, right?" Sebastian could feel life coming back and flowing in his veins. He was feeling like himself; holding the stick shift and putting his foot on the gas as he leaned back into a pillow of leather brought back feelings of comfort, control and power.

"You didn't tell me how nice your car was. I'm going to ask Nick for one of these for Christmas. Or as a wedding present."

Sebastian laughed, "Sure, I'm sure he has that kind of money to burn, Love."

Adjusting to a little slice of heaven on four wheels, Sam began to think about lunch. "So, what's your favorite restaurant, Sebastian?" She watched the dry landscape whip by on the long road into town.

"It's called 'La Posada.' You walk through this crazy, old hotel and out into the garden area. They have a fountain, a fireplace and the landscaping is amazing. Then the food! The flavors, the bread!"

"Sebastian, are you still going to Napa?"

"Do I still drink wine as if it were water? Yes!"

"You seem so at home here. That Iza- I've never seen the scholarly side of Dr. Rosenthal. And Iza, she's like a hawk! Is she going to tear us limb from limb?"

"I think that's her specialty. I was feeling like a weasel spotted by a ravenous hawk."

"Then why are you here, Sebastian? I've never seen you speechless before."

"Love, I'm like a cupcake in the desert. I'm letting the heat melt me so that I can see what I'm really made of."

"There you go again, showing me up!" she smiled. "You're on a psychological trip, eh? Traversing the open, dry lands of your subconscious?"

"Yeah, something like that. Nice one, Love."

"Well, I guess that's an explanation for why you aren't being yourself."

"In some ways, I haven't been myself since I left the magazine. Then in St. Martin I realized that I no longer am the fashion, marketing guy. So, I'm looking in these wide, open spaces for who I am. There's no place to hide here."

"Not with Iza around. I don't know if I like her."

"You just need to get to know her. She's cool, love." In town now, they pulled up to the valet and got out of the car. "She hasn't been fun today, but she knows so many things." They headed in, walking past through the lobby toward the restaurant. Sebastian asked the hostess for a table for two outside.

Sitting down, he continued, "Sometimes I think she works magic, Love." He put his sunglasses on. The day was beautiful and bright. The restaurant was fantastic.

"Magic?" Sam knew Sebastian well, she knew no one could fool him. So, what the hell was he saying?

"Look," he said, pointing. "There's a butterfly over in the flowers."

Sam looked around, "Oh, this place looks like something out of a magazine. Nick and I should get married here!" She admired the fountain, the green grass the trees; she loved the detail of the stone floor beneath them, the unique architecture all around them. This would be a classic setting for a wedding: adobe buildings, quaint corners with benches, gardens. She looked to one side and saw a beautiful room with glass doors, a bar. She looked the other way and saw a bridge allowing passage over a creek leading away from the fountain. On the other side of the bridge was a spa, a beautiful sculpture at the entrance.

"This isn't a hotel, it's a get-away!" Sam's eyes ate up the delicious, colorful sights.

"That's why it's my favorite. When I come, it's like I've gone to another time when people still had gardens and they stopped their day to enjoy their meals."

"No wonder you like it here. Is all of Santa Fe like this?"

"Some, yeah. It really does have its charm."

"Actually, I hear they have a famous cooking school here. That might be sticking around for. I'm looking into it."

"I thought so. After all, you've already rented a home." She shifted in her seat, "I think it's a good thing, Sebastian. You're looking for what's next and food and wine are passions."

"They are, Love," he said, playing with the thought of his passions. He was re-wiring his brain to think of food and wine as more than lifestyle interests. Now he had to redefine himself: he was no longer a fashionista. Would he be a sommelier? A restaurateur?

Just then Sebastian's phone rang. "Hi honey," he greeted. He looked up at Sam and lifted a finger, asking for a minute. She nodded in agreement.

"What? Really?"

"That's wonderful, honey. I'm sitting here with Sam at La Posada. You remember the hotel with the restaurant in the garden? Yeah."

"Uh-huh."

"I just started Iza's Moon Process. Cindy is here, Sam. So, you have perfect timing honey. I'm sure you'll love it."

"Uh-huh."

"No, no need. I'll ask Iza if there is an additional cost and I'll cover it. Don't worry honey. Can't wait to see you tomorrow!"

He hung up.

"William coming back?"

"Yes, tomorrow morning. Poor guy, I'm hoping he'll help take some of the heat off of us!"

Sebastian and Sam had the best lunch they'd had together since Key West. The food was exquisite and Sam couldn't get enough of the ambiance. They lingered as long as they could, soaking in the warmth of the day, the coolness of their iced-teas and each other's company before they had to head back to the ranch.

14

Adam, Eve & Energy

Sebastian pulled into a parking space at the ranch. He and Sam headed into the X casita and saw that the witches were already gathered. Katriana's dog too. It was quiet. He and Sam came in without a word and sat.

Iza took a few deep breaths and then began.

"First let me tell you a little about energy and gender," Iza began. "You see, everything in our universe is either masculine or feminine. These are the two ways in which energy flows. Masculine energy is assertive, it goes. It focuses and tends to be more linear."

"I am good ezample. I jave the mos masculine *energia* in de room." Katriana said, her accent thick again. "But you and Iza are close," she said to Cindi.

"No more being assertive and jumping into my explanation," Iza commanded.

Then she turned back towards everyone, smiling gently. "There you have two examples of masculine energy at play. She inserted herself into my conversation and I gave her a command.

"The feminine energy is receptive, it moves inward. It directs, but does not lead. It is not focused, but rather has a broad watch. Masculine is vision, focus; feminine is intuitive, multi-tasking.

"Masculine energy flows and asserts into feminine energy, which receives.

"Sebastian, you are gay – I know. Generally, a masculine body has masculine energy and a feminine body has feminine energy. People have both energies and generally, men have more masculine energy

71

and women have more feminine energy. However, in homosexual people this usually is not true. In any relationship, homosexual or heterosexual, the masculine and feminine attract. Gay or straight, one person's dominant energy is masculine, assertive energy, and the other's dominant energy is feminine, or receptive energy.

"You, Sebastian, are on the masculine side of gay. Your boyfriends are usually more feminine, right? You are the provider and you take care of them physically and financially?"

Sebastian thought about this for a moment and nodded.

"And they are more feminine, providing you with nurturing and emotional well-being."

"Yes," Sam answered for him, "But Sebastian's the one that cooks and decorates. How does that make sense?"

"Everyone is their own unique mix, angel." Iza answered warmly. Sam couldn't help but notice that Iza's tone was so different from the inquisitor who had been in the room before lunch. "Cooking or not, Sebastian takes the role of protector and provider."

"Oh..." Things were beginning to make sense to Sam in a new way. "That is one of the things I love about him most. He's am amazing person, but he protects me."

"And I love Sam because we are family."

"Yes, he provides the masculine contribution and, you see, angel," Iza said, turning to Sebastian, "she provides you the feminine nurturing, which you call family.

"This is a perfect relationship for you both because you have great emotional intimacy." Iza looked to Sam. "It will ruin your relationship, and you just got engaged."

Sam's jaw dropped. She had been waiting for the right time, like at dinner, to put her new engagement ring on and announce the engagement to Sebastian and Cindi.

"How did you know? I haven't told anyone?" She took her ring out of her pocket and put it on. "He proposed!"

"Sam!" Cindy and Sebastian jumped up and went over to hug her and see her ring.

"Dear, you'll have to tell us all about it later on! What a sly boy, that Nick! Scooping you up so fast!" Cindi hugged Sam again and then sat back down.

"Felicidades!"

"Congratulations, Angel. That is some ring. We can talk about how I knew later, but I could see it."

"Now, where were we?" Iza said, bringing the focus back on topic. "Oh, yes. Sebastian, you are avoiding opening in your life, being vulnerable. You are avoiding true intimacy."

"No. Iza, that's not what I am missing in my life. I had intimacy in my last relationship with Roby. I came in search of my life's passion. I want to have something for myself, a career."

Sam put her hand on Sebastian. "She's right, cupcake. You said you knew things wouldn't work out with Roby. Also, he betrayed you," now she looked to Iza, "which is connected to the intimacy."

"Of course," Cindi's therapist voice was back. "He experienced betrayal because what he most wants is someone he can trust."

"To open up to and be vulnerable with," Iza picked up Cindi's words. "Creating intimacy in your life is the only way you will get more intimate with yourself, Sebastian. And that is the only way you will know yourself well enough to know what it is that you want to dedicate yourself to in your life. That is the only way to find your passion or meaning or purpose."

"I have to be intimate with a man in order to know what I want to do with my life?" His voice was confused, angry.

"Close, you have to be intimate with yourself, angel."

"And no thing else matter," Katriana explained. "Not you karma, no pass life or past. Do understand? Not you pass and what happen. All that *es importante*, importan, is you intimacy with you."

"And what does intimacy have to do with the masculine and feminine?" Frustration danced around Sebastian's head.

"We'll get to that angel."

"I am incredulous. I am impressed, ladies." Cindi looked to Sebastian to see how the client was taking and processing the day, which normally would have been at least a couple of years of therapy combined. It wasn't that therapy always had to be a slow process, it was that a client generally needed years to shift and adjust how they saw themselves and their issues. More often still, generally a client had to come to see that they had issues, as opposed to just denying them.

"Tell me ladies, can you work at this pace with anyone?" Cindi asked.

"Oh, no! Most people have breakdown!" Katriana looked to Sebastian and waved towards him, "Is that we could see he could go. Generally it take time for people for this level *de* awareness."

"Yes, he is special." Cindi agreed.

Sebastian, dropped his head back on the couch, certain he'd found the 7th ring of hell. Unless he'd just been given the recipe for everything he wanted in life, according to Iza. He got up and lay on the floor, arms and legs extended.

"Does this mean that Sebastian and I should change our relationship?" Sam asked.

"No, we'll take care of that, angel." Iza turned to Sebastian, "Welcome to your 'Walking Under The Moon' process." She smiled. "You are doing great! Let yourself be vulnerable."

If Sebastian had come west seeking something different in his life, he found it. Different, but better or wrose— right now? Maybe worse. When was the last time he'd felt so raw, so cut-up, so unloved? His anger had now given way to something a little more helpless, a little darker. He almost felt like he did when he was 6 and his father was yelling at him, belittling him; his father had made it clear what a yellow-bellied bastard his gay son was.

He lay for a moment, eyes closed. The world was spinning. He didn't blame Iza, though a part of him wanted to. After all, she was the one cutting into him. He sighed, his feelings overwhelming him.

"How are you angel?"

"Never better."

"Sarcasm, good. You haven't lost your edge." Iza looked up to Katriana. "I think they are ready. One last thing. Stand up where you are. Sam, go up to him. Face him."

Katriana and Cindy quietly observed. Iza waited a bit, letting Sam and Sebastian just stand in the middle of the room next to each other.

"Look into each other's eyes. There's a connection between you two. Katriana says it is karmatic, that you've lived other lives together."

"Hi Love." Sam smiled and began to get more comfortable at Sebastian's greeting.

"No talking." Iza monitored them carefully. Not that they were doing anything, so what was she monitoring? "Just be with each other; just look into one another's eyes."

Sam and Sebastian gave each other a, "OK, what up with this?" look. The look was meant to make fun of Iza, but it really acknowledged their discomfort. On display, not talking. Just looking at one another was awkward, at the very least. *What are we supposed to be doing? What is the point?* He raised an eyebrow.

A minute passed allowing them to ease into this. As they did, they found that they were more comfortable looking into one another's eyes. Initially the staring felt like an invitation of privacy but then it began to feel easier, and a connection began to emerge. The look on their faces didn't change, though it relaxed. They began to smile at each other with their eyes.

"Good, we're almost there." Iza whispered.

Sebastian felt a nice connection with Sam, the one he'd always wanted. He felt like he could be himself, his real, true, imperfect and different self. He hadn't realized how much he wasn't himself around other people until now. It surprised him because he prided himself on being authentic no matter what.

Huh, he thought, *I hadn't realized. Things are so different with Sam.* He didn't really have words to express how he was feeling right now, but then he thought, *Accepted, I feel accepted. Comfortable, maybe.* Since he didn't know exactly what he felt, he savored, *Just feeling good. A different kind of good,* he told himself.

"Now, for the sake of Sebastian and this process, for the sake of increasing your awareness and his, and for the sake of going deeper into the energy you have at play with him, let him kiss you."

"What?" Sam asked, turning to Iza.

"You are a psychologist, angel. This has deep work beneath it. Look at him again and be receptive to him. Sebastian, wait until I tell you."

Iza waited for them to get comfortable looking into each other's eyes again. She knew Sam was uneasy, but there was no way around that. "Kiss her, Sebastian."

Confused, but trusting the process, Sebastian leaned forward to kiss Sam. As he did, he felt further drawn in and before he knew it, he was embracing her and kissing her passionately. To his further surprise, Sam was not only allowing this, but she was reciprocating the depth of the kiss. For a minute, the Hawaiian Orange casita vanished; Cindy, Katriana and even Iza's transfixed eyes all seized to exist. As if this were some fairy tail romance, Sebastian's kiss stopped the world and all that he knew and all that he cared about was Sam. When he finally pulled his lips away, he felt an urge and didn't stop holding her. In all of himself all that mattered was Sam. He wanted to be one with her, to be with her, to merge with her; he wanted to fill himself, his breath, his heart, his sight - with Sam. He looked into her eyes and saw that she felt the same way.

"There. That's it, angels," Iza whispered. "You didn't know you felt this way about each other."

Cindy's jaw dropped. Katriana smiled at Cindy and patter her knee, reassuring her that all was well and as expected.

"I feel so drawn to her." Sebastian was still in that other world so his words were faint. "I never knew I felt this way about you-"

"You don't." Iza stood and walked up to them. "Sam feels the same way, but you are both wrong." The look of hunger on their faces and the craving they each felt for one another contradicted Iza's words, beyond a doubt.

"Notice yourselves. Notice the way you feel, how you long for one another. Notice how your mind is consumed with questions and an intense desire to figure out how to have the other in your life forever. Notice, most importantly," and now Iza touched Sebastian's abdomen, breaking their embrace, as Katriana did the same to Sam, having slipped up behind her. "Your body. Your chemistry is going crazy and it is pulling for the other person."

I can't believe— Shocked at how well Iza described what he was experiencing, Sebastian started to turn to Iza. "No, stay there. Remember this mad addiction. Feel and experience this sensation so that you will recall it later."

Sebastian and Sam started to take a few breaths. "It hurts a bit." He began to weaken.

"Sebastian-" Sam's voice sounded like that of a whimpering, hungry orphan pleading for food and love.

"You too, angel. Be aware of what is going on in you. This runs far deeper than psychology."

"Fascinating." Cindy stared, having never seen anything like this before.

"OK, sit for a minute - in separate chairs. Katriana, sit by Sam, no?" Katriana nodded and took Sam, who was discombobulated, by the hand and slipped an arm behind her back, leading her to the couch. "Sebastian, sit in my seat."

"Let's talk a bit about what just happened."

"I thought I loved Nick!" Panic began to rise in Sam. She was just beginning to lose it, so Katriana placed one palm on Sam's knee and the other on her shoulder, which instantly took the panic down a notch.

"You do, angel. Let's talk about what really happened here."

"What the hell?" Sebastian's big brother was emerging to protect Sam.

"It's OK, Sebastian," Iza said lifting her hand, and with a 'These-aren't-the-drones-you're-looking-for' kind of Jedi-master voice. It worked, because it kept Sebastian, whose hormones were going crazy, from jumping out of his seat.

"Sam," Iza turned to her, "you asked me if you needed to change your relationship with Sebastian. I promised we'd take care of that and that's just what we are going to do now."

"My God, man," Iza said, turning back to Sebastian. Admiration emanated from her now. "You are the full package. What a defender! Are you sure you are gay?"

"No," he said, looking to Sam. "Not sure of anything right now."

"Except how you feel about Sam. If we let you, you'd consume her right now." Sebastian didn't respond but the subtle expression on his face agreed. Iza took a step, drawing the attention away from Sam and onto herself. "You would have the best sex of your life and then you'd wake up tomorrow morning knowing you'd made the worst mistake of your life." Now her voice dropped, "Both of you."

"I see that!" Cindy was amazed.

"And that is best kind." Katriana said, remembering. "A few weeks ago I met someone and we had the same pull. Sometimes it just fun."

"I thought you were married, Katriana." Cindy turned and whispered to her.

"Yes. We have open marriage. Freedom."

"I see," whispered Cindy.

Iza took a step, looking away. "This is what people call 'chemistry' and they confuse this with attraction and genuine love." Now she looked at Sebastian again. "Of course you are gay, angel. Don't let anything, and certainly not a craving, dictate who you are. Only you know who you are."

Sebastian lightly shook his head, "But I don't. Not after that—" His voice trailed off, *know who I am, after that?*

"We unwound who you *thought* you were. Now you will have an easier time *finding who you authentically are*. Otherwise, you wouldn't have looked for the authentic you. In time, life would have made you look, we have just sped this up."

Sebastian sat in Iza's chair with the high back, shifted in his seat and breathed heavily.

"What you both experienced just now was an energetic hole. Like a black hole in space, it wants to suck and pull in whatever is nearest, especially dysfunction. You two are perfect for this reason: Sam the provider of love, Sebastian the provider of protection and reassurance. Deeper still, you both have issues around intimacy, so you share karmatic energy. There is nothing your holes want more than to get filled with the other and this is why you two are so tied, so bonded."

Ugh, Sam noticed the panic she had felt being replaced, *I don't know about this! I don't like this! Holes?* her resistance shouted in her head. She looked to Cindy, the happiest kid in the world's largest human-behavior-candy store. She looked to Sebastian. His nose may have flared with disdain.

"Ok, let's fix those gaping holes. Katriana?"

"Vamos," Katriana said as she stood and motioned for Sam to stand. This way." Katriana took Sam out of the Hawaiian casita. "It would be good, good sex, I know. But tomorrow you be unhappy. Trust me, *yo se*," she said, her voice trailing off as they left the building.

15

Black Hole Healing

"Alright. Dr. Rosenthal, you'll need to stay in the background for this." Iza pointed out a place for Cindy to sit. "Angel, grab those two chairs and place them here in the center of the room."

Sebastian did as he was told, still feeling gruff and tasseled.

"Ready?" she asked. He nodded. She turned the chairs to face each other and she sat, motioning for him to sit too. "Close your eyes. B-r-e-a-t-h-e," she said slowly. "You are feeling a ton of things, most of which are almost foreign to you. Tell me what is going on in you, angel."

Her words alone helped Sebastian realize that she was right, "Yes! How do you know?"

"Don't worry about that right now. Go on."

"I have this anger, this crazy draw to Sam that I've never had, not even the night we might have slept together."

"You didn't angel. Otherwise, you two would be tied together and you're not. Go on."

Sebastian had so many thoughts, feelings and overwhelming charges of energy that he didn't even know where to look in himself. "I.. I..." He looked around, looking for a clue and began to tear up. "I..." now his voice, like a balloon, was deflating. Cindy watched as this big, beautiful, strong man shrank. She looked more closely, not believing her own eyes. He was smaller, shorter.

"What is happening to him? He's..." she doubted her eyes, "...smaller?" She couldn't help herself, she had to ask.

"He's discarding some of the energy he is not."

"You mean he is shrinking?"

"Only for a minute. He's going to fill his own energetic hole now."

The world had been like an echo, present but dull and faded in the background until Iza said these words. Sebastian looked up at her, hopefully and helplessly.

"One last thing. How do you feel?"

"Awful." He opened his eyes.

"Yes, angel. I mean what is missing?" She paused, letting him find out. "Would Sam coming back in the room help?" He nodded yes. "What would she have to do or say or be to make this better?"

"Fascinating," Cindy whispered.

"I feel so empty - it hurts, Iza." Sebastian crumbled and shrunk again.

"It will change, angel. What would Sam do to make it better?"

"She would come and love me. She would tell me that I'm wonderful. She would make me feel like it's OK that I'm gay, that I'm smarter than her and that my mom loves me more than him."

"Fascinating," Cindy whispered more lightly, so as not to intervene.

"Good. Alright. Close your eyes. Picture another you, a perfect you. Maybe it is your mom, maybe it is your God, maybe it is a bigger, stronger Sebastian. You walk in, angel. You see the you sitting here before me. Look at him, smile. Give him whatever he wants or needs. A hug? There," Iza said, watching Sebastian.

She turned to Cindy. "I'm watching his energy. Do you see how he is shifting? When he brought the other him in and when they interacted, Sebastian started to breathe again. He's beginning to shift things."

Cindy stood up and came up behind Iza to observe Sebastian, who was on another planet, completely undisturbed with their talking.

"Now, the bigger Sebastian, talk to the one sitting. Ask what he needs and listen but also watch to see what you think he needs. Tell me."

"He's a good person."

"Yes, of course. He's great. Tell him."

"He is so good at dealing with life, but he's sad. He needs love. He needs to know he's OK."

"Yes. He's just hurt, but you can help. Love him, no matter what. Tell him he's a great person just the way he is."

"It's hard, he's... bad."

"No, angel, no. He was told he was bad. Send him love and you will see that he is good. He is wonderful."

This went on for over 20 minutes. Iza kept guiding Sebastian to conjure the energy of acceptance to counter this energetic hole that craved acceptance. She kept saying that deeper than the reasons not to accept him, he was love and deserving of love or anything else he desired.

"You are doing so well, angel. Let's wrap it up. Look one last time. How are you?"

Sebastian opened his eyes and looked up at Iza. He was surprised. He looked around the room. "Everything looks different!"

"Yes, angel. You have shifted yourself, your energy and that changes how you perceive."

Sebastian looked at Cindy.

"Remarkable!" Cindy looked at Sebastian as though he were a shinny, new thing. "He looks different- How can this be?"

"Sam will be the same. They'll be coming in any time, I'm sure."

Iza stood up, "Let's take a quick break. I'll get Sam and Katriana then we'll meet back in here. Angel, can you put the chairs back?" Sebastian did and then he and Cindy sat and excitedly chatted while Iza stepped out.

"I can't believe it Sebastian, dear! If I hadn't seen it with my own eyes!"

"Hon, I feel different."

Cindy's face lit up with surprise again. "You sound different too! Just when I thought you couldn't get any better!"

"I do?" He looked at his hands, at Cindy and all around. It was a miracle. "I feel so good. I feel light, happy!"

Several minutes later Iza, Sam and Katriana walked back in. Sam looked different too.

"Sam, dear! Wow! You look..." Cindy searched for the right words. She wanted to say "fuller" but was afraid it would be mistaken for "fatter." Still, that's how she looked. "You look- like you are more here. You look amazing!"

"I feel great!" Sam had a vibrant glow about her, "This is incredible! I feel… alive!"

They all sat again and Iza motioned for Sam and Sebastian to sit on the love seat they'd sat at previously. This time though, they weren't lost in each other.

"Now you are bot so differen. How you feel?"

"Still want to jump each other?" Iza taunted.

Sebastian looked at Sam. They no longer looked like they were starved of love.

"No." He smiled, moving freely instead of being locked onto Sam. "I still love her, but I feel- well, it's like I was on a drug before. Now I just love her."

"It is a drug. When you have a hole, it creates an addiction that can be all-consuming and devastatingly destructive. It will cause all sorts of problems in your life until you fill it with the appropriate energy."

"How do you know what the appropriate energy is?" Cindy seemed like the hungry one now. She was hungry for information and to understand. "How did you know how he felt, what he was experiencing? How did you know what to do? How did you know how to handle him and Sam? Could anyone have kissed him?"

"My turn." Katriana said, tired of being quiet, which didn't suit her one bit.

"Iza and I can see the energy. They very connected. Iza could see the *energia* between them, so she know making them kiss would put them at their worse place. Then it a madder of filling the hole. You always fill holes with love, acceptance, approval. Always. People need help knowing how fill whole."

"Fascinating!"

"See now, angel. Do you still feel like you need to change your relationship with Sebastian to save your romance?"

Sam looked to herself. "No," she said, discovering how she now felt. She looked to Sebastian and then back to Iza. "I love Nick. I love Sebastian, but it's different. I can't believe I wanted to have sex with him!"

Sebastian sighed dramatically, "Thanks Love."

"Sorry, but you know what I mean!"

"I know," he chided.

"And I know what you mean, Iza. If we had slept together, it would have ruined so much! I can really see that. Wow though, because at the time, wanting him and that kiss, they felt so good. I can't believe it. I can't figure out what's going on psychologically."

"It's not psychological, angel. It's energetic. Simply speaking, we activated the energy of your holes so that you could fill them yourselves, which makes you more of a whole person."

"That's it!" Cindy said, jumping out of her seat. "That's exactly it! They both look more whole! It's like they were a ghost of themselves before!"

"That's quite literally true. They were missing a part of themselves, so it is a bit like being a ghost.

"Now, the trick is that you have more work to do on yourselves. It's possible that you won't kiss and feel the same attraction again, but whenever you have some of the crazy thoughts, feelings or that pulling in yourself, remember this: that is the black hole pulling. That will be when it is time to fill your black hole again. The black holes don't get filled in one session. You have to continue to feed yourself, to feed your soul."

"Fascinating!"

"Let's break for the day. I'm sure these two need some time to recuperate. This kind of work will wear you out. You'll probably both sleep like babies tonight. Sam, angel, you'll feel more in love with your honey tomorrow too."

"Really?"

"Yes. You are clearing your ability to experience love, so it will be stronger."

"Fascinating!"

♥

Part 2

16

Kissing Therapy

Everyone left the Hawaiian casita. They'd all agreed to get back together in a couple hours. Sebastian had offered to cook, but Iza said he should rest and process the day's events. She and Katriana would make dinner. Sam went to her room to call Nick. Sebastian was about to leave.

"Honey," Iza said, holding him up.

"Honey? I'm no angel anymore? Was that my initiation?" He chuckled.

"No, she wan sometin. When she say 'honey', she want sometin." Katriana spoke as she tidied up the room. Cindy was helping her.

"Honey, William has asked to come back. I'm happy to say I'm at full capacity right now. Can he stay with you at least until the guest space is empty?"

"Sure, hon. Actually," Sebastian smiled, a bit of a devilish look on his face, "I might prefer he stay with me."

"Oh. Uh, angel, I need you to stay celibate until tomorrow when he's here."

Sebastian's expression was a cross between confused and controlled. "Honey, I'm gay. I was looking forward to--" He teased.

"I know, I'm sure." she interrupted. "It's part of the program."

"No problem then, he arrives in the morning. He should be here around 10."

"Ah, perfect." Iza now turned to the ladies. "See how things always line up for me? That will work out perfectly. So, we'll start at

10:00. If he's a bit late, it won't matter. Alright, we'll go take a break and then get dinner going. Bye angel."

"Good bye, my three witches!" Sebastian began walking out and called back, "Miracles, not just magic. My witches perform mi-ra-cles!" He managed to sing "miracles" with a high-pitched flare.

"That's the Sebastian I know and love!" Cindy said, smiling as if she were a cat with cream.

Iza used her sultry voice, "He is yummy! Too bad--" she smirked.

"You two!" Katriana waved them off. "Let's go Iza's house."

"Can you get your energy stuff and silent miracle junk to make him un-gay, dear?" Cindy asked in a provocative voice.

"I thought you were newly married, angel." Iza said, scolding Cindy with her finger.

"Well, Sam sometimes call him a 'cupcake'. I was just wondering what flavor that handsome body is! I can look, you know." Cindy was being uncharacteristically naughty.

"Well, angel, if only. No, we can't un-gay him. That's in God's hands." Iza said, disappointment on her face. "He would be so much fun!"

"Indeed."

"You two! Yuo like cougars! If he available, you would not be so bad." Katriana said slowly, pronouncing her words carefully. "Bad! You two are bad!"

"Yes, dear. But we are bad and he is gay, so there's no harm!" Cindy looked to Iza, "And it is soooo fun to be bad!"

Now all three witches cackled and squealed so loudly everyone on the ranch heard them.

♥

"Honey," Sebastian said looking around, having heard the witches cackling. "I just heard the strangest sound. Anyway," he had just poured himself a glass of iced-tea and was sitting in the big, comfy chair in his casita while on the phone. "William, I'm thrilled that you are coming tomorrow. You haven't met Katriana, she is like a 300 pound gorilla hiding in the body of a loud mouse! And Iza, well, she's a miracle worker. I call them my witches! Today was incredible, so I'm glad you'll be back to see it first-hand!"

"Miracles, witches and a gorilla? How promising! I can't wait to tell you some of what's developed here too. I'm going into a meeting in a minute to finalize and sign contracts!"

"Contracts? Sounds like it's big time! Oh, before I let you go, Iza asked if you can stay with me for now. She's all out of room. You don't mind, do you honey?"

William liked the way Sebastian had just said "honey." Had Sebastian changed his mind about their relationship?

"I can't wait. I'll see you tomorrow. Sweet dreams, tinker bell."

"Sweet dreams- and good luck with those big contracts!"

♥

"Hi Babe!" Nick jumped when he saw that Sam was calling him.

"Hey."

"It's so good to hear from you! You've only been gone a day, but I miss you like crazy, Sam!"

"Oh," Sam smiled, warming up. "It is so good to hear that, to hear you-" her voice trailed off.

"You OK, babe? You don't sound like your usual self. You don't sound like the future Mrs. Andrews!"

"I know." She took a deep breath. "Nick, baby, this seminar is like none I've had before. I'm learning a lot. I mean, a lot! But, it's also a bit uncomfortable."

"What do you mean, babe?" Having listened to his fiancee, Nick was starting to understand that something was wrong. Nervousness edged itself into his room, encroaching on him.

Sam hoped that Cindy wouldn't walk in the room, keeping her phone conversation private. They were sharing the "Green Bamboo" suite. It was small, but perfect for a short-term guest. The quaint room had two single beds, a leather love seat, a leather chair and a simple desk. The desk was under a large, picturesque window facing a rock formation that looked like Mother Nature had carved an abstract sculpture with the wind. The room was beautifully decorated: the walls were a light and comforting shade of sage-green and a photograph of an exquisite bunch of hibiscus flowers complimented the green walls perfectly.

She sighed and leaned back on the bed, but then her reception got scratchy.

"Hold on, let me go to the chair and see if the reception is better." She walked over. The chair was like an inviting teddy bear, hugging her as she sat. Ah, that felt good.

"Baby,"

"Yeah? You're scaring me a bit. What is it?"

"They had me kiss Sebastian."

Braced for a car accident, Nick waited for the crash. Nothing came. "Is that it? What else? Did they have you sleep with him?"

"No, no! What do you think I am? A puppet?"

"No, of course not, babe. It's just that your tone and your words, you were freaking me out!"

"Well, you don't go around kissing other women, do you?" Sam now wondered why Nick wasn't going crazy-mad. *Is this what our relationship will be like, an open one? That'll be the day!* Her mind shouted.

"Babe! What are you saying? No, of course not. Look, I'm not really thrilled to hear you say that you kissed Sebastian, but I'm sure there is more to the story." Then the news, which wasn't a car wreck, but certainly a slap in the face from a tiger with claws, started to sink in. "I'm sure there's a good reason why you have only been gone for one day and you're telling me someone had you kiss Sebastian." And, I thought he was my friend, Nick told himself.

"Baby, I love you. I'm crazy about you, I never stopped thinking about you." She stated with passion. "The workshop is on psychology and energy, as I'd said. Iza, the leader, was showing Sebastian what lust is." Oh, that didn't sound so good! Shit!

Sam could feel Nick's temper flaring. "Those were Iza's words," she said, backing out of it. "Iza says that lust in disingenuous." Sam was getting flustered. On the one hand, she wanted to be honest with Nick, the love of her life, because she didn't want to their engagement period to foster a lie. On the other hand, Iza wasn't trying to cause Sam problems. On the contrary, she'd told Sam that the intimacy she had with Sebastian had to change, for the sake of her relationship with Nick. Besides, the work she'd done with Katriana seemed to change everything. Still, Sam felt guilty.

"I told Iza I was engaged, well, actually she knew. I hadn't told anyone." Sam was trying to explain that Iza wasn't trying to cause Sam and Nick problems, but rather that she was trying to help Sebastian.

"What?" Nick wasn't a man for drama, so he kept calm. He loved Sam with all his heart, like he'd never loved another. He wasn't going to let life just steal her away, especially not to a gay man. None of this made sense.

If Sebastian had wanted Sam for himself, he wouldn't have invited me to Key West. He wouldn't have stepped out of the picture.

No, this didn't make sense, he thought again.

Still, she's only been gone for one day! One day and she wasn't telling her best friend, Sebastian, and business partner, Cindi, that she was engaged; she was kissing her best friend! What the hell was going on out there?

"I'm sorry baby. I wanted to be honest with you, but there's really nothing to be honest about."

"What?" The pitch of Nick's 'what's?' kept increasing in frequency.

"It's one of those things, it made sense here. I think you had to be here. I'm not in love with him, we won't be kissing again. I just wanted to be honest because I love you."

"Ya, I love you too, babe, but I think you hit the nail on the head. I had to be there. I'm flying out." Nick was a man in love. He didn't care what it would cost, he didn't care what was going on. He was going to go out and claim his place next to the woman he loved.

"Oh!" Sam's eyes started to tear up. "Really? That's so romantic! You'd come out to be with me? You're jealous?"

"Babe, I love you. You mean more to me than anything in my life ever has. I'm not jealous, but I need to come and be with you, see what's going on." Nick got up and opened his suitcase. As he spoke, he walked over to his computer and opened it, getting ready to buy a ticket west once he was off the phone.

"Baby, it's so not necessary." Sam was starting to think that the romantic notion was necessary though. "You don't have to drop everything and fly out, but if you do, I want to show you a restaurant that has a beautiful garden where we could get married!"

Nick stopped, his finger in the air. He was about to hit the 'Enter' key to awaken his computer, but now, as if he had just been given the launch code to push the button for a nuclear strike and then told to hold, he processed all the stress. OK, I'm marrying a lunatic. He smiled, his uncle Arthur had always said that Nick would know he was in love when the woman didn't make sense to him - and - drove him crazy. I'm crazy in love, he told himself.

"Babe, let's get married." He said, his heart restored.

"You already proposed, Nick. We set a date for next April."

"No, you found a place. Let's start to plan it and get married in a few weeks."

"Aw!" Now Sam was hit by a truck of love. She couldn't believe what Nick was saying. She couldn't believe how in love he was with her, Nick, this magnificent, handsome and big-hearted man. If this was a dream, Sam never wanted it to end.

His bride was speechless, but he could feel her heart inside of him and her heart was overwhelmed with love. Nick was thrilled. They had it all. He could see that their love was like no other and that it would never end. They would live happily ever after.

Nick pushed 'Enter,' booting up his computer to book his ticket.

17

What's Brewin' In The Kitchen

A great dinner was being planned for the next evening. Iza, Cindy and Katriana spent over an hour in Iza's not-so-big kitchen preparing a salad, pasta, chicken in marinara sauce, asparagus and more for tonight. At the same time they also prepared items for tomorrow's dinner party. That meant a lot of bumping elbows and near-miss accidents. Cramped or not, Iza enjoyed having other cooks in the kitchen.

There were also a lot of questions from Cindy, "So, could anyone have kissed Sebastian?"

"No, angel. Don't say anything, but tomorrow he'll do the same with William."

"Oh." Then Cindy would ponder what she'd been told, reconfiguring and shifting how she now saw human behavior. She didn't know what 'energy' meant still, and she wasn't sure how to describe it, but this she knew: she'd seen Sebastian shrink and then get bigger, brighter. She'd seen Sam glowing. Yes, she found this all fascinating, her new favorite word!

"How did you know that he and Sam didn't sleep together? You sounded like you really knew."

"I tell you." Katriana stopped chopping onions to talk. "There was no sexual energy bind in them. They not connected."

"Not connected?"

"Sex connects people energetically. You connected for life. I don let that stop me from fun. There was a hot guy a couple week ago."

"Keep chopping," Iza directed. "And it's cord. We are connected to everyone, but not corded in. You are connected by a cord to those you are sexually intimate with or with children."

Cindy stopped dead in her tracks.

"Honey," Iza looked to Cindy and the salad, "keep cutting. That salad isn't going to put itself together."

"It's just that, well, I believe you. Many of my clients, I've seen them change their behaviors once they sleep with their lovers. Before that, they tend to be more rational, more like themselves. They sleep with him or her, and all hell breaks loose!" Cindy thew her hand in the air for emphasis. "Then they want more, they become erratic with their lover or they sabotage the relationship. Ladies, are you saying that it is because they are energetically bound?"

"*Sí y no.*" Katriana stopped again and put her knife down. "See, when they go that deep and connect sexually, they also go deeper in themselves. Now their needs come up. Now their unresolved childhood issues come up. They lose control. Sometimes they lose control together because they have to have each other - like Sam and Sebastian were jesterday. They would have let Iza marry them if she offer. Other time, people become drive by their un-resolve issue."

A light bulb went off in Cindy's head. "Ah! That's why their inner child comes out!"

"*Sí.*"

"My God! That's why sleeping with some people isn't as problematic, right? You said Sebastian had to kiss the right person."

"*Sí.*"

"Well, if you slept with someone a couple of weeks ago, aren't you tied to them now?"

"No. Iza and I know how to keep our energy, how to undo energy if we have sex. And I like have sex with the right people!"

"Keep chopping. Ladies, stay focused." Iza said, authoritatively waving the cooking spoon in her hand that she was using to stir. "Cindy, angel, yes. Sex will cord you into anyone you sleep with but when the dysfunction matches like puzzle pieces, as it did for Sam and Sebastian, that's when people think they are in love. That's when they have to have each other. The hole is in their energy and it pulls to get attention. It needs what it needs. However, it never heals unless you give what is needed self-to self. People think that love will heal them, that Mr. or Mrs. Right will make them happy and whole. As you know, it never does. Still, the hole craves what it is lacking.

"Now, let's focus on dinner. Cindy, angel, you should come back again soon. Talking with you is great, it's fun."

"*Sí*, we love how into all of this you are." Katriana said, but then quickly went back to chopping to avoid Iza's cooking command.

"We do. Most people aren't interested in human or spiritual development to the degree that we are. We should coordinate our schedules and you should come back to gain more."

"*Sí*," Katriana said, stopping again. "She should come for long weekend."

"Yes, I would like that. I'd like to gather enough information to change my practice and write a new book."

"*Sí*. You should. *¡Que magnífico!*"

"We'll plan it. I'm sure coordinating schedules will take some effort. Ok, now, witches, work some magic in this kitchen! I'm going to invite Jonathan tomorrow night, who is in the Surfing casita, the white door. I think we have enough food."

"*Sí*, it would be good see him. I have not see him in a while."

"Tell him that we'll have a-" Iza cut Cindy off.

"Don't say 'fascinating' again, angel!"

"*Sí*! Say it!"

"Promise a fascinating time." Cindy said, daring Iza.

"Oh, you are a witch!" Iza glared. Then she laughed.

Sebastian had showed up early to dinner to ask Iza if she needed any help. She jumped on the offer, saying that his other nincompoop witches had dallied away prep time, so she could use help setting the table up for dinner.

"You know where the table is past the patio. The cushions for the chairs are in my attic on the left. Please set the table for us. I invited Jonathan, in the casita, but he wasn't able to make it. You still haven't met him, have you? He'll come to the dinner party tomorrow, you'll meet then."

Sebastian cleaned the table, placed the pillows and then set the table. The sun would set in about half an hour. Iza's land was breathtaking. After setting the table, he pulled a chair over to give himself a vista of her land. He could see the four casitas and the fountain in the middle of the garden. Off a ways to his left there were beautiful, large trees and an endless sky behind them. He also saw a small path just before the parking lot, to his right, and wondered where it went. He hadn't taken the time to explore the land yet. Maybe he and William would walk around and spot the coyotes they heard howling at night, the jackrabbits that Iza said they ate or the bats she said often took off at sunset.

He took a deep breath. He liked it here. Iza was amazing; Katriana was wise. *Witches in my life? Who knew?* He had had a good sense about Iza the first time they'd met. After today, he knew his hunch about Iza and heading west was right. There was something more to be gained here, on the ranch, from the witches and from this *enchanted* land. *Today has been spectacular, save feeling like the world was coming to an end,* Sebastian thought. *It was the most amazing and the scariest day* - Sebastian felt a stirring in his heart, no his soul. He'd never felt anything like that before. His soul felt… bigger. Lighter. "Ahhh!" He stretch his arms out, triumphantly.

Sebastian watched the sky slowly darken, *life is grand.* He took a deep breath of the oncoming nigh, *now I can start finding my passion.* He sat with the feeling of a warm heart and a happy soul before he was soon joined by the dinner party guests. Delicious food, drink and company under the stars was like love from heaven kissing them all goodnight.

Part 2

18

Kissing Frogs

"Good morning, Iza," Sebastian said, knocking on her door and opening it.

"Oh, hello angel! How did you sleep?"

"Like a baby! I couldn't wake up, so I slept in an hour. I guess you were right, I think yesterday exhausted me."

"You're just processing and it happens at different levels down to a cellular one."

Sebastian raised his eyebrows in surprise.

"Are you making breakfast?" she asked.

"Yes, but I also wanted to let you know that Sam will leave around noon to get Nick. We thought the 'Moon Day' was just one day."

"Normally it is. It just came together over two," Iza said, nonchalantly.

"Do I owe you any extra, hon? For the second day?"

"We'll work it out later, angel. I need to jump in the shower to get ready."

❤

Refreshed and ready to go, they all found themselves in the Hawaiian Casita again. William walked in right behind them.

"*Buenos días,*" began Katriana. "We glad you made it, William."

"Hello everyone. I'm glad to be back. Too bad I missed yesterday."

"Is OK. First, welcome." Kia, Katriana's large dog, sat up staring at the guests as if he were inspecting each one, especially the newcomer.

"William, you here now. Can we jump right in?"

He nodded, "Yes, please." Sam gave Sebastian a knowing look, saying "Poor guy, doesn't know what's coming!"

"OK. William, as you know, we working on Sebastian."

Wide-eyed, William was checking out 'the witches'. He was enthusiastic to see what would come since Sebastian had been so thrilled yesterday.

"We are working to *des-hacerlo*, to undo him so that he can bring his energy together."

"*¿Deshacerlo? No me había dicho, ¡qué placer!*"

Everyone stared at William!

"No way!"

"Hon, you didn't tell me you spoke Spanish!"

"His accent is as good as hers!"

"Oh," William said, delighted. "I've surprised you all." Then he looked to Sebastian, "I guess it just hadn't come up."

"What did you say?" Sam asked.

"Undo him? I hadn't been told. What a pleasure!"

"Honey, how do you speak Spanish so well?" Sebastian looked to William, more interested.

"I'm from Puerto Rico. Well, and Miami. I grew up in both places."

"*O, qué bueno, ahora tengo con quien hablar!*" Katriana sang, feeling at home. Now she had someone to speak to, she'd said in Spanish. William's Spanish was like music to her ears.

"I better take over here," Iza said watching things spinning out of control. "Congratulations, angel. Now, please stand up in the middle of the room. Just give yourself a minute to adjust to being up there." Iza looked to everyone else. "I know you are all excited, but silence, please. Let's get started."

William felt foolish, but only for a moment before he realized that he was having another unimaginable experience. "I feel pretty!" He said joking.

"You are, angel." Iza turned to Sebastian. "OK, go ahead. Eyes. Watch each other. And no words."

Once again, Sebastian stood, on display. He hadn't thought he'd be uncomfortable this time. Still, he looked into William's eyes.

"Breath, angels. It will help you settle faster."

Sebastian and William smiled at each other - while four women stared at them. They tried taking a few deep breaths and found that, sure enough, that began to settle them.

"William, angel, Sebastian is going to kiss you when I tell him. Is that alright?"

William looked at Iza smiling, "If you insist."

"Great. Close your eyes and just be there with Sebastian." A few seconds went by. "Sebastian."

Sebastian knew his cue. He leaned over to kiss William but stopped half way there. He looked at William to see what it was that felt different than it had with Sam. Then he put his arms around him and kissed him. This kiss was deep, the way yesterday's had been, but there were no sparks, there was no awakened hunger. There was no painful craving. Instead, the day grew dark. Suddenly, a summer storm shifted the mood bringing the focus inward. Sebastian leaned back, stopped hugging William and, when his eyes were open, he smiled at him. A new, different smile.

"You made it rain! OK, tell us about it - Sam, can you get them each a chair?"

They both Sat and then Sebastian looked at Iza. "Honey, how did you know?"

"That's my job, angel. How was it?"

"Gentle. Wonderful." He reached out to hold William's hand. "I have feelings for this man I didn't know about. He moves me." William smiled and lit up. Sebastian had never been so flattering before.

"Are you ready to jump him?" Iza asked.

"I could be, I mean, he does have a hard ass - and a great wand in front!" Sebastian never broke his gaze upon William.

"¡Cierto!" Katriana exclaimed.

"Hello," Sebastian said, extending his hand. "I'm Sebastian. I don't believe we've met before and I'd like to get to know you." He gave him a once-over. "I like what I see and I'd like to see more. Won't you go to dinner with me?"

William's energy toward Sebastian was opening more now. "You're a sweet-talker, eh? Dinner, I'd love to. But I don't go home with strangers after a first date, just so you know." William's words were flirtatious, gentle and seductive. He was challenging Sebastian, playing hard to get.

Sebastian lifted his hand and placed it on William's face then he leaned in and kissed him again. "How did I not see you before?"

"I'm glad you see me now. And, you'll have to wine me and dine me to make it up to me."

"It will be my pleasure."

"OK, you too, everyone's in love and I have no one. This is about all I can take!" Iza said. "Where's my love?"

She asked rhetorically, but William answered. "My door swings both ways. If things don't work out on my date…"

"Are you trying to make me jealous?" Sebastian asked, his voice getting husky, but playful.

William raised a flirtatious shoulder in response.

Iza didn't miss a beat. "Really? Well, I'll take it. If things don't work out on your date, my house is the dark one, at the end of the path." Iza fanned herself, as if cooling down her hormones. "Alright, enough fun," she said, but she blew William a kiss. "Now, back to business. Cindy, do you see it? William is the feminine, Sebastian is the masculine. Sebastian has to be careful because William has a lot of offers coming his way - and I'm not talking about mine. William has a great use of both flows. He is predominantly the feminine, creative flow and it is going to bring him success."

"Did you tell him, hon?" William asked Sebastian.

"No darling," he said, interest emanating from his eyes.

"I'm 'darling' now! I like that. How did you know Iza? I got a great big contract," he turned to Sebastian, "maybe I should take you to dinner and you can give me dessert because I'm in the money!"

"Congratulations, darling," Sebastian said, hugging William. He found himself wanting to touch William a lot more since the kiss. Everyone else congratulated William too.

"The script is called 'Lonely At Dawn'. I'll tell you all about it later. Anyway, they liked it so much they asked for a sequel. I'm going to be busy writing."

"Sebastian, how do you feel about William? Are you hot and horny for him, the way you were for Sam?"

"He did warm my body that way - but it wasn't like yesterday. Today my heart is open, I'm in my heart so much more. It's like the world is calm with William by my side."

"He could complete you."

"Yes! That's it. Also, William and I would *make love*, not have sex."

"William, yesterday we showed Sebastian what the addictive craving is with Sam's help. More specifically, yesterday we showed Sebastian what an energetic hole is like. He learned about the addiction that the hole brings forth and the way it can override and drive his behavior to the point of making him desire a woman instead of a man. This is true for anyone; anyone will have their energetic holes craving a hole-filler. Sebastian experienced it. So did Sam." She looked to measure William's reaction. "Angel, I hope that doesn't upset you. I'll use anything to help someone see and heal themselves; Sam was perfect for activating Sebastian's hole due to their co-dependency."

William sat silent, raising an eye brow and trying to understand all that had happened yesterday and was happening now. "I'm a little surprised, but I'm OK. If it helped him, that's great."

"Good. Glad you aren't worried. He and Sam have begun to heal this hole. Now they are freer to engage themselves in their romances. They are freer to seek genuine love, and not hole-filling. Yes, I know how that sounds!" She let everyone chuckle.

"Now Sebastian understands gender flow and he understands the attraction he'd had to Sam, the genuine attraction he has to you and, most importantly, he understand that it doesn't really matter whether he is with a man or woman. It's all about his partnering with a feminine, since he tends to be masculine. Happiness and fulfillment are all about finding love and not being driven by an endless addiction."

Now Iza turned to Sebastian. "Things have changed. You could now be more intimate in a relationship and with yourself." He nodded in agreement. "You can be yourself in a relationship, the way you just felt with William."

♥

Half the morning was gone and the rest of the time they worked on healing holes again and answering questions. Iza and Katriana moved around helping Sam, Sebastian and William with the hole healing as well as answering Cindy's questions.

Iza was talking with Cindy and Katriana was engaged with William. Sebastian saw a chance to speak privately with Sam.

"How are you Love? What do you make of all of this?"

Sam smiled at Sebastian. "It's been amazing. The work we did - the kiss. Are you over it, Sebastian?"

"That's what I wanted to talk to you about."

"Well, I guess it doesn't matter. Nick is flying out, so we'll be staying in the Bamboo room. I want him to see that restaurant you took me to, I'd like to get married there."

Sebastian looked down, nodding his head. "Yeah, why is he flying out again?"

"He wanted to see what was going on. I told him they made us kiss."

"Did you tell him what the kiss was like?" he asked, looking up at her.

"No, no need to upset him."

"Oh, I think you did that, Love. Kole? Flying out? Sounds like my friend is running out to make sure I don't steal you away."

"Yeah, well, he doesn't understand the work we did to heal the hole." They both nodded. "Is it healed all the way for you? Iza had said we might need more healing."

"I don't know. I mean, I'm more interested in William than I've ever been."

"Yeah, I'm excited about Nick flying out."

"Are we happy? Are you happy, Love?"

"Yeah. Sebastian-" she hesitated.

"Yes, Love?"

"I'm madly in love with you. Ha!" She hit his arm in jest. "Point for me. No, I get like ten points on your scoreboard."

"Good one, Love. You had me fooled for a minute there. I'll give you the points," and he raised his hand, marking a point on his invisible scoreboard.

"Well, I think I'm going to see where things go with William. He's handsome, right?"

"Yeah, right. I mean, not as handsome as Nick or you, but yeah."

Sebastian turned to look at William. He and Katriana were wrapped up in their conversation on healing the energetic holes. "He's cute. I'm impressed that he got a script accepted. Imagine, a movie that he wrote will be made."

"That's cool, Sebastian. Nick and I are going to get married when the restaurant has an opening, I think. So, I'll be hanging around. Do you think William will be around to attend the wedding?"

"I thought you were getting married next year."

"Nick surprised me, said he's crazy in love with me and that he wants to do it as soon as possible."

He is afraid I'm going to steal her away. He turned to look at William again. *I think I could be falling for William.* "I hope so, Love. I hope William's here to go to the wedding with me."

19

Sebastian's Morning After

That evening Sebastian carved out alone time with William. Sam and Nick were exhilarated with the idea of moving the wedding up and practiced for the honeymoon. Sebastian and William had been spending some time talking with the witches but soon went back to the casita.

Sebastian undressed William with his eyes the minute they walked into his casita. He closed the door, locked it and then turned to William.

"Wow, tinker bell. Can I ring your bell tonight? Or should I play hard to get?" William floated over to the couch and unbuttoned the top buttons of his shirt.

He pat the space next to him. Sebastian dimmed the lights and lit a candle. He took off his shirt and sat next him. At first they gently kissed but in no time at all, they were consuming each other.

Until the next morning when they talked.

♥

Sebastian was beside himself. His mind now swam with frustration and confusion. How could William be bisexual? And he'd been seeing someone? When Sebastian had found out that it was Katriana- it was like a line had been crossed. Sebastian couldn't believe that he'd taken a leap of faith by sleeping with William, and it had turned out to be even worse than Roby, who had betrayed him and broken his heart. At least Roby had always been gay. At least with Roby he'd never thought that he could build a life. He thought he was in love and he'd been having fun with Roby, but nothing else.

The problem was that after everything Iza had told Sebastian, after kissing Sam and William in the Hawaiian Casita, Sebastian had opened his heart and *believed* that he could have love. He had believed that he could have a future with a partner.

He came out of the bathroom. William was already dressed. He approached Sebastian, but Sebastian put his hand up, stopping him.

"Leave."

"Honey, Tink. I don't understand. This doesn't change anything. Sebastian, I've liked you since the first time I met you. I still like you. Last night was amazing."

"You should have told me that you've been seeing someone *before* we made love. And you certainly should have told me that it was a woman!" Sebastian felt crossed. Double crossed- and betrayed. "Get out!" His command came from deep inside of him, as if he were a lion whose roars come from a chest the size of a cave.

William hadn't really unpacked, so grabbing his things and putting them in his bag was fast. He left the bedroom and then Sebastian heard him leave the casita.

Sebastian now stood naked, his towel wrapped around his waist. He'd showered to try to calm down and to try to wash away the betrayal. He had chosen his lovers so carefully his whole life that there had only been a handful of men. He couldn't believe that William was now on his list.

He thought about what Iza and Katriana had said, that you become corded into anyone you sleep with. Sebastian would have never, never slept with William, had he known. Yes, William's withholding of information was unforgivable. Sebastian did not sleep with men who were screwing other men. He had too much self-respect for that- so he'd missed out on a lot of lovers, but he didn't care. He wasn't going to lower his standards. Not realizing what he was getting into last night, his standards felt like they were six feet under.

He sat on the edge of the bed. He refused to cry, hardly ever did. It was a point of weakness, one which his father had always looked for because once he'd gotten Sebastian crying as a boy, he knew he'd broken him.

"Damn!" He grabbed the closest thing, a pillow, and threw it across the room. "I should not have listened to Iza! I know better!" He scolded himself. *I know better*, he thought again. *I've always know what was right for me, why the fuck did I listen?* He began beating the bed, letting his anger out. "Why did I listen?"

He thought about the kiss with Sam.

Sam! He got up and went to his cell phone and texted her.

"Luv, can u talk? bad. Fight w Will."

He put his phone down and walked back into his bedroom to put boxers and pants on. He walked into the bathroom to comb his hair. His eyes were red. No doubt, he figured it was because he was seeing red. He went back to his phone to text Sam again to say he needed another a tequila night when he heard her voice at the door.

"Sebastian?"

He walked to the door. "Come in." She walked in. She hadn't seen his casita yet and noticed how cute it was. She also noticed how half-naked he was. Sebastian was getting softer, meaning he had extra padding around his waist, but his broad shoulders, muscular arms and his chest! Sam had never been so aware of his masculine form, not even at the beach in St. Martin.

"What happened, cupcake?"

Sebastian leaned in and quickly kissed Sam, just as he'd done when he'd first gotten to Philly to see her.

"Why did you do that? Now it's weird! And Nick is in our room!"

"I had to." He stepped back, grabbed her hand and led her to the couch. "Don't be mad. Please, Sam, I need you. Don't be mad."

"OK, OK cupcake."

"Don't call me that." He said, walking to the kitchen. "I hate it. I'm a man, not a goddamn pastry."

"Oh." *Did I just get off the tea cup ride?* at Disney, her spinning head asked. "What?"

"Call me something else Sam!" he said, raising his voice. He put water on to boil to make tea and then walked back over to Sam. "I'm sorry."

"No, it's OK. I can see that something is wrong. Really wrong. I've never seen you like this, Sebastian."

He sat by her. She rested her hand on his arm, his muscular arm.

"What's going on - honey?"

"Don't call me that."

"Pumpkin? Dear?"

"I hate it."

"Wanker?" They both laughed.

"That's better, Love."

"'Love'. I've always liked that you called me 'Love'. Makes me feel like we're, uh," she said, reaching for words to describe the feeling. "Connected."

He looked up at her from a soft place. "You can try calling me that."

"Can I? I'm engaged." She took in a breath, as if something hurt. "OK, how's this? Love, you need to put a shirt on and tell me what happened."

"Oh, yeah, sorry." He got up and went to his room, she followed. He opened the closet and reached for a red button up.

"No, that one," she pointed. "Blue. It brings out your eyes." That didn't sound like something an engaged woman would say. "The red's all wrong for you," she added, trying to sound like a friend and not someone watching his broad shoulders.

He sat on the bed and held her hand. She sat with him.

"William-" He backed up to start from the beginning of the story. "Love, William and I had sex last night and this morning he told me that he's been seeing someone else."

"Oh!" She squeaked. "No."

"It's gets worse. I've only had a handful of lovers, Sam. I thought things could really work with him, especially after these last two days."

"Oh my god, what a romantic you are." Her voice was soft. Her eyes grew deep with emotion.

"And, he's the wanker. He's been seeing a woman."

"What?"

"He told me he's bisexual. Sam, I would have never slept with him. I'm so angry- and betrayed. So heart-broken."

"I've never seen you hit by anything. Wow. Something deeper is going on; you've been different since you came here. Maybe you should speak with Iza, Love."

"Don't call me that." He looked up to meet her eyes. "It's not working. It's taking me back to that damned kiss. And I don't want to talk with Iza, I think this is all because of her."

"Yes, it has been intense." She paused, hearing what he'd just said. "Damned kiss?"

"Love, it's driving me crazy. I feel like Iza opened something in me that was never there before." Now he stood up. "Maybe you should go, Sam."

"Why sweetheart?"

"Don't call me that."

"Why Sebastian?"

"I like the way you say my name," he said, tilting his head to the side as though her words ran him over. "And if you don't go, I'm going to give in and kiss you again."

"But, Nick-" she said, not moving.

"Sam, I need you. You are so beautiful." He sat by her, put his hand up to her face.

"No, Sebastian, I'm not."She felt her cheeks getting warm.

"Love, you are." He reached behind her and pulled her hair loose from it's bun, letting it fall. He caressed her face. "Sam, something is going on, something I don't understand and I can't control." That was his last warning.

He took a deep breath, trying to gather his strength but when he opened his eyes, he saw her again.

"I just don't understand. I've always thought you were beautiful and that you hide your beauty-"

"You do?"

"But since the kiss, you're gorgeous," Sebastian's breathing was getting heavy. "That kiss," he trailed off as he leaned back. Then he looked into her eyes again.

"That's it!" He stopped trying to stop himself. Hell, she was still here and he'd told her to leave.

"What the hell did Iza do to me? To us? Sam, I still think I'm gay, but I-"

Sam leaned in, interrupting him and they kissed quickly.

They looked at each other. Hunger and lust were beginning to consume them.

"I know,- Love." She said.

"I have to-" his breath had quickened so that he could hardly breath. And that was all he could take, that was all she could take. She no longer had the excuse that Nick had abandoned her; she no longer was the psychological mess from the year's earlier issues. She was out of excuses - and still, she had to.

"Sam-"

Her eyes were on his lips and he finally leaned forward and kissed her passionately. He leaned her back on the bed as they embraced and kissed so hard, so hungrily that their mouths would soon turn red. Sebastian wasn't thinking at all. He let his body take over and one hand rose to cover and fondle her breast. They both moaned and, without the audience from two days ago, this kiss was more deeply reaching than the previous one. They had kissed before in St. Martin, but they'd been drinking and, frankly, neither of them remembered what it was like.

This was as if they were kissing for the first time, because it was the first time they let themselves be genuine about their desire for one another.

Sebastian pulled away and fell over on the bed next to Sam. He turned to face her.

"We can't."

"No," she said. "Not with Nick here." She looked into his eyes. "Love,"

Her words were like an intoxicating spell so he pulled her down to him and he kissed her passionately again. Then he stopped.

"Nick will wonder where you are." He said, pulling himself away.

"Yes, we have to stop."

"Sam." They sat up on the bed. He stood and reached for her hand and led her to the couch in the living room. The tea kettle was whistling, so he turned it off and then sat on the couch next to Sam.

"The first time I saw you I knew you were special. Sam, I want you. You're my family. I know you're engaged and I really- I'm gay."

"It doesn't feel like it to me," she teased lightly, still trying to catch her breath.

"I need to sit with this because if you want me half as much-"

"I do." A tear formed in Sam's eye.

"Oh, Love," he said, embracing her.

"I love when you call me that." Sam was now crying. "I feel so bad, Sebastian. I love Nick, I do. But I love you more. I always have, just in a different way- which is becoming so irresistible."

Sebastian was coming to his senses. He embraced Sam, being the protector that he was, and that she loved. "Sam," he said, gently lifting her chin and kissing her lips. "Sam." He kissed her again, opening his mouth. Tasting her as she felt his powerful lips, as her body began to heat up again and as her heart opened. Sebastian had a way of calming Sam and making her feel so safe, so loved, so cherished.

"OK," he said, pulling away from the kiss. "Love, I'm gay, but I want to know." He stared at her. "I want to know why I want to kiss you, why you touch my soul."

"Sebastian?" Sam couldn't believe what he'd just said. "I- you touch my soul too. I've never felt that before. Maybe Katriana was right, maybe we are connected beyond anything we can see or that we know about."

"I know you have to go," he said, still holding her and she nodded in agreement. "But, this feels so incredible, Sam. I've never been attracted to a woman before." He looked up to the ceiling, "And, God! I want you."

Sam reached for his face and pulled it in closer to her, kissing him again.

"Sebastian, I'm scared. Where do we go from here? Are we going to-- but you're..."she didn't want to say it. "Are we ruining our lives? My wedding? I'm scared."

"No, Love, don't be scared. You're always so up tight- which I love about you." He sighed. "I know what you are saying though. Where do we go from here? Kiss me again."

"No, I'm risking the man of my dreams by being here with you."

"I wouldn't do this lightly. Love, I've never touched a woman's breast before. I am mad about you. I want you. Mmm." He moaned with sexual frustration. "Love, I would never want to hurt you. I'm confused too, I still swear to you that I'm gay- and I'm still upset about the whole William thing."

"Sebastian, the way we feel, the things that are going on and -" She paused. "But I can not walk away from this. I've never been so drawn, and I like it." Now she bit her lip. "I don't think you can say you are gay anymore. You might be bi, like-"

"No! Love, don't say it! I can't be bi."

"Why not? And what do you call kissing and fondling me?"

"Love, I call it a spell. You've cast a spell making me desire you." That was all it took for them to kiss deeply again.

"Sebastian, I don't want to lose you. You're my best friend." She stood up.

"Love, Sam, you will never lose me. I'll try not to kiss you in front of Kole."

Sam walked to the door and opened it. "I'll see you later," she said with love-filled eyes.

"Go, Love. I don't want to be close to you at the door because I'll kiss you again and, with any luck, Kole will be walking by. Now," he said, looking down at his lap, "I need a cold shower." He looked up at her, "Join me?"

"Don't invite me! It's tempting."

"Next time I may need to thrust myself into you," he warned, almost feeling her.

"Ahh," she moaned, almost having felt it. "You're... I need to talk with my therapist!"

"Cindy? No!"

"I'm joking, sort-of. Who will I talk to? You?"

"Of course, Love. You've always appreciated my insights on you and your patients. And I have some new insights for you," his voice was lusty.

"Ugh!" She smiled. She blew him a kiss then stepped out and closed the door.

Sebastian sighed and fell back into the couch. What the hell was going on? He had to figure some things out. He was a gay man! Always had been! So, why was Sam suddenly bringing new life and excitement to his world? Hell, why was Sam now the center of his universe? He was mad as hell at Iza for all of this, but at the same time, maybe he should go to her. She'd probably know how to help.

He tried doing the healing exercises she'd taught him. Then he tried again, and again.

Getting nowhere, he finally gave up and went to the bedroom to masturbate, thinking about Sam.

20

Dinner Under The Stars

Tonight's celebration was about the completion of Sebastian's 'Moon Day,' but truly, Iza took advantage of any excuse to have guests. She carried dessert toward the group, but stopped to look out to the two tables placed side by side to accommodate everyone outside. The table was lively with all her guests. She loved having people over but it never happened as often as she'd like. Nowadays people always went out to eat at great, but impersonal restaurants. They hardly ever went to one-another's homes and they rarely ever enjoyed home-cooked meals. Iza always wondered where people found the small fortunes to pay for such over-priced meals.

She was bringing dessert over, but she stopped to watch the party. Jonathan, who lived in the Surfing Casita, had brought a friend, Eric. Kole, who Sam called Nick, had arrived and he sat to Sam's left; Sebastian sat to her right and then Cindy. Iza noticed that William wasn't next to Sebastian, but in between Cindy and Katriana's seat.

"*¿Qué pasa?* Why you not walking? The ice-cream is going to melt before it on the pie."

"Look at that, Katriana. Sam has those two hunks, one on either side, and they both adore her."

"Oh, yes. They do anything for her."

"It's not fair. She's lovely, but so weak."

"Yes, but she feminine and they both masculine, so they like her." Katriana put the ice-cream down on a ledge. She put her hand up to Iza's arm. "Listen, remember I tell you I had great sex partner? A handsome young man?"

"Yes, you lucky bitch. Rubbing it in?" she semi-joked.

"No, no. It was William!"

"What?"

"Yes. William. He come to my casita. He and Sebastian, uh, I think broke up. William ask me if he stay with me. I like him so I said 'Claro.'"

"Really? No wonder Sebastian's energy is more tied up with Sam tonight." Iza was getting the picture now.

"Oh. You think something between them?"

"I don't know. Her fiancé is here, but they are very bound."

"Sí, energetically, he sending her sparks."

"Where's that dessert?" Jonathan called.

"Coming!" Iza called and they both walked over.

Sebastian stood and collected the dinner plates. "Iza, dinner under the stars just doesn't get old."

"No, angel. It's always full of surprises too. How are you doing since the Moon Day?"

"I'm great, no complaints. I'll take the dishes into the kitchen."

"No, angel. Don't worry about them."

"Please, it's no biggie. Besides, hon, there's no room out here."

"I'll help you," Sam sweetly offered. She turned to Nick, "Baby, I'll be right back."

They carried the plates into the kitchen and put them down. Their hands weren't free for half a second before they kissed deeply.

"I missed you today," they both said at the same time.

Sebastian began rinsing the dishes to occupy himself; to keep himself from Sam. "Do you think we can get some time alone tomorrow?"

"I'll try. We're supposed to go to La Posada tomorrow."

"Can I come?"

"Really, love?" Sam asked, surprised. "Sure, Nick won't mind."

"I'm sure I'll find an opportunity to kiss you tomorrow too. Might feel you up again while I'm at it, Love."

"Stop, sweetheart. I'm starting to feel guilty."

"Don't call me that."

"Alright already!"

♥

Back at the table Jonathan was telling Cindy all about his art exhibit in one of the galleries that represented him. He had been in Portland.

"Yeah, it's crazy out there. It's fun too. Anyway, my art was very well received and, what means most to me- I sold seven paintings!"

"That's fabulous, dear."

"You have no idea! Eric went with me this time. He's got quite the head for business, and he wanted to see Portland."

"Don't believe I'll be doing any business there after all." Eric said.

Katriana saw a spark in Eric. "What you do?" she asked, joining the conversation.

"I'm a businessman. I own a few companies." Eric looked at Katriana observing her small frame and big presence carefully. Katriana looked right back, seeing something special in him. Eric was tall, probably a whole head taller than Katriana. He had short, dark styled hair, as you would expect from a businessman. Out under the stars they were surrounded by nature. The tables stood on a deck. Beyond the deck nothing was landscaped. Nature decorated with a few tall trees, several shrubs and small boulders. Eric looked to be in his 50's, maybe early 60's and he, too, had so much presence that he looked as pronounced and heavy as one of the small boulders. Not that he was fat; he just looked like a significant force of nature. Katriana could sense wisdom and understanding within him.

"I am like Iza. My specialty is dreams." This caught Eric's attention.

"Yes, she's a great dream interpreter." William said, gaining interest in the conversation. "She interpreted my dream from last night."

"No, I told you. *No es interpretar.*" She told William. Now she turned to Eric. "I speak the language of energy. Dreams are energy and you must know sensation of energy to know what a dream is truly about."

Eric nodded in agreement. "I like that, Katriana. I've always been great at business but the more I learn about energy, the better my businesses do."

"*¡Claro!*" Katriana said. She smiled at William and then looked over to Iza. "Iza, *dale* desert, pie to Eric."

Iza turned from the conversation she'd been having with Cindy and Jonathan. "Pie? Ice-cream, angel?"

Eric hadn't met Iza tonight, save being introduced, because she'd been in the kitchen and at the other end of the table. His eyes met hers and she instantly got his attention. "If you recommend it, Iza. What kind of name is that?"

"Come on over here, angel. I'll serve your pie and tell you." She smiled flirtatiously, as she did with all men, regardless. Eric stood up and came over. Iza looked to him, he had presence in his cowboy hat and mustache. *Rugged,* she thought. "Here, let's sit on the bench. Are you into spirituality, angel?"

"Yes, Iza. That's how I know Jonathan."

"Do you live in town? I give a weekly meditation class, you should come."

♥

On the other side of the table, Nick and Sam were talking about possibilities for themselves. After hearing about Sebastian and William getting together last night, Nick - or Kole - was feeling comfortable with things. He had also talked with Sebastian, which made him more comfortable. After all, he and Sebastian had met in New York and they had planned to be business partners. Additionally, it was Sebastian who had brought Sam and Kole back together. Nick had nothing to worry about and there had been no need to fly out.

"Babe, I haven't had a chance to tell you," he said to Sam, stroking her hair. "I interviewed for a job, a great position, and I should be hearing back in a day or two."

"Really? Wow, Nick. Why didn't you tell me?"

Katriana called over, "Kole, you want pie and ice-cream? I have William take it to you."

"Share babe?" Nick asked Sam, knowing that she always wanted just a few bites. She smiled. "Yes, thanks-" he hesitated, having forgotten Katriana's name.

115

He was having a hard time remembering so many names, but everyone was confused about his name, too. He had finally started to introduce himself as "Nick-Kole," but when he heard himself say "Nichole," well, that didn't work either.

"Thanks, Katriana," he called. He leaned into Sam, "Thanks babe." He kissed her gently.

"Mmm. You are dreamy." The pie arrived and he fed her a bite and then tasted it himself.

"Blueberry-apple," his mouth full, "different, but so good!"

"Did you fly to Boston for the interview?" Sam asked cheerfully.

"Did you fly to Boston for the interview?" Sam asked cheerfully. *He's such the business man!* This voice liked the idea of Nick making good money. Then another part of her wanted to ask herself *what* she was doing because she had a great thing with Nick. *I'm so in love with Nick,* it reminded her. The time they had spent together since Key West had been so fantastic: *we had fun, the four of us having the best time in Key West... Key West, Candy West.* Sebastian's words ran through her mind, stealing the lime-light from the memories of Nick. Her thoughts now went back to memories of she and Sebastian on that trip.

He had been *so* gay, but he'd also taken her to a special dinner at the Rusty Pelican in Miami- *it was been so romantic there. Was Sebastian testing to see if I was interested in him?*

Sam's mind began do deliberate an argument, each side presenting different evidence:

The voice against spoke, *He slept with William but, he drooled over every man that walked by.*

He's not into me -

Then one side argued, *or, was he overcompensating?*

The other side opposed, *He drooled over Captain America when we went to the movies-*

Again, the side arguing, *Or wasn't he the sweetest to me? He's always been so attentive to me; he came to my rescue in St. Martin.*

She looked over at Sebastian, who was sitting next to her talking with Cindy. He turned, saw her looking at him so he smiled warmly at Sam before returning to his conversation.

He's hot for me: he's always been so great to me; he came to my rescue in St. Martin.

She looked over at Sebastian, who was sitting next to her talking with Cindy. He saw her looking at him so he smiled warmly at her.

Stop! She looked back at Nick. Then she thought about Sebastian kissing her, saying he was going to thrust himself into her, "Excuse me, baby. I have to go to the bathroom!"

"Oh, OK." Nick was surprised to see Sam jump up. "Too much wine, babe?"

"Maybe," she said, heading for Iza's house and bathroom. She needed a moment to herself because her thoughts, her imagination and picturing Sebastian naked... it was all overwhelming her. In a good way. She wanted to be alone for a minute - or would Sebastian come to Iza's house, seeing Sam leave the table?

"Ugh!" she moaned. She was driving herself crazy.

No, stop! she screamed.

No, don't stop- her mind raced over and over Sebastian kissing her. *What is wrong with me? Nick is drop-dead gorgeous. And mad about me. And I'm mad about him!*

She went into the bathroom and sat on the toilet, seat down. She put her head down onto her hands which were supported on her knees.

"Love, you ok?" She looked up quickly at the closed bathroom door.

"Sebastian, why are you here?" She opened the door and kissed him.

"Iza sent me to fetch something from the kitchen. Great timing, right?" He saw that she was upset. "What's wrong?"

"I just keep thinking about you. I can't get you-"

"Out of my mind. I know," he looked a little worn out now too. "I know. I'm going crazy too. But I just can't-" he kissed her again. "I can't help myself and I don't wan to."

He kissed her passionately. They were in the bathroom with the door open and were listening for the front door, just in case. Feeling that they had a private moment, Sam's hand traveled down, running and rubbing on the outside of Sebastian's pants.

"Oh!" He said, surprised. "Oh," he now moaned. "You like that?"

"I don't know yet. How do you like being felt up - by a woman?"

"Do it more and I'll let you know." They kissed again, both fondling each other. Then he pulled away.

"Woman, you are driving me up a wall." She smiled proudly and now he caressed her face. "Love, let's not get crazy. I don't want you to be upset. You have Kole, I'm gay. Don't feel guilty. We haven't crossed that line yet. For now let's think of it as best friends with a few kissing benefits we aren't going to tell anyone about."

"Yet?" She asked suggestively.

"I want to make sure that finding out is what we both want."

"I'd always want to know if we didn't find out. I'd have a question hanging over my marriage if we didn't see."

"I know, me too. Do you want me to talk to Iza, Love?"

"Maybe."

"Let's go before Kole comes looking for you. I'll leave first." He kissed her goodbye and left.

Pretend that it is no big deal, Sam told herself. She closed the door to the bathroom and sat on the toilet seat again. Her insides tugged in two directions. She had fallen in love with Nick; now she was being seduced by Sebastian. How could this be? *Sebastian's always been my best friend. Now we just kiss- and want to tear off each other's clothes! Some therapist... Ugh! Maybe I should talk to Iza, maybe we both should.*

Now a new idea entered Sam's mind. It made no sense, but, consumed by desperation and guilt, she believed it was a good idea. It is at times like these that even the most self-aware make a choice that is not who they really are, a choice that they would never make, under normal circumstances.

Why not just have them both? Sebastian seems fine with it, someone offered.

Sam got up and walked up to the mirror.

"Who are you?" she asked the reflection.

No judgment, Sam. *You can have them both, why not?*

"Whose voice is that?" Sam hadn't heard this super-confident and unscrupulous voice before.

Why not? it asked again.

"Because I'd be lying to Nick!" she answered.

You already are, the unscrupulous voice pointed out. *And you can't stop now. Nothing can keep you from exploring loving Sebastian. You don't just want to have sex with him, you love him. So, don't bother fighting me. You can't help yourself, nor do you want to.*

Sam sighed looking and leaning down on the counter. "You're right. I can't stop myself" she looked up into the mirror again. "I don't want to." She stared at her reflection. "I might as well ride the wave."

Sam saw a tube of lipstick on the counter. She looked in the mirror and put it on. The color accented her lips. *You're beautiful,* she heard Sebastian's words echo in her mind. *You downplay it. Let your hair down.* Beyond the echo of his words, he now spoke in her mind. "I have to have you."

Sam puckered her lips. The lipstick looked good on her. What if she started waring makeup too?

Her mind was made up. BFs with benefits. After all, that was the only way she could have her cake and eat her cupcake too.

♥

21

Of Twins & Twitches

Cindy entered the Bamboo room where she, Sam and Nick were staying. They had come in just a few minutes ahead of her.

She entered the Bamboo room where she, Sam and Nick were staying. They had come in just a few minutes ahead of her.

"What fun! Now there's something we never get to do at home, dinner under the stars. I think I'm going to miss this place."

Sam and Nick smiled at each other because everything Cindy said sounded so scientific as opposed to experiential.

"Cindi, thanks again for letting me stay here." Nick, or Kole, was staying in the Bamboo room with Sam and Cindi. Since his trip was unplanned, where he would stay had been an afterthought. Cindy had insisted that he stay with them. She didn't want them to have to pay for a hotel or to have to leave the ranch to go to a hotel in town. Being with these wonderful people and enjoying the spellbinding land needed to be a whole experience.

"Please, dear, don't mention it. Do you two need some time alone? I can go talk with Iza for a little while."

"No, Cindy, I'd feel terrible making you stay out," he responded in a gentlemanly manner. "Besides, if you ladies don't mind, I'd love to take a quick shower."

"Take your time, baby." Sam looked to Cindy who nodded.

"Great! If neither of you need the bathroom for a little while, maybe I'll soak in the water a bit. Try to rehydrate my skin. I think I've aged 5 years in two days."

"Lotion, baby. I keep telling you, you have to bathe in it here."

"Men don't do that, but I'll take a few more minutes in the water. Oh, and I'll warn you, Dr. R., sometimes I sing in the shower."

"How cute!"

Nick entered the bathroom with a towel and some clothes and turned the water on. Cindy looked to Sam as she sat in one of the two small club chairs. She motioned for Sam to join her as she spoke, "That's some red lipstick you are wearing, dear."

"You know I want to talk."

"Uh-huh. Talk."

"Perhaps you truly are becoming like the other witches," Sam said sweetly. She sighed, "Cindy, Sebastian kissed me." Sam had previously looked like a fox with a secret that she could hardly keep in. Now she lit up.

"Give me the context, sweetheart, because you know how I feel about you. I want to know what's really going on."

"We're drawn to each other. Every time he kisses me I want to beg him to be inside me." Hunger was written all over her body.

"What about Nick, dear?"

At this question, Sam sat up straight. Cindy could have sworn that Sam's red lipstick then got redder. "I know." She looked away, toward the window and took a deep breath. "All those years, I never felt like anyone could be interested in me, not seriously." She looked back at Cindy. "I dated one Fred after another. I always knew that they didn't really care; they were just having fun. Fred never bought me jewelry, never took me on vacation. Sebastian takes me everywhere and never lets me pay for anything. Nick bought me jewelry - and they are both-" now her whole body spoke, "so gorgeous."

Cindy had focused in on Sam, whose words were almost moaned instead of spoken. To bring Sam back to her rational mind, she casually agreed, "Yes, they are hunks."

"I never thought I would have a man love me, really love me." Now Sam was in a world all her own, eyes glazing over. "I never had a man want a future with be that went beyond the weekend." Sam now sat, starring. A minute passed before she continued.

The look on her face changed. Her eyes came into focus and, with a resolution Cindy had never seen before, Sam looked straight at her.

"I want them both. Sebastian touches my soul. I can't be without him, and I won't be. Nick is my dream, I think he's the one. How would I choose? How would I live without my heart and soul? Without the man of my dreams?"

Cindy was stupefied. It was rare to work with a client *in this state* in their lives. It was the stereotypical state in which men often had an affair, bought a hot red car- and wreaked havoc their lives. It was a dangerous state, one which psychologists referred to as 'the sabotage state,' since people usually destroyed their lives.

Cindy took a deep breath. What did she want to say?

"Sweetheart," a term she reserved for special times, special people. "I understand. You are compensating some: you had no love and now, well, you have twice as much." She smiled. She knew to offer Sam understanding. *Sam? Was this Sam?* The expression and the hot red lipstick made the woman before her look like a different person.

"Will you tell Nick or feel guilty?" Cindy asked, trying to bring the old Sam's senses back.

"No. I decided I won't. I can't. Besides," Sam said, with complete confidence, "this way we're all happy. We all get what we want, for now."

"Uh-huh," Cindy nodded. This was no time for her to disagree or push Sam. Sam was nuts! "Well, sweetheart, you know that all I want is what's best for you. I'm here for you, you can talk to me anytime."

This relaxed Sam. Instead of stiffly sitting up straight, she curved her back and the expression on her face eased, "Oh, thanks!"

Agree with a client's insanity and they speak to you sweetly, Cindy stood.

"Well, dear," now Cindy was back in her usual mode, discarding the therapist and dear friend hats. "I need to go out for a while to give you and Nick some time together." Sam tried to say something but Cindy put her hand up. "Uhp! I want to. I think it's important. I'll go talk with Iza and Katriana. They've answered so many of my questions so cryptically that I understand less than before I asked. Since I'm leaving tomorrow, I want to take advantage."

"Oh, OK." Sam agreed.

Cindy's timing was perfect because she was at the door just as Nick came out of the shower.

"I hope my singing didn't bother you," he said.

"Dear, we didn't even hear you. I'll be back. Off to confer with my witches!"

22

Three Witch Wine

Cindy headed to Iza's where she saw William outside the front door, Katriana in the doorway.

"No, no se puede, William. Dame un beso y te veo después."

"Am I interrupting?" Cindy asked, not understanding the language or what was going on. She saw William say something, kiss Katriana and squeeze her breast before he turned around to leave.

"Good night, witches!" He called. *"¡Apúrate, querida!"*

"No, you not interrupting. Come in, you are just in time." Katriana said, holding the door open for Cindy.

"In time for what?"

She looked inside and saw Iza sitting on one of the two purple velvet couches. Around the couches were a couple of large amethyst crystals and several tall plants with tiny Christmas lights which created a fairy feel in here. In between the couches was a maple coffee table with an opened bottle of wine, one that hadn't been opened yet and three glasses of wine. Iza picked up a third glass and extended it to Cindy.

"You in time for this."

Cindy took the glass. She sat in the matching purple velvet club chair with light-colored wooden arms. Oh, this was comfortable, Cindy thought settling in. Her chair sat on the far end of the room near the plants which allowed her to see Katriana, sitting on the couch to her right and Iza on the opposite couch. It was relaxed and welcoming.

"What's the occasion?" Cindy asked, sipping the wine.

"You. We knew you coming." Katriana answered. She poured more wine into her glass.

Cindy looked at her with surprise, "What?"

"Silent Knowledge, angel. We knew you'd come about twenty minutes ago."

"That why I told William he can't stay. Just witches because we need to talk about Sam and Sebastian. Right?" Katriana's wine glass was half empty again.

"Don't worry about the details. Just enjoy your last night, the wine-" Iza said.

"The company. We no have many friends we enjoy like you, Cindy. No many witch friends." Katriana said. She raised her glass, "To witches!"

"To witches!"

Cindy laughed and quickly got on board because this was a rare treat for her. Being at the ranch had been such endless fun.

"So, angel," Iza motioned with her hand, prompting Cindy to go ahead and bring up anything she liked.

"Well, first let me say that you two are amazing. I need more witch friends, so I want you to expect phone calls after I'm gone."

"Of course we do." Iza went over to her desk and brought a couple sheets over for Cindy. "We expect you back soon. Here's your certificate of participation and a flier for the journey to Bali." Cindy looked at the flier and read the title, *In The Temple of Life*.

"Fascinating!" She looked at Iza to see if her 'fascinating' was irritating her. They all laughed. "I'll have to talk with my honey, but I'd love to go, dear. I've never been and I've heard so many wonderful things, not to mention everything I'm sure I'd learn."

"Great, angel. Now, the wine is meant to help you with whatever is weighing on you. What is it?"

"How did you know?" Cindy asked in surprise, but then she waved her hand saying, "I know, 'Silent Knowledge.' " Cindy took a large swig of wine and extended her glass, "May I?"

"*Sí, claro.*" Katriana poured more wine in both their glasses and topped off Iza's.

"Well," Cindy began, looking more serious now. "There is a state of mind that people sometimes enter. Psychologically, we don't know exactly what triggers it. Sometimes people are loosing control over their lives, so they are on the edge, but that's not always true. In this state, which psychologists lovingly refer to as 'the sabotage state,' people behave erratically. It's common for them to behave in extremely uncharacteristic ways." She took a deep breath and saw that Katriana was nodding her head. She looked to Iza, who didn't look surprised at all. "It's not a good place to be," she emphasized

This is a grave state! Are they understanding? "At that point we often lose the client or they change and their lives are never the same." .

"Yes, angel. We know."

"Oh?" At this point, she decided to never let the witches surprised any more. ??She'd even decided to expect that they'd have something to say about this, since they'd been waiting for her to come over tonight.

"You are worried about Sebastian and Sam?" Iza's question was rhetorical.

"Well, yes. Of course," she said, nudging her glasses up the bridge of her nose. "Especially Sam. I just spoke with her. She looked crazy. She was wearing a red lipstick and saying things I never thought I'd hear her say. Her eyes glazed over and, well, if I didn't know better, I'd say an evil twin has replaced her. Yes, I'm concerned."

"It's normal." Katriana said, refilling her glass and offering to refill theirs.

Cindy couldn't believe that such a small, slender woman could drink three times as quickly as she could. *Where does it all go, because she doesn't seem drunk at all.*

"Oh, I'm European. We know how to drink wine," she said in perfect English. Cindy was amazed at the mind reading and the perfect English, but had to stay focused on the conversation about Sam.

"Angel," Iza said, taking her cue that Cindy was ready to listen. She took a deep breath, "We need to explain what's going on energetically. You're a psychologist, so think of the craziest case you may have studied in school, one with unfathomable circumstances. Think of a young boy who was kept locked in a room and never fed; think of a woman who is sexually abused and belittled to the point of madness."

"Alright," Cindy shifted uncomfortably in her plush chair. "Humanity at it's worst."

"Yes, angel. Well," Iza waved her hand almost conjuring an image of such a miserable person. "The reason people go crazy, become animalistic, savage, is because their core needs have not been met. Depriving any being of basic needs, like dogs that are forced to fight, keeps them from being whole. We've talked about the three basic needs for love, acceptance and approval; these are words and things to you and I, but more significantly, they are truly energies. These energies can manifest in one of many ways, forms. A dog or a human that is beaten is taught that they are not valued; this can starve them of love or acceptance- or both. When they are always scolded or punished, with or without reason, they are left craving approval. Do you understand what I'm saying? That love, acceptance and approval are lived in various ways? A baby that is loved unconditionally, that is held, coddled and praised all of the time grows up having those needs met. Such a baby becomes a happy, wholesome person who tends to be loving, generous and understanding.

"It's like building a house. Imagine one that lacks a foundation or one that is built with nails instead of screws. The integrity of the house will always lack until it is rebuilt. The house will never know the strength of good materials and good workmanship so it may sway in the wind or get knocked down when the big bad wolf comes and blows it away.

"People are like houses, in this way. Their foundation, good materials and good workmanship are energetic but look like things to us. Love, food, being cared for and given compassion as a child. This is why formative years are so important. When something is lacking, and karmatically something is always lacking in our time frame, then people have weaknesses. The question is always to what degree.

"Katriana and I saw the lack of integrity in Sebastian and Sam. Like two houses with similar structural problems, they have a lot in common. The energetic lack in them is a part of what attracts them to one another."

"You're saying love is based on-" Cindy searched for words. "From our darkest parts?"

"Yes, simply put." Katriana answered as if this wasn't the worst and most depressing thing Cindy had heard in a long time. She and Arthur had fallen in love and gotten married - because of their weakest parts?

"How can that be?" She cawed. "When we fall in love we are so good to the person we love. We think they are better than pie!"

"Yes, at first." Katriana said, refilling her wine and still speaking perfect English. "Once the honeymoon period is over, the cute little things we initially liked are the ones that annoy us; we go from feeling as though we'd give our own lives for the other to arguing and bickering in public. Not everyone, sure, but it speaks to the point. Once the initial attraction brings people together, then the work starts."

"Uh-huh," Cindy said, starting to clue in.

Iza continued, "Romantic relationships are the hardest part of most people's lives. This is because it is the most intimate aspect of our lives, the one in which all of our issues come forward, forcing us to deal with them.

"I brought Sam and Sebastian to their rawest place, the most wounded part or the greatest energetic hole that they each had. As you saw, it hardly took any work on my part. Truth is, those homes were already shaking lose. A kiss alone, can you believe it Katriana? Have you ever seen anyone fall apart and get so sucked into their hole so quickly?"

"No, it was remarkable. One for the books!" She laughed. "Oh, you're book!" She said to Cindy.

"Fascinating. So, you are saying that by knocking on the door of their weakness, Sam went crazy?"

"It's not weakness, per say, angel. You must understand that it is karmatic energy. Everyone has karma. It sets and determines the issues someone will experience in life."

"And those two are karmatically connected. They've known each other in a past life, maybe more."

"Should they do a past life regression?" Cindy wondered if there was anything to help them.

"No point, angel. This life is the only one that matters. Life brings everything you need to the 'here and now.' Past life regressions should be nothing more than entertainment."

Cindy took a deep breath, held out her glass. She blinked, stared... The second bottle was three-quarters empty and she did not remember it being opened.

"How does this explain the evil twin? Oh," Cindy understood the answer to her question the minute she asked. "She's now in a fragmented personality, like the boy who was kept locked up."

"You've got it, angel. It sounds like a strong energy fragment."

"Everything is energy to you two, isn't it? Cindy asked.

Katriana bowed her head, "Even science recognizes this now."

"True," Cindy pondered. "Well, Sam looked Cybil-like tonight. The look in her eyes, the confidence, the red lipstick. I thought you had both helped them fill the energetic holes you said you saw in them. Did you make a mistake?"

"No angel, we just need to go deeper, as they have. Their depth was remarkable. Rare." She paused, taking a sip of wine. "Sam is of greater concern. She has chosen to take on an energy," Iza said carefully, leaning towards Cindy. "She's using the energy of pretension, which you might call ego, to mask. That's why you said she is saying things that are uncharacteristic. As long as she is hiding how she truly feels, she will behave this way. And as long as she wants to keep both men, she'll hide how she feels about cheating on Kole, thinking that feeling loved by them both is more important."

"Fascinating!" Cindy admired.

"I need a pillow to throw at you, Dr. Fascinating." Iza said sarcastically. They all laughed, the wine making things funnier than they may have been.

"I don't know if it is the wine, but the way you explain things makes perfect sense. Energy or not- what am I going to do to help my dear friend?"

"Angel, just be there for her. We've done all we can. Now it is time for the universe to take over. Perhaps they will fall madly in love, perhaps this will bring them to their knees," Iza said, serious again.

"Oh, they will be on their knees," Katriana said, raising her eyebrows. "And perhaps they will fall madly in love."

"Pst," Iza crooned, "is there something you aren't telling us Katriana?" Iza stared at her. *She knows something, I know it!*

"No, claro qué no."

"Back to Spanish, eh?" Iza turned to Cindy. "She turns into a different, English speaking-seer when she drinks. Unless she doesn't want to answer my questions. Then she's all Spanish!" Iza watched Katriana for a clue as to what Katriana had foreseen. Realizing that she wouldn't be finding out right now, she thought, *OK, I'll let it go. For now.*

The three ladies enjoyed each other immensely, cackling until midnight.

23

Identity Crisis

The next morning Sebastian was up bright and early. He put on his Docker shorts and a different blue shirt. The red one he dropped on the floor. If Sam said red wasn't his color, then it was out.

"Shite!" His British pronunciation was the official "shit" in his home growing up. *I'm gay, why am I thinking about Sam non-stop?*

He put his shirt on and walked out of the bedroom to his cell phone, which was at his desk.

"Cin come over. Quiet" He hit 'send'. It was convenient having everyone on the land at the ranch. He could leave and be in his own casita or see them in minutes. He put water on to boil for tea.

He buttoned up his shirt and put his socks and shoes on. He looked out his window. Cindy was coming. He opened his door.

"That was a cryptic text. What's going on, dear?"

Sebastian made sure the door was closed before he began.

"I think I'm in love with Sam. Tea?" He went over for the tea. "English breakfast or green?"

"What's new? You've always loved her." Then it dawned on Cindy. "Iza's magic made you un-gay! You don't love her, you want to bone her!"

"Cindy!" Sebastian said, looking up at her in surprise. "How crass! No, I don't- well, yes," he said, raising his shoulder in agreement. He carried two mugs and several tea bag choices over.

"Ha, ha! You are smiling like the Cheshire cat!" Cindy's laughs were so in her head. The only time he'd ever seen her laugh from her belly was the night they drank two bottles of tequila. "Green, please dear." She took her mug, "Thank you." Cindy began to tap into her psychologist mode.

"Now, Sebastian. What seems to be the trouble? Iza, Katriana and I know you're in love with Sam. I'm sure that kiss, that hot, smutty kiss-"

"Smutty?" That was crossing the line.

"Oh, you are taken with her!" She quickly shifted from surprised to sassy. "Everyone knows you just slept with William. Aren't you becoming the man-slut?" She adjusted her glasses. "I'm impressed. If it weren't for you and Sam-" She put her hand to her chest, bracing herself. "You two are so HOT! Arthur and I are going to take a tantric sex course together. I can't wait."

"Really, Cindy? That sounds pretty hot too." Sebastian said, moving around in his seat.

"Right now you're thinking you could learn some sexual positions for you and Sam!"

Sebastian turned red. "It's bad enough being hot for a woman, but I have no idea how to - um, do her."

"I'm sure you'll do just fine, that lucky thing," she whispered under her breath. She turned to look at Sebastian. "Well dear, I could help you with this, but Katriana is taking me to the airport in ten minutes."

"Oh, right. Yes, you should go."

"I'll say this, Sebastian. You and Sam have always behaved like a couple, so it's really no surprise."

"But is it right? I'm gay and Kole— ugh! I feel bad, he's my friend."

"Well that one's your own fault. Setting them up!" Cindy stood up, chuckling. "Give me a hug, dear. You can call any time. Whatever you do, be careful. Don't hurt my business partner." Cindy raised an admonishing finger for emphasis. "For now, go talk with Iza. Your witches told me that energy zings were zapping between you and Sam last night. That's why she sent you in for the pink ice-cream scoop out of the kitchen. She was giving you a little private time. She doesn't have a pink scooper!"

"Ah, I wondered." Sebastian raised his eyebrows.

"I get a point on your scoreboard, dear." She motioned for Sebastian to give her a point.

"Oh? You? How's that?" They hugged and Cindy headed to the door.

"I'm a witch and Iza's my friend! That's two points, dear."

"Love you Cindy. Come back soon."

"Yes, dear. Love you too - and your cute ass!" This she added as she turned the corner, disappearing outside.

Sebastian sat again with his tea. It was time to go to Iza's and make breakfast. "Maybe I will talk with Iza. Why not, what do I have to lose. Sounds like she already knows anyway."

He put the mugs in the sink and headed over to make breakfast at Iza's.

♥

Nick wanted to skip breakfast at the ranch, spend time alone with Sam. She knew of a country restaurant with farm-fresh eggs just up the road.

The restaurant was clearly the older, converted part of the ranch-house. They were greeted by peacocks and chickens outside. The royal, shimmering blues on the male peacocks caught their attention. Not something they saw in the city. They could see a feed store, cages with other animals and hay behind the restaurant. A true, ranch restaurant!

Inside they were seated among western photographs on the walls of horses, roosters; next to them was an old country stove that served as a waiter's station. Sam could see that all of the chairs and tables were unique, a true collection that had obviously grown as the restaurant expanded and took over the house.

"Welcome," the middle-aged waitress greeted before they'd sat. "What can I get you to drink?"

"Do you have iced-tea?" Nick didn't know how people lived here, it was so dry.

"Black or Prickly-pear?"

Confused, he just opted for what he knew. "Black."

"Two, please. We're both so thirty," Sam added.

"I'll bring you a pitcher," the waitress smiled. "I'll be right back for your order. Chalkboard over there," she said, pointing at an old stove, "has today's specials." The board offered: broccoli quiche, breakfast burrito bathed in red, green or Christmas salsa; pancakes, eggs with biscuits 'n gravy and today's soup, minestrone.

Sam was going to pick from the menu, but Nick had something else to talk to her about. "Babe, I received a call this morning while you were in the shower. I have a surprise, good and bad. I got the job! It's a great position, but I have to fly to Austin today to start training tomorrow."

So many things raced through Sam's mind she didn't know how to react or what to say.

"Babe?" he asked, worried that she wasn't saying anything.

"How long will you be gone?"

"I'm so sorry I didn't talk to you about it, but this way we'll have the money to pay for a wedding. You can still stay and plan it. The training is for two weeks."

❤

Sebastian was cooking up breakfast, as usual. Iza was finishing getting ready. It felt good to be back in his groove, cooking breakfast in Iza's kitchen.

"Do you want to eat outside or inside today, hon?" he called to her.

Iza laughed to herself. "He's ready to talk," she told Peppermint. "No surprise."

Iza walked out of her bedroom, down the hall and into the kitchen. "Why don't we stay inside, angel. I think you'll appreciate the privacy."

"Privacy? Oh," he said, figuring her out, "you know I want to talk. Is there anything you don't know?" He walked the plates over to Iza's table as she brought a glass of orange juice over for him and a cup of joe for herself. It was a great café table and perfect for two people to have a cozy meal. It was a high table with a glass top, beautiful wrought iron, curling legs which held it up. They sat at the table's bar chairs which were a deep purple fabric. A tall plant next to the table provided ambiance and a sense of the outdoors inside.

134

Before them was a window looking out to the garden. Iza's house had the best views.

"You shagging her?" Iza asked, chuckling.

Sebastian let Iza make fun waving her on. Then he thought he'd turn the tables. "No, I want to fuck her," he said casually. "I guess your healing didn't work out so well because all you did was make a gay man want to screw a gorgeous blond."

"Oh, you have it bad, angel." Iza laughed again.

Sebastian hung his head low, "You have no idea." He lifted his head and looked to Iza. He was grateful that things were quieting down around the property - glad that no one else was joining them for breakfast today. "In St. Martin she wanted me, Iza. I wasn't tempted at all. So, what the hell is going on now? What kind of black, sex magic did you perform on me?"

"Sex magic? If that had been what I was up to, you'd be shagging me now, angel."

"Yes, well- And you were so wrong about William!"

"I have to admit, angel, things have surprised me a bit. I know you worked with your energetic hole. So there's something else... You know who would know? Katriana."

"No! She's the one William's shagging. I am angry that he didn't tell me he had been seeing a woman before we slept together. I kicked him out. At first I was hurt, still am, but then Sam came into my mind. She's all I can think about, Iza."

"Angel, Katriana is a master at reading energy. She could tell us-" she paused. "She did say that you and Sam were karmatically bound. Maybe that connection is larger than I thought it would be." She went on eating.

"So, what do I do Iza?"

"What do you mean, angel? Oh, and I wanted to tell you, the help you gave me for the other day, it worked! I've had more people sign up for the trip to Bali. Will you help me with my web page? I have an event in a couple of months that I'd like to get people to come to."

"Yeah, sure. I enjoy marketing." Sebastian looked out the window. He saw Jonathan heading towards his casita. "Iza, I'm a gay man lusting after Sam, that's not right! She's engaged and I can't get her out of my head. What the hell? What do I do?" He was exasperated.

"Nothing angel. Nothing at all." She looked at him seriously. "If you are really so hung up on Sam now, then there's more going on. We just have to dig deeper. Anyway," she said, leaning back and drinking her coffee, "what's wrong with wanting to screw the cute, little blond?"

"I'm gay." His nose flaring, he huffed. "This isn't me. What's going on?" I'm so confused, frustrated. Mad.

"Right. Angel, give it a few days, see how you are doing and if you are still as horny for her as you are now. If you are, we'll talk more. In the meantime, I keep telling you to come to class. It would help."

"I'll wash the dishes. I'll give it a few days and I'll come to class. By the way, hon, who were the two new men at dinner?"

"Why, did you think they were cute?"

"Sure," he winked. "Of course I did," thinking about something else, he felt better. But I mean the gentleman, the one who doesn't live here. The one with the dark hair."

"I met him for the first time last night. That's Eric, Jonathan's friend. He said he'd come to class too."

"Uh-huh. He likes you, you know."

"Not as much as you like the blond. Oh, and angel, you are welcome."

"For what?"

"For sending you in to fetch the pink ice-cream scooper. I'm sure you found it." Iza smirked knowingly at Sebastian, who smiled at her as though he'd been gifted something devious but delighting.

"I'd say I did."

"See, you already feel better angel." She stood, "After the dishes, come help me with my event."

24

Dark Shadows

"*¿Qué pasa?* What you want talk about?" Katriana asked as she came into Iza's house, Kia right behind her.

"Hi honey, here, grab the drinks. Let's sit." Iza had been preparing in the kitchen. She had made soup and sandwiches for lunch and invited Katriana over to talk. Iza placed the plates at her high coffee table. Each plate had half a turkey and Swiss sandwich with a cup of tomato soup. "Grab a couple of spoons angel, the napkins are on the table.

The ladies settled in and began to eat.

"You call me 'honey'. What do you want, what going on, Iza? *Veo que es algo importante.*" Katriana gave Kia a piece of turkey and then Kia settled on a throw rug.

"All I understood was 'important'. I'd say, yes. Katriana, did you unleash a monster?"

"You taking *Sebastián?*"

"Yes, angel. I lined things up so well - he was supposed to enjoy William." Iza looked Katriana in the eye, "I think you poisoned that well."

"Iza, that no matter. That had no to do with me. Sure, William and I - nos vimos - when he here before, but not this time. Until *Sebastián* broke with him."

"Mm," Iza believed Katriana but wasn't convinced. "In all of the years I've been helping people heal their energetic holes-"

"Decades! Many decades!" Katriana added.

"Thanks, angel. You're so helpful." Katriana was easily Iza's closest friend. They had so much in common and few other people could have conversations about energy the way they did. At the same time, Katriana had an abrasive side that could steam-roll Iza so that Katriana could also be Iza's least favorite person. Of course, Katriana felt the same way about Iza.

"No, Katriana, there's more to this and I want you to look at the energy, see what you see in this situation." Her tone deepened, "I'm seeing shadows."

Katriana looked straight up. This was serious. ¿Qué Sometimes the ranch had a bit of an infestation problem. It wasn't rats, per se, but dark spirits that lurked around.

"Mira, they watch us. Te lo dije."

"No Spanish."

"Sí. They watch but they no here." Katriana's words were confident. She saw in Iza's eyes that Iza wasn't convinced, so she turned to the dog. "Kia, ¿Qué hay? ¿Hay peligro?" Katriana used a hand command, asking the dog to look around. Kia sat up at attention and raised his nose, as if to acknowledge the request. Next Kia lifted onto all four legs and began sniffing the air. Finding nothing, Kia walked to the window that faced the garden and barked. He immediately walked to Iza's office, the east side of the house. Kai stood at Iza's desk, as close as he could get to the windows, sniffed the air and barked. Kia disappeared now, walking to the north side of the house where Iza's bedroom was and they heard a bark. Then Kia went to the kitchen, the west side of the house, and repeated the same behavior before coming back by Katriana, touching his nose to her leg and then retiring to the floor where he had been sleeping before.

"Kia say there nothing. You no have to worry."

On the one hand, Iza and Katriana didn't believe in demons, but they had experienced plenty of stuck and malevolent spirits who were roaming the earth. They were similar to ghosts because they didn't have bodies and could not participate in life. At the same time, they hadn't necessarily been human and they could influence people who's energy vibrated low. These shadows fed on the emotions of the living vicariously, people who were depressed or angry all of the

138

time.(??) When people vibrated that low, the shadows were able to connect frequencies, broadcast their thoughts and motivations, influencing a person's behavior. Most often this made a person angrier or even suicidal.

"Then how do you explain Sebastian? A gay man who worked with his energetic hole and was doing better. He left the workshop to be with another gay man- and is now obsessed with a woman? He is so hung up on Sam, Katriana. It's taken me by surprise. What is going on?"

"I told you, they connected, beyond what you see. *Mira,* it not dark shadows."

"I've been having those dark dreams again, I know they are lurking around."

"Oh." Katriana now understood why Iza was suspecting that Sebastian was being influenced by the dark spirits. "No, Iza. OK, look, where has Peppermint been sleeping? He not guarding you?"

"No, he's been at Sebastian's."

"Then that why you having bad dreams. They bothering you. I leave Kia here to guard you tonight. *Sebastián* is not being influenced. There is something bigger. He and Sam have something they working on together, that all."

"So, you don't see any dark energy, angel?"

"No. No that kind. Just the ones that come to your dream. No the other. But it - *es muy* - different. *Muy-* different. What *Sebastián* say to you?"

"He says he can't stop thinking about her. He's heavily addicted, insane for her. I don't think he cares that he'll destroy her marriage or the way he sees himself."

"Yes, big change to his self image. Well, you can give him a cleanse."

"An egg cleansing? Might not be a bad idea." Iza sighed, still feeling like something was off. "Different," she echoed Katriana's words pensively. "That's a part of what I'm talking about, Katriana. People behave differently when their holes are vibrating, differently than who they think they are, but Cindy's description of Sam and what I saw in Sebastian- I've never seen people be hit so hard. It's like we didn't do any energy healing even though we did. So, I thought it was you interfering with William or that the shadows were back. There's something else at play?" Her words trailed off.

"No. Mira, I will watch over them. When I see them together maybe I find out what going on between them." This relaxed Iza. "Oh, you worried about him."

"You know, I am. I like him, taking him under my wing I suppose. He could be a powerful man." Iza said, dreams in her eyes.

"*Si*, he have the energy of that. In the stars, he have very strong future."

"Back to me," Iza said, still concerned about the shadows. "I appreciate you offering to leave Kia, but I think Peppermint is better at night. I'll keep him in the house, since you aren't worried about Sebastian at all."

"You ready to talk about the shadows that follow you?"

This had been an on-going conversation that Iza hadn't liked. Katriana had repeatedly told Iza that she was attracting entities due to her overuse of masculine energy. Hating this conversation and topic, Iza often tried to skirt the conversations.

"There's nothing to talk about. I'm working on it." Iza picked up their empty plates as she walked them into the kitchen she called, "Let's talk about something else."

Iza came back, stopped to pet Kia and then called for Peppermint. "Where's my loyal kitty?"

"Meow!" He obeyed the summons and sat by his pet. "At least someone loves me."

"Iza!" Katriana scolded.

Now Iza looked up, ready to admit something. Katriana waited silently.

"I know why Silent Knowledge brought Sebastian to me."

"¿Si?

Iza braced herself with a deep sigh. "He wants what he can't have."

"Oh! You no think she's going to leave her *prometido*!"

"Promised? Kole, or Nick - I'm just not sure. I saw the way she looked at him when he left. She's in love with them both, and Sebastian wants what he can't have."

Just then William walked in. No one bothered knocking on Iza's door. He greeted them. He leaned over and kissed Katriana. "We need to go in 15 minutes," he said.

"OK, but go. Iza need to talk with just me for few more minutes."

"Sure. Don't be long or we'll miss the movie!"

Once William was gone, Iza looked at Katriana, a disgusted and jealous expression on her face. "How come you get to be a cougar?"

Part 3

25

Playing It Out

Sebastian was working in his casita, well, trying to work. His one-track mind made it hard- that is, it made concentrating difficult. But, if you were thinking that he was constantly aroused thinking about Sam, that too was true.

He decided to distract himself by going up to Iza's house.

"Knock, knock."

"Come in angel," she called back from her office nook at the far end of her house.

"Can I make dinner over here tonight, Iza? I need something to distract me."

"It sounds like a treat for me, angel. Tell me, what will you cook for me?"

"Lemon-dill salmon. And a butter-leaf lettuce salad."

"Great!" She still sat at her desk but turned to face him. "Oh, honey," she asked in a serious tone, lowering her glasses to see Sebastian clearly, "you spoke with Eric at dinner?"

"Yes, great chap."

"More angel. I could get 'great' from Peppermint here."

"Meow!!!"

Sebastian walked a few steps into the living room where the cat sat on the deep-purple, velvet couch. "Hello, Peppermint," he said, scratching behind his ears. "He's smart, Iza. I've dealt with enough sharp business people to know the signs. Also, he's quite spirited and he's interested in your teachings. He said he's thinking about going on your upcoming retreat. Where is it to?"

"Angel," Iza said, which sounds ed a bit like 'dip-shit.' "You helped me work on the website a couple days ago. It's to Bali, remember? Tst!" She made a scolding sound.

Playing with the reprimand, Sebastian raised his hand to stoke his hair, "I know, I've been a bad boy lately."

"Oh my God, angel!" Now she raised her finger, pointing with great authority and thinking: *Time to rope him into helping more than he'd agreed.* "Number one: you need to come to Bali. I'll give you a discount for helping me organize and market it." She lifted a brow, "Number two: are you still hung up on the engaged girl?"

"Engaged girl," he exhaled his words. "Er," he bit his lip. "It's so bad, Iza. I'd shoot her straight into my veins if I could."

"Oh, you have it badder than BAD. Her honey left, you know. Packed his bags."

"Really?" He looked up with great interest. "Why are you encouraging me, Iza? I thought you wanted to shag me and that you always did what was best for people."

"Oh, I do, angel-" she took a breath. "Still, at this point, you have to play it out. Sebastian, I saw the energetic cord between you two, I just helped you activate it. It was already there and you two jumped to experience it. There's something more going on and it's bigger than you and Sam, so you might as well ruin things sooner rather than later. That way things can come back together as best they can."

Sebastian looked down and then up at her again. Normally he listened to no one, save Sam. Iza though, well she was wise beyond anyone he'd met before, she knew what she was doing. And Sebastian trusted her.

"*Ruin*? You think she's ruining her marriage."

"I think you are both ruining things. But angel, 'ruin' might be the wrong word. Let me clarify: at this point, I see that you two have to see what it's like to be sexually intimate with one another, so be sure to be *intimate*. It would be good for you, don't just have sex."

"I couldn't just have sex with Sam. It's already intimate." Admitting this brought on a wave of light headedness. Facing how vulnerable he was before Sam was going to either cause a physical

144

response, or an emotional one of fear. He sat down and rested his head on his palm to help his light-headedness, avoiding the fear.

"You look paler than usual, angel." Iza went to the kitchen and came back with a glass of water.

"I think I need some tequila therapy."

"We can arrange that, easy."

"Tomorrow night. Invite Eric."

"Well you're clear on what you want in this case," she said, surprised. "Alright, later you can tell me who else, since I'm guessing that William and Katriana won't be invited."

"Ehk."

"OK, is that British? Because that's a new sound for me." She sat on the arm of the couch and put one hand on his back, which instantly seemed to calm him. She was, after all, a witch, he thought.

"Anyway, Sebastian, I can't tell you what's best for you or for Sam - I mean, sure I thought I knew, but there's more at play here. I need for Katriana to see you and confirm before I say more about the energy. Still, you are both going to do this sooner or later. Frankly, the sooner the better. Maybe you can have a fling without Kole finding out and they can still get married as planned. It would be out of her system then. You can play with heterosexual sex and come out knowing yourself better. That's what life's about, angel."

"Iza," he said in disbelief, "you'd condone her having an affair and then getting married?"

"No, not necessarily. Angel, I don't believe there is any force on earth that will keep you two from being together. Afterwards, if she were to decide to proceed with her marriage, well, why ruin things for her and Kole?"

"It's immoral. She'd be lying. I'd be lying to him." He looked up to read her face. "What are you saying Iza, that you have no morals."

"No angel, I have no judgment. I already tried to help. You and she are bonded in a way that isn't normal. I sped up what was there so that you could heal the energetic hole that was driving the attraction. Believe me, angel, you were attracted to her before this, too, you told me as much the other morning at breakfast. I tried to help you skirt the whole issue."

Sebastian thought about this. It was true, she was right. She had done so.

"But you sent me looking for the ice-cream scoop–"

"Yes, because at that point it was clear that you were hung up on her. You were sending her energetic zaps all night. If Kole could see energy, he would have beat you silly."

"No judgment?" He echoed, thinking about this, trying to adapt the mindset.

"The best thing for you both is to go through this storm and then rebuild from there. At this point, the sooner you come out of it, the less damage you might have. No judgment, but since you insist on going through the storm, I'm seeing how I can facilitate things."

Sebastian nodded his head, seeing clearly how Iza was truly helping them. "Thanks." He stood up to leave. "Bali, yes. I'm there. I just wasn't sure which event, you have so many."

"Oh good, angel. You add good ju-ju to my marketing and events."

"What will it cost?"

"Is your little blond coming? Or just you?"

"Yes, she wouldn't miss it. She's getting Cindy to go so that they can have you issue another professional development certificate."

"If there are two of you in a room, then between air, lodging, the retreat fee and food, you'll be looking at four to five thousand for your portion."

"Wow, that's steep!"

"That's why we go in November, angel. It's the least expensive time of year. At other times, it would cost the same just for the air."

"Really?" Without hesitating, he enlisted, "Well, I'm in." He ignored the price. "It'll be a priceless trip, I'm sure."

He took a few steps, saw Peppermint sitting on the love seat across from the couch he'd sat on. He leaned down to pet him, "Oh, honey?"

Iza had been heading back to her office nook, but turned around. "Yes?"

Now Sebastian stood up and faced her. He had a masculine look of determination. He was the one that knew this time and the look on his face was masterful, which Iza liked.

"I lied," his voice was husky now. "Eric's got something going on. Oh, he'll come to Bali because he's after you."

Sebastian walked out leaving Iza frozen.

"What?" her faint words falling on no one other than Peppermint.

"Meow-row!" he responded.

Iza was shocked. Sebastian knew a lot more than he was letting on - *and Eric? After me?*

26

The Longevity Cafe

Sebastian went home, put on sneakers and decided it was time to walk around Iza's property.

At this point you're going to play it out. He kept repeating her words in his head. What did he think of that? Did he want to play it out? Was Iza right about a storm and cleaning up afterwards? Were they doomed for disaster?

Sebastian walked over to the trail that began at the end of the driveway. It was an uphill walk through short, dry shrubs and a lot of junipers. Iza had said at dinner one evening that gin was made out of juniper and that people were highly allergic to the pollen it put out. Sebastian watched juniper after juniper as he walked along the path. Their leaves were similar to that of a pine tree, but they weren't tree-like in their shape. The junipers were like huge balls, never too much taller than six feet and always wide.

Aftermath. Sebastian didn't believe in aftermath. He always strove to make the best choices for himself to avoid repercussions that he didn't like. This had enabled him to trust life, to let go and always enjoy life, no matter what.

Fifteen minutes later he was back at his computer doing research. The walk around the ranch had given him what he was after - clarity. He thought he might have spotted a jackrabbit, though it was just a dark blur to him. He had heard several birds cawing at him too, and these had been just the whispers from that inner voice he needed.

He wanted to see Sam. If Kole had left, the pressure would be off, they could spend some time together. Alone. She hadn't rented a car, but had ridden in Cindy's rental, and Kole's car was gone. Was she home? He could text her, but no. She'd come over sooner or later. He turned back to his computer research.

Forty-five minutes later there was a knock at the door. Sebastian was hungry for it to be Sam. He'd seen her in passing in the last few days, but hadn't been close to her since the dinner party and their bathroom rendezvous. He looked out the window, Sam!

He opened the door. Sam's hair was down, fluttering in a gust of wind, the way it had in St. Martin. What was more striking and arousing though was that she wore make-up and red lipstick. Her blouse hung low in the front, a lose neck that almost looked like a long necklace - she couldn't have been wearing a bra. Her black blouse was tucked into a fitted skirt that ended above her knees. Her elegance and seduction were topped with red, high-heeled shoes that screamed for attention.

Sebastian got the message. He put his finger up to his lips, indicating for her not to speak. He took her hand and led her in his house. He closed the blinds for privacy and then turned to her. For a minute he stared into her eyes, reading her expression and connecting with her soul. He didn't wait long at all before he sat her on the couch, leaned her back and gently pulled her panties off and pushed her skirt up. He knelt on the floor before her and spread her legs. He looked at her, measuring her response. Her heavy breathing gave him permission. She stretched her head back when she felt the touch of his mouth between her legs as he turned *her* into the cupcake.

She moaned and gasped- since this was his first time, he listened carefully to make sure that these were sounds of pleasure, as pain and pleasure can sound so similar. No, she's not stopping me. *If she were in pain, she'd tell me*, he thought.

When Sam was satisfied she reached for his shoulder. He raised himself, wiping his mouth, and then sat by her.

They kissed. He put his hand in her blouse, the long neck providing the easy access that was intended.

"Obvious, aren't you Love?"

"I had to entice you somehow. I thought you might be having second thoughts."

"You've de-virginized me, you know. I've never done that before."

Sam realized what he meant. She was the first female body he'd explored. "How was it?"

"Well, Love," he said, kissing her, "You are *my* cupcake now."

"Sebastian!"

"I get a point for that," he said raising his finger to his invisible scoreboard. "Or would you give me five points?"

"Sebastian!"

"I liked your filling," he said suggestively. "You were delicious. Can I do that again?"

"Sebastian!" She slapped him playfully.

"I need practice, Love."

"Now?" She leaned back. "I thought we might move on to you. Or that we might talk."

He pulled her panties up. "Yes. Let's go into town, Love. You are right, we need to talk. Unless," he began to pull her panties down again.

"Sebastian!" She stopped his hand.

"OK, but I want to tell you - I wanted to taste you, see what it was like. Make sure that I'm OK with your parts." He leaned in kissing her neck. "Since they are new to me." He kissed her ear, licking it - measuring if she was excited. She leaned her head back, accepting him on her neck. "Some gay men are turned off, I wanted to make sure."

She stopped and pulled back to face him, realizing what he meant. "And?"

"I asked for a second serving of dessert, didn't I?" His free hand traveled back to her thigh under her skirt toward her panties, "Can I do it again?"

"This is weird." Sam said, flatly at first and then laughing. "This isn't how most men do this. They usually get right to-"

"I'm sure. Gay men too. But I want to discover you, Sam. I want to," he began kissing her neck again. "To go slow, make sure you want to have an affair." He moved his mouth to hers. "I want to make sure that I want to make love to you because I don't know how to think of me anymore. It makes no sense, my head is spinning— I've only been attracted to men, but now you're all I can think of…

How you feel in my palm, kissing you." He kissed her again. "About thrusting myself inside you."

Sam was getting worked up again. "What are you waiting for, love?"

"I want to savor every discovery of you." She placed her hand on his crotch. He felt so stiff and she wanted him, but he stood suddenly.

"Let's go talk. Town! In town! I'm going to go shower. Give me two minutes!"

Satisfied, but hungry again, Sam was left wondering why Sebastian hadn't even unzipped his pants and why he jumped away from her. She felt a little uneasy. Her red lipstick and new clothes gave her the courage to be a *sexy Sam*, but his reaction made her worry. *Am I making a mistake?* She stood, ignoring her doubts. He was going slow to be sure they both wanted to cross this line. She wanted to cross it, and could while Nick was away. He'd never know. She could hear the shower water running. She stood and walked to the bedroom.

"Sebastian?" She called, warning him that she was coming to the bathroom.

"Yeah?"

She pulled the shower curtain back and stared at his naked body being rained on. *Yes, this will happen.* She felt better, he hadn't changed his mind.

"I just wanted to see. Nice," she turned and walked away.

♥

Sebastian drove into town holding Sam's hand to keep her from running her hand over his pants. He had never guessed she had such a sexually forward side to her, although it matched her new look. He was enjoying every minute of it. They even got into town too quickly, he'd thought.

The Longevity Cafe was downtown in the middle of the historic buildings. As they entered Sam walked around looking at all of the tea canister labels that lined the wall at the entrance with the register. She looked at the cute tea pots and mugs that were displayed for sale. The cafe was dark, due to the lighting and the smaller windows.

"What will you have, Love?"

"Americano."

"I should have guessed." Sebastian ordered their drinks and then took her by the waist, pulling her into him and kissing her. "I'm liking having you all to myself. Let's get a table."

They walked past the entrance and into the section of the cafe with tables, booths and a stage.

"Wow!" Sam exclaimed when she saw that one of the booths had a hammock chair. Everywhere she looked there were big, colorful pillows. She pointed and then saw another booth that was a raised platform: the table atop it had short legs and long pillows served as seats. This booth was a Russian-styled table. "Oh, that's so cute, let's sit there."

Sam continued to look around at the walls. They were painted a light orange, which surprised her because psychologically orange was a color for creativity. She would have expected a subtle, calming color like a dark blue or gray, but it looked great in here. The cafe's 'longevity' theme was new age, so the decorations were a large planter, a Buddha statue, a framed photograph of the Dali Lama and other typical items.

The booth Sam had picked was perfect. The wooden bottom was padded with a bench cushion to sit on and one to rest your back on. Colorful pillows adorned each seating area and made it inviting. The tall back to the booth gave a great sense of privacy, which they craved. Above the table hung three blue lanterns with beautiful glass and metal work.

Sebastian went into the booth first and then opened his arm for Sam to come lean against him.

"I love you, Sam," he whispered in her ear. "And I'm scared."

Sam turned to face him, which wasn't easy in this booth. The man at the register, brought their drinks over.

"Here you go." He saw that they were a bit squished. "You look like you need a little more room," He reached down to a handle on the side of the raised platform. He opened it and pulled out a smaller table with short legs and switched it out for their larger one. The smaller table fit well on the end of the big, square platform so that now their table was to one side, allowing them to stretch their legs.

"Thank you. This is so great." Sam watched him go and then turned to Sebastian. "Why are you scared?"

Sebastian avoided the question. "Love, are you sure you want to have an affair? What about Kole and your marriage?"

"I know, but I made a choice the night we were in Iza's bathroom. I decided that I could have you both- can't I?"

He felt a bit relieved and kissed her. "Yes." Something was on his mind, she could tell, because otherwise he'd be kissing her more, fondling her.

"What aren't you telling me, Sebastian?"

He sighed and looked away. *I might as well be intimate and tell her everything on my mind, he thought. Like Iza had said.*

"I don't want to ruin your life. You were so in love with Kole."

"Love-"

"There's more," he interrupted. Sam, I would take you here and now but,"

"Yes?" Sam's inner voices started to go crazy. Was he changing his mind? A tear fell down her cheek.

"Love, why are you crying? Don't cry."

"Sebastian, I decided to have you both because I don't know what else to do." She looked at him, "I have to have you, you're my best friend and now-" She looked for a napkin, wiping her tears. "I feel like a different person because I was always a little attracted to you, but it's so much stronger now."

"I know, Love. I feel the same way. Look, I'm scared because Iza said we have to play this out."

"You talked to Iza? I don't think she likes me."

"That's because she can't figure out why I want to tear into you or why Kole wants to."

"Sebastian," she trailed off. For the first time in her life Sam was feeling pretty and desired.

"Iza thinks that after we have sex, we'll lose interest in each other. I don't want that to happen. I don't want to lose you. If we have sex and then you marry Kole-"

"I don't want to lose you either. It doesn't feel like I'll get over you. It's always been like this, I've never wanted to lose your from my life."

"I'm sure we'll stay connected, but would we stay close?"

"Kiss me."

He did so.

"When you kiss me, I feel like I can breath again. As if I've been submerged under water."

"I love you, Sam." He felt his love for her run though his veins and his soul. "I always have." He held her cheek and raised it to meet her lips again. "I love you." *Tell her. Be intimate*, he heard Iza's voice in his head. "I'm afraid I wont want to let you go after. I think I'll want you more."

This was music to her ears because she felt the same way. She wanted him to want her.

"Have me."

He looked deeply into her eyes.

"Alright, Love." Feeling brave he went on, "This isn't just sexual. I know it's more, I don't know how I know, but I do."

"I do too, my love."

"Then we need to talk about some other things, Love."

"Yes, I think we do. Nick left."

"I heard. Where did he go?"

"He got a job, he's going to their headquarters to be trained for two weeks. I'm glad. That put off the wedding planning and, since we don't have a home right now, he figured I could stay here, work and plan the wedding."

"Stay with me." He stroked her arm. Her skin was so soft. "In my casita."

"I'd love to."

"I'm enrolling in a cooking school."

"That's great, Bass!"

"*Bass?* I like that. I'm so happy, Sam. I feel so good when you are next to me, you make the world better, more inviting."

Sam was feeling calmer. She had both men promising their love. "Bass." He kissed her again. "Sebastian, are you going to stay here? In Santa Fe?"

"I don't know, Love. We'll see what happens. All I know is that you need to be near me- all of the time."

"I need you too."

Just then Sam's cell phone rang. She pulled it out of her purse and saw that it was Cindy. She looked to Sebastian. She swiped to answer the call.

"OK, what are you two doing, dear? Put me on speaker phone."

"Hi Cin," Sebastian greeted.

Sam looked up from the phone and into his eyes. Her mind was silent, she realized. Mmm, she relished the peace and quiet. *Bass makes everything so wonderful.*

"Hi yourself, dear. When I left it sounded like things were getting saucy. Sam, dear, I want to make sure you know what you are doing. Let me know if you want to talk."

"Do you think we're doing the wrong thing, Cindy?" Sam asked.

"There's no 'wrong thing.' You know that, dear. You two have something special. A turtle could see that. The question is, is this what you both want? Are you fooling around or are you two serious?"

"We're-" Sam began.

"No! Don't answer that. That's for you two to decide. Sam, dear, I just want you to know that I'm here to talk with you. Sebastian, I'm not as worried about you. So you think you're swinging both-" This time Cindy was cut off.

"I am gay!" He retorted.

"Yes, dear. Right," she appeased. "Well, when I left, Sam was looking like a Barbie Doll."

Sebastian put his hand over his face, "Yeah, I know. She looks drop-dead gorgeous."

"Anyway, Sebastian, you didn't let me down. Iza and Katriana are phenomenal. Iza invited me back, and I'm arranging the trip to Bali now. She and Katriana did say you two have quite the energy between you. 'Energy' isn't my department, but it may account for a gay man wanting a woman." She chuckled, which sounded like a frog croaking. "You two are something else! I could write a book on you as well."

"A book? You can't, you don't know how things are going to end." Sam said, feeling uncomfortable at the thought.

"I'm sure I'll be finding out."

"Cin, hon?" Sebastian leaned into the cell phone. "We're having a tequila night tomorrow. Won't be the same without you. Miss you, honey!"

Sam looked directly at Sebastian, an accusatory look on her face. "Now you sound gay."

Sebastian tilted his head slightly, raised his eyebrows quickly saying, "I told you I am."

"Alright you two. I can't wait until your first fight. It will be so juicy! You'll call me when it happens, dear?"

"Yes, Cindy." Sam answered. "If I can, I'll put you on speaker phone to hear the whole thing."

They hung up. Sam reached over to Sebastian's pants and rubbed.

"I have an early appointment tomorrow, with a client. He's on the east coast and the call is at 7 am his time. So, I can't stay out tonight. Also, I'm supposed to talk to Nick tonight, I better stay in my casita."

Sebastian looked disappointed. He looked down at her hand and took a deep breath. "Alright Love. Then tomorrow I want to take you to lunch and then back to my place." *Conflicted or not, I'm going to find out.*

Sam leaned in to kiss him, whispering "Sure, but no lunch."

27

Cooking School

The next morning Sebastian was disappointed to wake up alone when Sam was just fifty feet away. He hadn't jumped into bed with her because he had wanted some time to adjust to the idea of doing something so un-gay, by his definition. He also knew that, as much as it was torturous, taking it slow was making this experience last. It was like biting into the most delicious dessert and savoring it for days.

His hair tussled, his bed unmade, Sebastian sat at the edge. *OK, ol' boy. It's time to do something today*. He yawned. He'd been wanting to check out the Santa Fe Cooking School for some time, and today was the day. As far as his finances went, he was still working part-time for the magazine, but he didn't love it and he knew it wouldn't last forever. Rent would be due next week, so it was time to focus on his career. The reason he'd come west.

He wore his pajama bottoms, no shirt, into his kitchenette. He put water on to boil for tea. Once the tea was done, he sat on the couch. He'd enjoy a few quiet minutes to himself before getting his day going. The first thought that popped into his head was Sam. Thinking about tasting her for the first time excited him, so he quickly refocused.

Sam. How could this go? How do I want it to go? It sounded simple: boy meets girl, boy falls in love. But 'simple' this was not. Sebastian had spent 38 years being attracted to men; he had identified in a community, in a mindset that saw life through a certain set of eyes. His life story was about him, and being gay was who he was. It was like finding out you were a martian all of a sudden. You'd always believed you were human, but no. Turns out that everything you know and the way you thought about and defined everything in your life, was now changing.

Sebastian wasn't a dramatic man- it's just that he felt like he didn't even know his own body, which had never been excited about breasts before. Now he couldn't wait to fondle Sam again, to kiss her, to taste her... *My Sam, my cupcake.* Bollocks! He reminded himself, *She's not mine.*

The deeper truth was that Sebastian thought he was falling in love. Sure, he'd told Sam that he loved her, but he was gay! He told the baker at the grocery store that he loved him too. *Falling in love,* that was different. She wasn't his, she was engaged to Kole. They had both said that they thought they'd want each other more, as opposed to losing interest, but Sebastian knew that you can't control things. You have to let the cards fall where they may. Sam wasn't exactly breaking off her engagement and he wasn't asking her to. But what if Sebastian fell in love and she went back to Nick? What if Sebastian let go of who he was, a gay man, and still lost the woman he longed for? *I could lose it all.*

Focusing back on money, to avoid thinking about losing it all, Sebastian debated Iza's rental choices. He could rent the casita month to month or he could pay for a year at a 20% discounted price. Should he commit to a year? He liked it here. Before he kissed Sam and after sleeping with William, he'd thought he might keep moving west on his own. Now he wanted to know where Sam would be. *Give yourself some time to see where things go,* he told himself. *Yes, of course.*

Cooking school! He went for his laptop to look up the directions to the school again. It was in town! Near the Longevity Cafe!

An hour later Sebastian headed into town to check out the cooking school. On his way, he received a text from Sam. She had a couple of clients and didn't think she'd be free until the early afternoon. This meant that Sebastian was no longer in a hurry to get back, so he planned to go by the grocery store too.

♥

Sam finished up with her first client and had a little time before the next. She went outside for some fresh air. The Bamboo room was hidden behind the Hawaiian casita, so she didn't have a view of the garden. Outside she saw the fountain and walked down to sit on a bench by the plants to watch the water and the occasional bird fly down to bathe.

Lost in thought, William surprised her, "Good morning, Sam."

"Oh!" she jumped. "William!"

"Sorry, didn't mean to spook ya!" He pointed to the bench. "May I?"

"That'd be nice, I don't see you too much lately. How are you?" Sam genuinely liked William.

"Good. Work is going great. Wish things were better with Sebastian, but you two seem to be doing well."

Sam blushed and looked down, "Yeah, I can't believe it. Sorry things didn't work out for you two, but yes. Yes, uh-"

"You two are connecting. We all know how close you are."

"I understand you and Katriana are quite the item too."

"Yeah." He paused. "I really like her, but-" he looked at Sam, who was listening. He looked down. "She lives in a different world and she's introducing me to that world. I wouldn't have ever dreamed-how I see life is changing. The thing is," he grimaced, "I feel like the town simpleton."

"I know what you mean. I'm not sure Iza likes me and I feel uncomfortable a lot of the time."

"No doubt. I'm right there with you, Sam." He looked up at the leaves in a tree above swaying in the wind. It was a warm day for fall, but the mornings and evenings were getting colder. "They both have strong personalities. I used to, not sure what happened to me. I feel a bit off kilter."

"That's a good way of describing it." *Yes! I'm not the only one!* "I guess it's worth it. How have you changed how you see life, William?"

"How hasn't it? Everything Katriana sees or is told, she doesn't believe. 'Nothing at face value,' she says. She looks at the energy every time."

Relief poured over them both. It was good to have someone to talk with, someone who understood how they felt. They talked until they each had to return to work.

♥

Sebastian paused outside the entrance to the cooking school. The building was like a condo for businesses crossed with a mall. Different stores occupied each shop space, the name of the shop hanging above the door. Walking through, he could see into each store through its corresponding window. There was no natural light inside and the space was small. It hadn't been designed as a place for people to sit or chat. Sebastian found a directory and headed to the second floor. He walked by a nice fountain on his way to the elevator but he shook his head wondering who would design such an uninviting space. Oh, well. He rode the elevator and saw that the school had a shop straight ahead. He'd look in there afterwards. Then he spotted the main office, a much smaller space next door. The shop had taken two store fronts and the office just a small, single space.

"Good morning," he greeted. "I want to find out about the cooking school."

The woman at the desk looked up at him. It was 10:00 am and her hair was disheveled. A pen stuck out of the sloppy bun on her head and her glasses hung on the end of her nose. The top of her blouse was unbuttoned and she sat hunched over. She looked like she'd been working all night.

"Class schedules are inside the shop," she said in a dull voice as she pointed toward the store next door.

"In the shop? Oh," Sebastian was surprised. This didn't sound official or organized, it sounded more like he was signing up for a tour, like he did in Key West. "I thought this was a cooking school-" His sentence hung in the air. He didn't know whether to ask or state that "Santa Fe Cooking School" had led him to believe that they had a *school*.

"Yes, we offer over twenty classes on different types of New Mexican cuisine. A full list of the classes being offered for the next few months is next door, but generally you need to reserve your party's class several months in advance."

Sebastian got the picture: this was a tourist thing. "Great, thank you."

He left the frazzled lady in the office and went into the Cooking School's shop. Inside the light changed from the dull lights that lined the halls of this building to bright store lights combined with the natural light that came flooding in from the glass wall at the end of the store. Oven mitts, frying pans and specialty mincers and lemon squeezers caught his eye. He saw ornate over sized serving platters and specialty wine pouring spouts; shinny silver spatulas and silicon-coated whisks.

"Hi, can I help you find something?" A cute, young lady with long dark braids asked from behind him. He jumped, not having her come up to him. *She was quiet as those jack rabbits!*

"Oh, uh, hi." He looked down, as she was short. "I'm just browsing right now."

"Well," she wheezed, "what kind of cooking do you do? Sorry," some more wheezing, "allergy season."

"Oh, yeah, the junipers, right?"

"No, they're in the spring. It's other things in the fall."

"Fall?" Sebastian was lost to time. "Might be nice to cook a turkey for Thanksgiving this year."

"We have turkey bags, recipes for the brining your turkey and specialty canned chilies for making stuffing, if you like New Mexican-styled turkey. You do New Mexican cooking?"

"Well, no."

"Oh, you a baker? We have a great class on making tres leches cake," she said with a great accent.

"Tres what?"

"It means three milks. You're not a baker either." She looked at him the way Sherlock Holmes looked at crime scenes, but saw no crime. "I give up, what do you cook?"

"Uh, well, I was here to learn how to cook. I mean, I cook, but I wanted to get professionally trained." As an afterthought, he added, "And, I cook. American dishes, Italian meals-"

"Yeah, I get it. Sometimes the name throws people off. We're for tourists or home chefs and our classes are specialized. The most popular classes are the flan class and the hatch green chili class."

"Can I take a schedule of your classes?" He liked the idea of private parties coming to classes. Maybe this hadn't been a wasted trip, maybe he could learn something about how they ran things.

"Sure," she walked over by her register and pulled out a sheet of paper. "The classes with the "X's" are already full."

"But the whole month's classes are exed out."

"Yeah."

Then Sebastian looked at the pricing, $85 to $99 per class, with a note saying that the class included a full meal. He looked to the class duration, 90 minutes.

"How large of a party can you take, say if no one has signed up for class yet."

"Forty Five."

He quickly did the math in his head, almost $4,500 for a couple of hours worth of work. Not bad.

"Thanks," he said as he left with his head filled with ideas.

On his way out of the building he ran into the Longevity Cafe. He hadn't realized that the coffee shop was in this building because he usually entered the coffee shop from the street entrance on the next street over. He still had some time before his date with Sam, so he went in for a latte. He sat for a while dreaming about what kind of cooking he liked best. What would his specialty be? Would he like to own a restaurant, a B&B? Could he give high-end cooking classes and charge enough money to be happy? Ideas, questions and wines pared with meals danced in his head.

♥

On his way home he bought the best looking deli meats, bread and other ingredients he could find. Back at the ranch, he showered and then prepared lunch, in case Sam would be hungry. He also bought a couple of avocados and other ingredients to make guacamole, which he preferred over mayonnaise, on his sandwiches. His cooking space and counter were narrow, but the boxed chicken broth and frozen vegetables made the chicken soup easy to cook. He'd bought fresh cilantro to add at the end, making sure that the casita smelled fabulous when Sam arrived.

You'll ruin things, Iza's words had echoed in his head earlier, but now he'd gotten over them. Yes, he stood to ruin her marriage and his own heart depending on how things went, but he was compelled to risk it all. He was obsessed with her, reducing the weight of the risk. At this point, he just wanted her and felt like he'd waited for days since they'd first kissed. And she hadn't changed her mind. She wanted him too, so to hell with it all.

"Oh, it smells fantastic in here."

"Obvious again, aren't you love?" he asked, as he pointed to her. She'd been wearing make-up every day and her hair was down again. Her short, dark blue dress was held up by spaghetti straps, was fitted on top and then loosened in an A line skirt on the bottom. "I love it," he moaned.

Sam smiled. "What do I smell?"

"Chicken soup. I guessed you would be hungry."

"Starving," she said. It was early afternoon. "All I've had is a cup of coffee."

"Spend the night here, I'll feed you in the morning." He embraced and kissed her. "Cup of soup before I devour you?"

"No, I'm starved." She reached down and unbuttoned his pants.

"As you wish, Love." He undressed her as he felt her hand over his pants. "Bedroom."

She turned, dropping her dress and then her panties and bra. He ripped his clothes off and followed her into the bedroom, closing the door.

He put his hand to her breast tasting her for a minute before he lay her on the bed. "Dessert after." He said and he thrust himself inside her, feeling sensations he'd never felt before.

Later when they were both satisfied, sweaty and out of breath, they laid (lay) on the bed. Sebastian brought his finger to his mouth, asking Sam for silence. He pulled the sheets up to cover them and then gazed into her eyes, stroking her hair. She gazed back, grateful that her inner voices were giving her a respite. Her awareness was in her body, not her mind. This allowed her to feel the moment, feel her pleasured body - and receive the love coming out of Sebastian's eyes.

Several minutes later, forgetting that they were no longer in their 20's, Sebastian ran his hand under the sheet over her breasts caressing her nipples and then down between her legs as she reciprocated the caressing. She tried to taste him, but he wanted to feel what it was like to be inside of her again.

They satisfied each other again.

And then again.

28

Playing House

Exhausted from the day before, Sebastian and Sam slept in. At 9:00 Iza came knocking on the door looking for her breakfast cook who was an hour late.

Knock, knock.

Then she rang the doorbell, stirring Sebastian from his sleep.

"I was having a peculiar dream," he said out loud in bed. *Mmm,* he delighted in waking up next to Sam. It wasn't that he'd forgotten that she was there, It was still a new concept to awake with her in his bed. Naked in his bed. He was ready to start the day making love to Sam again, but he'd have to get rid of Iza first. He got out of bed and threw his pajama bottoms on and then went out to open the door.

"Morning Iza."

Iza gave him a look-over, "How fun for you, angel. Sleeping in, your hair is a mess- and I see you're ready for Sam," she said looking down at the tent in his bottoms.

"Oh!" he said, jolting himself backward and covering his crotch with one hand. "Sorry, you surprised me, I was asleep."

Iza turned and began walking away. "Feel free to come by for breakfast- if you two get out of bed at all. Tequila night: dinner at 7 to start the evening. And, I invited Katriana and William. He's back from LA and I knew Sam would help you forgive them."

Sebastian closed the door and went back to the room. Sam was sitting up at the end of the bed, her finger motioning for him to come over to her.

"Breakfast, Love?"

She nodded and pulled him forward as she began to lower his bottoms, pleasuring him.

"I meant are you hungry, should I feed you- ohhh," he moaned.

At 1:00 they were finally able to successfully make it out of the house, after several attempts at getting dressed and then undressed all over again.

By that time it didn't make any sense to go to Iza's house, where Sebastian did most his cooking. They wanted to enjoy time alone as new lovers, so they headed into town for lunch.

♥

This was fun. Kissing, being aroused, flirting, touching and then savoring each other. It was intoxicating! Sebastian could feel his addiction deepen, realizing it was becoming too late to break this habit, he was hooked. Sam glowed from having been showered by the many attentions Sebastian was giving her, sexual and otherwise. Her whole body tingled as though she were on a new drug called 'love and attention'. Nick's training was rigorous, so he had little time to text, let alone call. That made it easy for Sam to put her life with Nick aside, treating life with Sebastian like a separate reality. In Wonderland Sam could tell herself she was in a fantasy, a dream. No harm. As long as she didn't wake up, she could wear her red lipstick and live between both worlds.

"I can't get enough of you," Sebastian whispered as he kissed her in bed again. "But my lips hurt and Iza planned the tequila night at my request."

"Yes, Bass, let's go." She turned away from him and sat on the side of the bed, turning her head back to look at him. "Besides, that will let me tease you so you can't wait until we're back."

"You'd torture me that way?" From where he lay, he leaned over and kissed her side.

"I would."

"I see, you just want to drive me crazy." He kissed her side again, "You just want me to want you."

She blinked an acknowledgment. It was true, his desire for her was the exhilarating high of the drug.

"Love, I'm only leaving to let us catch our breath." Now he sat up next to her and brought his mouth to her ear. "I never saw this sultry, seductive side of you before."

"You brought it out in me, Sebastian. You told me I was beautiful."

"Good. You are, and I'm going to devour you." He began to kiss her again, but they both pulled back, their lips hurting.

"Pain's always a great motivator. Now I'm more willing to go to the party," she told him. "I need to stop by my casita and get something to wear."

"Another one of your eye-catching outfits? I've never seen you wear clothes like that before."

"I went shopping," she said shrugging her shoulder. "Just wait until you see what I'm wearing tonight."

"I can't wait- until I'm taking you out of what you're wearing tonight."

Yes, his desire for me is ambrosia, something I won't go without, she thought. Then she noticed that she hadn't been experiencing as many of her inner voices lately. The quiet had been so freeing! It felt good not to second guess herself. *The only problem,* she suspected, *is the likelihood that this is avoidance,* a defense mechanism meant to avoid the voice of guilt, logic, integrity. Not that it mattered, she turned her focus off and went back to watching him dress.

29

Tequila Night

Sebastian had said that he was still mad at William, but... he was plenty distracted, enough to not care that he and Katriana were at his tequila night. Katriana and William had placed chips, nuts, vegetable sticks and ranch dressing in bowl on the coffee table. They sat on one couch, Iza and Eric sat on the second, close enough to the coffee table for Eric to play bartender. Several bottles of tequila had been purchased for the evening, which they had coordinated to ensure variety. Eric had brought the tall, cobalt-blue bottle of Corralejos, a new favorite. Iza and Sebastian had several bottles, including a Patrón, they'd bought when shopping a couple weeks ago. The glass table was topped with a city skyline of bottles of varying height and color.

They drank quietly as they listened to William's captivating story-telling of his screen play. He said that "Lonely At Dawn" was a story of Arcadigo, a man in the US who looked old, slow and mundane on the surface, but had lived a secret life beyond imagination. In his youth, Arcadigo had traveled to exotic foreign lands when he enlisted in the army. Upon fulfilling his commitment with the army, Arcadigo had stayed in a small country in the Mediterranean initially as a guest of the king. Later in the king's employ, Arcadigo, headed up one of the king's enterprises, a coffee plantation, which required he travel the world in search of the best coffee plants. He was often invited to the most exclusive events everywhere he went, putting the world's best at his fingertips, William told.

"Arcadigo's travels and adventures provided him great wealth and connections that lasted him throughout his life. At the end of the movie we find out that looking old and frail is a cover. Arcadigo is still running secret trade missions for his friend, King Baltizar. The movie has given us this amazing look behind the scenes of this man and the riches that the world offers anyone but few embrace, the way he has. He's then summoned by King Baltizar, who is dying and wants to see his friend one last time. The king, seeking wise words to comfort him in death, asks Arcadigo if he has any regrets or if he's lived life to it's fullest. Arcadigo tells the king that his life has been beyond his dreams in every way save one: that his one love married another. Understanding this, the king responds that he'd initially sent Arcadigo out in search of the perfect coffee bean as a panacea for his ailing queen's condition. The king tells Arcadigo that after the death of the queen, he'd come to think of him as the son the never had. The king continued to sending him out on missions, hoping that Arcadigo would find love, the only gift the king couldn't bestow on Arcadigo."

"Angel, that's a fantastic story. The only thing he couldn't have - that which is the fabric of creation, love."

William looked happily surprised, "Oh?"

"Love is the energy that everything is made of," Katriana repeated, placing a chip in her mouth.

"And you tell the story so colorfully," Sam complimented. Everyone agreed.

The room broke into separate conversations. Every now and then Katriana would glance at Sebastian and Sam to read their energy, as she'd told Iza she would. She couldn't be obvious and stare. The energy around them was different than most of the energy she'd encountered around couples that were energetically connected and pulling toward each other. The energy between them was more dense and thicker now. It was clear: they had had intercourse, which increased the energetic cording. She decided she'd have to take a more direct approach and talk with them.

"*Sebastián,*" she pronounced in Spanish, "*¿Cómo estás?*" She asked warmly.

"Katriana," he took a breath and told himself that there was no reason to be mad at her about William. It would be immature. Besides, right now he didn't care because he was enraptured with Sam. "I'm good, how is my witch? Any magic going on?"

"Magic? Let's make some!" she laughed. How are you doing in your casita? It is one of the most beautiful, no?"

"Actually, I love it. I sleep like a baby!" Sam turned away from her conversation with Eric and Iza to listen to Katriana. Sebastian leaned over and put his hand on her knee. Since they were in individual club chairs, space was forced between them. Katriana now saw her chance:

"Why you no sit here?" She said standing. She pulled William's arm up too. "William want to speak with Eric, we switch, yes?"

Surprised, but feeling the push, Sebastian and Sam got up and switched to the couch. "OK." Sebastian barely said as Katriana guided his arm, sitting him down. He looked at Sam to see her reaction. Her expression said, "Weird, but OK." She smiled and, glad to be closer to her, Sebastian placed his arm around her. Now there was no space between them and Katriana could see the flow between them better.

"Actually, I had a dream, Katriana-" As if switching had stirred his memory, an image from last night's dream came forward.

"¿Ah, sí? Tell me, maybe we have a little magic tonight." She could see that he had a foot in the door to his dream. Great place for him to relay the dream's energy, she thought.

"I- I, am in a room. I don't know the room. It has wood paneling, it's surprisingly warm and inviting even though it's not what I would normally think was nice decorating."

Katriana waved him forward with her hand. Iza saw this and jumped in to help, "Go on, angel," her words gently invited.

"There's a light-colored heart in the paneling, like it's part of the natural wood. I like it here, I feel relaxed. I also see another thing, a railing. I only see the top - I can't tell what it goes to. It's only so wide, a couple feet, and it has bars coming down off of it, but I can't any more than that."

Now he snapped out of the dream, the gaze in his eyes gone. "That's probably not enough of the dream for you interpret," he looked into her eyes now.

Katriana scanned them both, reading Sam just as carefully, taking them both in.

"Mmm… Yes…" she said slowly. It was her turn to step into his dream. Her eyes didn't glaze over, like his had, but Iza could see that Katriana had caught something. She waited to see what she would share. Sebastian noticed too.

"Well?" He tried reading her expression, looked to Sam and then looked back to Katriana. "Can you interpret it?"

"No," she whispered, pulling on William's arm. He read the cue:

"Ah. She 'no interpret,' " William said in her accent. "She taps into the energy." Everyone chuckled.

"You found home. You said you came to Santa Fe looking for your purpose." Katriana spoke in perfect English. "Purpose isn't one thing, the way people think. It isn't the one thing you do in life that will make you happy; it isn't something that the universe, God or Silent Knowledge want you to do. No, purpose can change - because everything is energy."

Iza motioned for William to get Katriana a drink. Confused at Iza's cryptic sign language, he looked clueless at first. Then Eric leaned into his ear.

"Get her drink." He growled.

Ah! William went to the table with the tequila bottles and grabbed a shot glass and turned to Iza, *what kind of tequila?* She saw that he wouldn't know what to do, so she whispered in Eric's ear. He stood, seeming taller than when he'd walked in the door, and went to the table. He handed William a whole bottle and then motioned for him to take it back. *Oh, right!* William sat, poured tequila into the shot glass. He stared at the glass of tequila, who's contents disappeared before he'd finished pouring. His eyes widened at the empty shot glass; he stared hard, deciding to pour again. And then again. Somehow the liquid in the shot glass went down Katrina's throat without him even seeing her picking it up. He stared at the empty shot glass.

"Energy can manifest in many ways. Meaning gives a person substance in the universe. It helps them gather energy, fills them with energy. Your purpose is always to find meaning in your life. People use meaning and purpose the same way, that's fine. You can live your purpose to give yourself meaning in many ways: as a screenwriter, a businessman, a cook.

"Then there is meaning in energy. There is what we do, like being a businessman, and then there is what we *be, our being*. We must bring meaning to both of these, filling ourselves with energy in our being and in our doings."

Now Katriana focused her eyes and looked at Sebastian. "Your dream is telling you that you have found meaning in your being. You came seeking meaning, and you have found it."

William's mouth hung open, *found meaning? So fast?*

Really? Sam's eyebrow's raised high in disbelief.

Iza squinted, *what aren't you telling us?*

Hmm, Eric grumbled.

Sebastian furrowed his brows for a second, questioning her words. *Meaning? What's been meaningful? Meaning? What have I found? What..* He rapidly searched the hidden recesses of his mind seeking the buried treasured of meaning that she described. He discovered the treasure: *Sam!*

"And that meaning," Katriana continued, "will lead to a part of your purpose. A part of what you are meant to live in this life. That purpose, that doing, will then help you develop yourself, as you are meant to in this life."

"You saw all of that in a wood paneled wall?" Sebastian was amazed and incredulous at the same time.

"Angel," Iza jumped in, "when Katriana sees energy, there can be a lot more than what an image would reveal. The energy behind the image can be far reaching; it can be telling, deep and it can unfold, telling more than we think any one image or message can give."

"Sounds like you have found a gem," Eric spoke. His words were rare and carefully chosen, so Sebastian looked at him for a minute. He realized that this was all true, he'd found a gem in Sam. He'd always known she was special, but he'd never understood how special. He nodded in agreement. He looked at William now- they'd left things on such a negative note. Sebastian smiled at William now, admitting to himself that William had been instrumental in leading Sebastian to Sam. It was William who suggested they come to Santa Fe and find a fortune teller. *Shite!* Sebastian thought. I owe him. It was time to let go and forgive any ill feelings that may still linger toward him or Katriana.

Picking up on Sebastian's shift in feelings toward him, William spoke to him for the first time since they'd slept together.

"Honey, it sounds like everything you came looking for has found you."

Sebastian looked down and then up, "Yeah, I think so." He had to chuckle, he certainly hadn't left Florida and headed west to find an affair with a woman, or to meet witches. This trip had been filled with all sorts of surprises and gifts.

The group's conversation broke up into individual conversations again. Iza spoke with Sam to check on her and see how she was doing. She'd promised Cindy that she'd report back as to how Sam's evil twin was behaving.

Eric faced Sebastian, "You came to Santa Fe looking for something?" he asked.

"I used to be in the fashion industry, marketing."

"Iza said you help her."

Sebastian nodded, "I headed west looking to see what I wanted to do with my life. I have a passion for wine and food, so I thought I'd head to Napa Valley."

Eric laughed. His laugh was deep and hearty. "I don't see you making it there. What were you hoping to do?"

"Get more into the world of wine, maybe become a sommelier." Listening to himself, Sebastian now thought this sounded a bit crazy, like he'd been chasing a fantasy. "Sounds off to me now," he smiled, "but it brought me here. Or, I guess William did. We were driving out together and he wanted to stop in Santa Fe."

"Good thing." Eric said from under his eyebrows. He poured Sebastian and himself another tequila. "Try this, you can't buy it here. It's from Mexico." He poured a light, gold-colored liquid into Sebastian's shot glass.

Sebastian lifted the shot glass, looking at it for the first time. Every shot glass Iza had was unique. His had the words "Xel-Ha" on them, a logo. Below it read "Mexico," so he assumed it was a memento from one of Iza's many retreats. He sipped the tequila, "Wow!" Sebastian loved it.

"So, what have you found, because you're not a sommelier."

"No, I've found that I'm as passionate about food. I've been falling in love with tequila too." He said, raising his shot glass. "This is fantastic, thanks." Eric nodded and then Sebastian continued. "I tried to enroll in a cooking school, but I guess I didn't find the right one."

"Santa Fe has a lot of restaurants, but only a handful compete with top restaurants in big cities. There's room for us to compete. Would you cook for me?"

"Cook?" As though someone had uttered magic words into Iza's ear, she threw her attention in their conversation. "Is Sebastian cooking, because I want in! Angel, he's an amazing chef."

"Yeah?" Eric asked, reading Iza's endorsement.

"Well, yes. He's better than lil' ol' me!"

Eric smiled at her. "Who cooked dinner the other night, when we ate at the table outside?"

"He was forced to rest, so it was my witches and I. He's better though." Iza had a feeling. She knew Eric's interest couldn't be arbitrary.

"Does he have a kitchen or can he cook at your place? I'd like to try his cooking. I'm always looking to invest."

That's all Iza had to hear. "Come!" Iza stood, nudging Eric by the arm. When he stood, she interlaced her arm in his and led him to the kitchen. "It's small, but since we have events I have a full kitchen. When we need to, we can accommodate up to 50 people."

"Your kidding. Where?" he looked at her in disbelief. She had several acres of land, but the building's sizes were modest.

"Not in the house, in the Hawaiian…" Their conversation trailed off as they left the living room for a kitchen tour.

Sebastian turned his attention to Sam. He grinned. Just looking at her filled his heart, maybe this is what Katriana was talking about. Sebastian felt as though someone had poured tons of liquid love into him and he was about to overflow or burst in a wonderful way. He leaned in to her ear, "Is it time to go home, Love?" Just asking her warmed his body. He couldn't wait to take off her jeans and top. Her cotton red top matched her lipstick, and the V neck was revealing. He couldn't wait to peel it off her.

Sam squeezed his hand, but Iza and Eric came back just then.

"I'd like to talk to you, if you can spare a few minutes." Eric said to Sebastian.

Sebastian looked to Sam, who nodded in agreement.

"Sure," he agreed.

"Kitchen." Eric pointed and Sebastian got up and followed him.

In the meantime, Katriana and William had been talking with each other. Katriana now looked to Iza, bringing her into their conversation.

"William is heading out to LA tomorrow," her English still perfect thanks to the drinking. Iza caught William's transfixed eyes upon Katriana. Iza could see that William was falling in love. 'Poor thing', she thought. 'Katriana doesn't really fall in love.' She assumed that Katriana would break his heart.

Enthusiasm replaced admiration as William spoke, "I've been called to a meeting about the sequel. Sounds like they are jumping on a contract."

"I'm guessing you are coming back, angel. Will you be joining us for the Bali retreat?" Iza had a way of making people feel included and as though she was always looking out for them. This had been especially comforting to William when Sebastian had withdrawn his friendship.

"Are you kidding? I wouldn't miss it for the world!" He looked to Katriana, who was smiling at him, then he looked back to Iza. "I'll be back in a week or so."

The evening lasted a bit longer. Eric asked Sebastian to plan two dinners for him. He wanted to have a small tasting of different dishes with Iza and Sam to select a menu, and then a larger dinner with people he'd invite. Sebastian said it would be a pleasure. He told Eric that he'd seen the cooking class model and thought that private pop-up dinners or classes could make a great business. They agreed to work on their ideas and have the first dinner soon.

Sebastian floated back to his casita. Coming home with Sam still held a high, and tonight, their was also the promise of new opportunities. He loved being here on Iza's land, loved having wise witches to confer with and now he was excited at the prospect of a new business partner. What more could he ask?

♥

30

Propositions

"Iza, time flies." Sebastian said, bringing groceries in the house. He'd been shopping for the first dinner that he was cooking for Eric.

"No angel, time doesn't exist." She said from her desk. "It slows down when you are out of the flow of life and speeds up when you are in the flow," she said matter-of-fact-ly. "So, what kind of food did you and Eric settle on?"

"Two kinds, Italian and American. We want to have a mixed-cuisine feel that includes flavors and health-conscious foods."

"That's a good trick, angel." Iza left her desk and came over to help Sebastian unpack his groceries. "Would you like a glass of lemonade?"

"That would be great. I'll cut up some fruit for us too."

They sat outside on Iza's porch. "Thanks for the fruit, angel." She drank in the blue, cloud-filled skies. "The weather is changing."

"Yes," he responded, looking at her land. "It's getting colder at night."

"High desert, angel. It will snow at Thanksgiving."

"Snow? I didn't know it could get so cold."

"It's due to the altitude."

Sebastian drank from his glass and then turned to look at Iza. "Sam has to go to Boston for a couple of weeks."

"Oh? How are things going? Are you still claiming to be gay, angel?"

Sebastian looked properly annoyed, as he was supposed to. "Yes." He said flatly. He might have given her a point on his invisible scoreboard, but he wasn't feeling like himself. He was doing better, but he hadn't been feeling like himself since he came to New Mexico. First he'd been preoccupied with finding what would be meaningful to him in his life career-wise then he'd been obsessed with Sam. Their love was all-consuming, or it had been. His posture dropped a bit, just enough for Iza to notice out of the corner of her eye.

"Kole is getting done with his training and Sam needs to go and take care of some business with her license or something. She's going to stay with Cindy, but I think she's going to see Kole too. It'll depend on the assignment they give him."

"How's that, angel?" Iza could see Sebastian's uneasiness.

"Well, it will just depend on how much time they give him before he needs to show up at work. It also depends on what city they place him in. Could be Boston."

"Are you nervous about her seeing him?"

"Sure, but I know she's not done with me."

Iza watched a raven flying by. "What about the retreat? Have you booked your reservation? It's coming up quick."

"No, just waiting on Sam. I'm going to try to book us together, if I can. She's figuring how long she has to stay in Boston and whether she can come back here to fly out with me or if she'll have to leave from Boston with Cindy."

The conversation is weighing on him, Iza thought, so she changed the subject. "Has William told you if he is coming on the trip, angel?" She knew the answer, but that wasn't the point.

Sebastian was surprised that she'd ask him. "No, wouldn't Katriana know?"

"Maybe. Between us, angel, I think he's falling for her, but she doesn't fall in love."

"Is she going to Bali?"

"I'm sure she is, but I should double check." Iza looked around to see if anyone was outside their casita. "Oh, angel, Katriana had asked me to let her know if a casita opened up. I think she'd like for William to have his own. Will Sam keep the casita or stay with you?"

"She's keeping up appearances for Kole."

"So she told you she's keeping the casita?"

"Actually, no. I'll ask. Hasn't she arranged the casita with you?"

"No, but I don't see her much, unless she's with you. How are things going?"

"Iza, hon, she's challenging my gay. The more we have sex, the more I want her." Now he was grinning.

"Well," Iza said, surprise in her voice, "it sounds like you've tried getting her out of your system plenty."

"I'll say. I keep trying," he smirked, his usual playful self coming through.

"What, having sex with the little blond?"

"No, that's come quite easy." He said, smiling and thinking about sex with Sam. "No, I mean me. I've always been a gay man, Iza. Now I'm having to change all of how I think about myself, how I see myself."

"Your self-image."

"What?"

"Your self-image, angel. I keep telling you to come to class. Tomorrow night, come. Sam will be gone, you'll need something to distract you. Besides, it would give you time to talk with Eric after tonight's dinner."

"How is it going with him, Iza?"

"Great, angel. He's coming to Bali too." Now she leaned over and put her hand on his arm. "You have been great for my business, angel. We have a great set of people signed up for the trip. I'm making good money this time."

"That's fantastic, Iza. I've never been, I'm really looking forward to it."

"Angel, I know you'll be watching to see how things go when Sam goes back to Boston. I might be jumping ahead here, but what are *your* plans? Will you stay here after the retreat?"

Sebastian leaned back in his chair, sitting with the question for a moment. Just then Peppermint jumped up on the armrest to the patio couch that Iza was sitting on.

"Meow!" He said, looking at Sebastian, sitting to Iza's right in the matching patio chair.

"Demanding, aren't you?" Peppermint made his way over onto Sebastian's lap, purring and making his neck available for petting.

"I'd say I feel at home, like Peppermint here." He gave Peppermint a few good scratches and rubs. "I guess 'home' is another thing I really came searching for on this trip. I've always been on the east coast, and I love it. It's home, but-" he paused, feeling his way through, "I don't really have a home."

"You will. Angel, there's something else I wanted to talk to you about, a proposition."

Sebastian had been watching the fountain, a bit distracted thinking about Sam. Now he looked to Iza, interested in a different topic, which promised an offer. "Yes, hon? You've got my ear. Sam's still got the rest of me, but I'm listening," he said, giving himself a point on his scoreboard. The one thing Sebastian sensed about his life right now was that, in most ways, things were going to go back to being wonderful. He was feeling more at ease, joking again. He was feeling a touch more like his old self. Something had changed, something in the air. Something was bringing back the playful, easy-going version of himself. He gave himself a point on his invisible scoreboard.

"What was that?" Iza mocked.

"My invisible scoreboard. Things are feeling better in life." He took a deep breath. "East coast fall smells different, but it smells great here." He paused a minute, feeling good. "I don't know, Iza. I'm enjoying living here right now, though my heart is flying out tomorrow."

"You have it so rough, angel," Iza said, mocking him again.

He looked down, laughing. "Yeah, well, you might not make fun of me tomorrow when I'm missing her." He looked up again. "Seriously, I have a good feeling about Eric and a feeling, like money is coming my way. I like the conversations I'm having with Eric. Also," he added, rubbing it in, "Love has never felt so sweet." Iza noticed that his tone, his body and the energy in his words changed when he spoke about or referred to Sam. He looked at Iza, "What is the proposition you mentioned?"

"A business proposition. You could be a man of power, a warlock. You could be a great counterbalance to us witches."

Peppermint jumped off his lap, walking away. Sebastian moved in his seat and looked at Iza trying to understand what she was saying.

"What does that mean?"

"Once Sam is gone, let's take a trip to Chimayó overnight. I want to see how you do with the energy of a powerful place."

"I'm intrigued and, with Sam gone, I'll need a distraction anyway."

That was all the explanation he got out of her. He had some idea of what she meant- ah well, he needed to focus on dinner and his last night with Sam.

31

Many Small Plates

The nights were getting chilly. Sebastian couldn't decide where he wanted to serve dinner tonight because Iza's breakfast table, the glass-topped coffee table, was small and really made for two people. Outside there was plenty of room, but the wind was kicking up. A part of the idea was for everyone to taste various dishes, so he needed a surface for several, small bowls and serving platters.

OK, he thought to himself, I'll use the coffee table in the living room even though it's not my first choice. I'll make it look nice- Now, where did I put that scarf from the market? He ran home to find the deep blue, silk scarf he'd found at one of the many weekend artisan markets downtown. It was wide, perfect as a table cloth, and had waves of deep blue, light blue and white running through, like the ocean or the Santa Fe skies. At the time when he was at the market, he had no idea what he'd do with the scarf, maybe gift it to Sam. Compelled, he'd bought it anyway and now he was glad. It brought a splash of color and a Sebastian flair into the room. *Perfect!*

Time to cook. In the kitchen he listened to "OneRepublic,"one of his favorite bands, on his wireless headphones. He sang along as he took what he and Sam had prepped earlier, putting it all together. He'd made fresh sourdough for a bruschetta appetizer. He chopped the beautiful, plump heirloom tomatoes with fresh basil that he'd gotten at the farmer's market. He had placed some of the dough aside to make 4 garlic-mozzarella knots. These were coming out of the oven now. He planned to drizzle his Italian-spiced olive oil on top right before serving them. His third appetizer was a small salad made of avocado, olive oil and spices. Simple, but it offered a rich flavor. His 'main course' dishes included chicken in a mango chutney sauce: just the right amount of sweet from the mango, just a hint of heat from the peppers. Glazed asparagus and yellow rice accompanied the chicken. The second was a salmon dill with the same yellow rice, this time with diced cucumbers and tomatoes.

It had taken a lot of prep time, but his sous chef, Sam, helped out immensely this morning. As Sebastian finished making dinner, Sam was packing. It was only Iza that Eric didn't want in the kitchen. Eric said he wanted to taste Sebastian's cooking, see his ideas and measure his ability to direct his kitchen. Sam could assist, but Eric knew Iza wasn't capable of just assisting.

Dinner in the living room turned out fine. Although Sebastian now missed Judy's dining room (Sam's mom, where Sebastian had held several dinner parties), he made Iza's space work. He placed a couple of bottles of white wine on the glass table in front of the window, the 'breakfast' area. This was just a few feet from the living room where he served the dishes on top of his blue silk scarf on the coffee table. In this way he mimicked the food and drink placement as they had done the night they'd had the tequila party.

His dinner guests arrived.

Eric stepped into Iza's house breathing the aromas. "This smells great." He walked into the living room, " I like the color, the presentation."

Sebastian couldn't quite tell if Eric meant it or not because his poker voice gave nothing away. So, he took it as a compliment.

"I was in marketing; I believe how something looks is as important that how it tastes because the look will affect the taste."

Eric looked up from under his thick, bushy eyebrows, "You've got that right."

Sam, who was obviously distracted by her trip to Boston tomorrow, leaned over to kiss Sebastian. "Everything looks delicious, Bass."

"Thanks, Love." For a split second he could feel her hesitation about leaving him and possibly seeing Nick, or Kole, again. He would bring it up after dinner when they were alone. For now, he had to focus on the dinner. Everything was served, but he still had to be a host to his pop-up restaurant.

"Oh, fresh bread. I'm going to help myself, angel," Iza said, grabbing a side plate and a napkin. Sebastian had put all of Iza's side plates out so that everyone could take a fresh plate and serve themselves a taste of all the different dishes. Iza took a garlic-mozzarella knot and began to moan. "Oh, I love bread!" Eric followed her lead. He took a bite of this, a bite of that, but revealed no expression.

"Wine?" Sebastian offered.

"I'll serve," Sam said. She figured she'd pour her glass first. Tonight she wore one of Sebastian's favorite outfits of hers, a dark blue, fitted, sleeveless dress. He noticed that the silk scarf would match perfectly, so he made a note to give it to her after dinner. He watched her for a minute before turning his attention back to Eric.

"Cowboy, you can cook." Eric had already put some salmon, chicken and bruschetta on a couple of plates, with Iza's help. He'd already tried these, save the chicken he was about to taste now.

Sam handed a wine glass to Iza and Eric. She went back to the glass table and drank from a glass with her lipstick on it and then brought Sebastian a glass.

"Great. Let's talk some more after we eat, now that I've tasted everything," Eric growled as he reached to serve himself more salmon. "What do you like best, Iza?"

They talked and ate until everyone was full, except Sam. Sebastian noticed that she hadn't been eating as much. At one point he'd leaned over and asked if she was feeling OK, to which she'd replied that she was nervous about leaving. They agreed to talk later.

Eric and Iza had a great time, laughing more often than not.

"That's a lovely necklace," Iza said, noticing the energetic luster on the pendant Sam wore.

"Thank you, Sebastian gave this to me." Sam put her hand up to the stunning aquamarine stone that hung on a sparkling silver necklace. "It's the color of the ocean in St. Martin, where we met."

Iza could see. She saw more than a necklace, she saw Sebastian's attempt to give Sam something to keep connected with him; she saw Sam's need for his protection, which he had now materialized as a talisman for her to wear. This was no ordinary pendant. Whether Sebastian knew it or not, he'd imbued it with his energy to accompany Sam until he saw her again.

"I found it when I was looking around on Canyon Road. They have some unique jewelry shops there. I saw this and I just had to get it for her."

"Quite a find, angel."

"Where's Katriana tonight?" Eric asked.

"William left and I think she's been talking with him on the phone at night. Sometimes she does this, spends time alone."

Eric turned his attention back to Sebastian and Sam. "You two need to go home now. We'll clean up." He looked to Iza to see that she agreed and then he looked back to Sebastian. "Cowboy, you can cook. I was going to pick from what you cooked tonight, but you go ahead and pick the menu. We'll work details out later. Go enjoy your time with Sam." Now he turned to Sam, "Sweetheart, thank you for spending your night with us. You have a good trip, ya 'hear?"

"Cowboy?" Sebastian had ignored the name the first time, but now it hurt his ears. "You do know I'm gay, don't you?"

Eric raised an eyebrow and looked at Sebastian, then the other eyebrow to look at Sam.

"Sebastian, I don't get it! Why do you keep saying that?" Sam asked sharply. "Do you think he's going to talk to Nick or are you so bothered to be sleeping with me?" *Enough was enough already!*

Sebastian was taken aback. "Love, it-it has nothing to do with you, I've always been gay."

"Well, it *should*, don't you think? I mean, after all, I'm the one you've been screwing! But, if you're gay, what's the point?" Sam stood up.

"It's just who I am-" Sebastian defended himself as he realized that he'd hit a deep nerve with Sam. "Or who I was. Sam, I-"

Sam fell back on the couch, "Fuck you, Sebastian," she said crying. "It's like I'm just an experiment to you. I'm risking my dreams and you aren't- You aren't doing anything different, just your usual gay self.'"

Sebastian knew that Sam was upset because she was going back to Boston. She'd said she wasn't sure she was going to see Nick, but now Sebastian figured she knew she would. "Love, I'm sorry. Maybe you're right, maybe I can't say I'm gay any more because I love you."

"I'm overreacting- I'm nervous about seeing Nick, nervous about everything. I had put the guilt aside- I can't ignore it anymore. It's in my face and I have to deal with it." Sam looked up, realizing that Iza and Eric were still here. She stood, "I'm sorry."

"Not at all." Eric responded.

"Angel, you have nothing to be sorry about. You are handling everything beautifully." Iza's voice was as loving as Sam had ever heard it.

"Sebastian, I need to stay in my casita tonight. I should probably have someone else take me to the airport. I need some time alone, time to sort through things."

Sebastian's heart felt heavy as he smiled supportively, "Yes, of course."

"Angel, what time to you go out tomorrow?"

Sam turned to Iza, "My flight's early. At 6:00 in the morning, I believe."

"Oh, you'll have to leave before 4 then." Iza got up and went to her phone, pushing buttons. "Katriana is picking William up tomorrow. I think that poor boy can't stand to be away from her, so he's already coming back. Let me ask if she can take you, since she's going anyway."

To busy himself, Sebastian got up and started taking dishes to the kitchen. When enough plates were cleared, he took the blue scarf off the coffee table.

"She says she's going in the morning, so taking you is not a problem." Iza's words were still as sweet as ever.

"Thank you. Good night Iza, Eric." She walked to the door, "See you in Bali."

"Don't worry about clean-up. Go." Eric shooed Sebastian towards the door with his hand. "Go on."

"Thanks," Sebastian quietly spoke as he turned to follow Sam.

"Sam!"

Sam was walking towards her casita, but turned. Sebastian held the scarf up, offering it to her.

"I'd like you to have this, it'll be colder in Boston." His words were quiet, weak- very uncharacteristic of him. He realized she was waiting for him to continue talking. "Sam, I love you. I know you need to go and take care of things. Gay or not, I'll be waiting for you to come back." Feeling more comfortable, he approached her and held her. "I love you more than anything." He kissed her gently as tears began to fall down her cheeks.

"I'm scared, I don't- I thought-" she was shivering with the cold wind. "I just don't- know- what's going to happen." It was hard for her to admit this, but doing so unleashed some guilt and fear she'd been keeping tied up.

"I know." He embraced her again. "Please, don't forget that I love you, no matter what happens." He held her face in his palm, kissed her one more time and then turned around, walking away. He knew he had to go, otherwise he would start to feel that he couldn't let her go.

Sam held the scarf, watching him for a minute before heading into her warm casita. She could see Katriana waiting outside to coordinate tomorrow morning.

"I'm scared, Love." Sebastian told the wind, as he stood outside his casita door, staring into the dark night in the direction of Sam's casita. He sighed, his heart aching because he could sense that things had changed. "I love you." Now a tear formed in his eye as his heart broke. He cool feel her slipping away. "I was afraid this would happen. I love you more than I thought I could love a woman."

Sebastian's soul ached. All he had now was his faith, his hope that she really loved him, even half as much as he loved her. Knowing that she would be seeing Kole, his faith was tousled in the wind.

32

Traditional Scones In Cuisenarts

Sebastian slept in the next day, avoiding coming back to life with Sam gone. He would adjust his attitude soon enough- for now though, he let himself feel sorry for himself.

OMG, shite! Get your self-pitying, wonky ass out of bed and shower. He went to Iza's without a shower.

"Morning." It wasn't a greeting, so much as it was an acknowledgment of day. "We going to Chimayó today?"

"Hello sunshine, don't you look happy?"

"Mmm." He groaned, admitting he missed Sam.

"Katriana is spending half her day in Albuquerque, so she asked that we wait until tomorrow. That way she can bring her puppy."

"Kia?"

"No, angel. William. She's picking him up, you know."

"Puppy, eh?"

"So, we'll head out tomorrow. Is that OK?" her question was rhetorical.

"Yeah- uh," he took another step in the house. "What time is it?"

"Eleven. You just getting up?" she said looking to see if she should be concerned.

"Uh, yeah. Do you want me to make lunch? Or I could make scones, a treat for Katriana and William when they get in."

"Scones? Sounds like dessert. I don't think they'll be here for a couple of hours."

"Perfect. Can you throw a stick of butter into the freezer? I'll make my mum's traditional recipe with the Cuisinart."

"Traditional? Cuisinart? Freezer?" she chuckled.

"Do you have blueberries?"

"Yes, angel."

"I'm going to shower and then I'll be back in 20."

"Alright," Iza said, still sitting at her desk. "They better be good though, I'm skipping lunch."

"I am too." He walked out. "And, they're fantastic," he called from the other side of the door.

♥

Sebastian came back after a shower and started baking. Iza let him toss flour around for a while before poking her head into the kitchen.

"Honey, as long as you're in here," she said sweetly. Sebastian looked chef-like with his apron and flour on his cheek.

"Yeah, I'm hungry too. I'm making us sandwiches," he responded without even looking up.

"Good. Can you make lemonade too?"

Now he looked up at Iza, a bit surprised. "Yeah."

"Great." Iza pulled her head out of the kitchen to leave but then looked in again. "Scones are notorious for being hard to make."

"Good scones, yes." Sebastian had a ball of dough in his hands, debating whether to add more flour or not.

"Well," Iza said, waiting to see if he'd look up, "there's no point in making bad scones. Those we can get anywhere." She wanted to see if she could make him smile.

He looked up at Iza. "Hon, you aren't really talking about scones, are you?" He paused, reading her expression.

"No, angel. I just want to make sure you make good sandwiches," she smirked.

"No, try again," he sighed. He looked down at his dough again. "You want to know how I'm doing. Fine, I'm fine, hon."

"Well, now I know you're not. How much longer will you be in the kitchen? I think you need to come and talk with me."

"Not long. The sandwiches will take the longest."

"Longer than the scones, angel? I thought you were making good scones."

"Delicious, flaky, traditional scones. Mum's recipe." He kept working the dough.

"In the Cuisinart?" She watched him.

"Mm," he scoffed. Sebastian cut the dough in half. He added blueberries to one ball of dough, cranberries and orange zest to the other. He finished preparing the scones. He placed them gently on a parchment paper-lined cookie sheet and placed this in the oven. "About twelve minutes." Now he went back to the sandwiches. His bread was waiting in the toaster, lightly golden. He added a spread, sandwich meat, tomatoes, cheese and spinach.

She saw the spinach, "What's that?" she asked accusingly.

"Get out of my kitchen, hon. Lemonade and sandwiches coming up. Let's eat outside."

Iza backed off: the rule when someone was preparing food for her. She went to her bedroom, put on a sweater and went back to the kitchen. The weather was cooling down. The fall days were marking the change in events and activities. She saw that the sandwiches were on plates, so she gave each plate a napkin and then carried them out. Sebastian came out a few minutes later with the lemonade.

"Lemonade on a fall day, hon?" he asked.

"I like the way you make it." She bit into the sandwich. "Oh, this is delicious, angel." She took another bite and let herself hear and feel the fall breeze; she watched a couple of ravens flying by and noticed that, with the changing winds, they, too, changed their flight patterns.

"Row!" Peppermint cried, announcing his presence. He jumped on the couch Iza sat on, pawed at the cushion, settled down and looked up at her.

"OK, but it's good, so I'm only giving you a little piece of meat." She reluctantly shared a morsel with him. He took it, swallowed it whole, then closed his eyes.

"Angel, how are you?"

"I don't want to talk about it."

Iza nodded her head as she ate her sandwich. "It? You mean Sam?"

"Hum."

"You look a bit cold, angel."

"Yeah, I don't have any of my sweaters. They are all in storage. I need to go shopping. Any place you recommend?"

"Yes, but talk to me about how you are doing first."

Sebastian scoffed again. Then he lightened up a bit, thinking that maybe it would help to talk about it. "She'd been uneasy the last few days, but I think I made it worse. Done?"

Katriana's car pulled up then. She and William got out and waved at Iza and Sebastian. Iza waved for them to come on over.

She called out, "We've got scones!"

"I made them, they are fantastic," Sebastian added.

"Modest, aren't you angel?" she asked, turning to him.

"I have to focus on something good that I've done right." He stared forward, not wanting to talk about this any more.

"Hi, strangers!" Obviously William was thrilled to be back.

"*Sebastián, gracias.* After all morning in the airport, I looking forward to scones."

Sebastian smiled, "Thanks for taking her."

"Here, sit here." Iza stood, giving them the couch. "Let's take these plates in and bring the scones, Sebastian."

They disappeared into the house.

William took a deep breath, "It's great to be back."

"*Apenas te fuiste.*" Katriana lit up a cigarette, even though she knew William didn't like her smoking.

"I know, but I like it here. I missed it," William smiled and then he kissed Katriana. "I missed you."

"Oh, angel," Iza said as she came out the door holding a serving tray with a tea pot and four mugs. "Sanbusco, that's where you should go shopping for a sweater. Just put it into your navigation system, it's just downtown."

Sebastian held the door for Iza. He carried out a tray with blueberry scones, cran-orange scones, honey and clotted cream.

"Oh, hon, are you going shopping?" William's eyes lit up enthusiastically.

"Yeah, I need some warm clothes."

"Can we come? I'd love to shop downtown."

"No. No me. I'm have scone and go to bed." Katriana reached for a cran-orange scone.

"Sure," Sebastian said. Right now he'd welcome about any diversion.

"Angel, these are amazing! I'm going to tell Eric about your scones. Oh, I'll save one for him."

Sebastian smiled. After a restless night and feeling bad about Sam, it felt good to make something sweet. His night had been sour.

"Yeah, hon, these are fantastic. Can I try the other kind too?" William put three on his plate. "Travel makes me hungry," he explained sheepishly.

♥

An hour later, Sebastian and William were in his Mercedes heading to town to shop.

"Hey hon, after we shop, let's go by the St. Francis hotel. I hear they have a classic pub. I'll buy you a drink."

Sebastian was still a bit on edge with William. He weighed William with his eyes. *Bullocks!* A drink sounded tempting. Several drinks he wouldn't refuse. He quickly decided that he had nothing better to do, that tequila-therapy might be just what the day called for. Besides, not being home to think about Sam? Yes! He needed that escape.

"A drink?" He huffed. "In the mood for several."

"Great, it'll be a blast!"

"Yeah, sure." Sebastian tried to sound nonchalant, but it affected the speed at which he shopped.

Sanbusco, they learned, was a converted, old barn, though it didn't look like it. The small shopping mall had a lot of character, not that William got a good look. The minute they stepped out of the car, Sebastian spotted a shop with men's sweaters in the window. He went straight in, racing like a roadrunner. William had just started to touch a couple of items he was interested in when he saw Sebastian hand the cashier his credit card, looking at his watch. Sebastian raised his eyebrows, pleased. "Close enough to being past five, we can head to the bar!" He told the cashier. She smiled politely as he signed for the charge and took his bags.

William was far enough away that he couldn't hear what Sebastian had said, but he got the idea. He picked up the things in which he was interested and headed to the cashier. "Can I try these on at home?" He handed the clothes to the cashier.

"Sure, you have 7 days to for a refund or 30 for an exchange."

"Great." He paid for his clothes and looked at Sebastian who was awaiting him, smiling.

"I guess you really need a drink."

Sebastian's smile fell on the floor. "Yeah," his lips pouting. "Don't really want to talk about it." He was looking away, showing that this was difficult for him. "Until I've had a few drinks." He smiled.

"Ah! Boy's night drinking. Good, I could use the boy talk and the drinking too. This will be fun," William said, partially lying. He was starting to wonder what he'd gotten himself into.

♥

33

Secretos de Tequila
(Tequila Secrets)

Had it been even thirty minutes later, they wouldn't have found the uncommon parking space in downtown Santa Fe. Maybe there was an upside to Sebastian's speed shopping. They parked, pleased that the St. Francis hotel had parking so close by. The one-way street had been a bit tricky, but Sebastian was proud to feel himself becoming a local who could navigate the downtown streets. He still couldn't understand such narrow streets, but he could see how they contributed to the 'old town' feel. They noticed a small restaurant across the street on corner with a line down the street. If this was any indication of the food, Sebastian, *I should come by soon.*

Feeling the dropping night's temperature, Sebastian put on the charcoal, Peruvian sweater he'd just bought. *Oh that feels good!* he told himself, stretching into it. William couldn't help but notice, Sebastian looked enticing!

The St. Francis hotel was earth-toned, like all the other buildings in Santa Fe. Unlike others, it had beautiful columns marking the entrance and giving it distinction. They walked through the columns delineating a charming outside seating area, to the stairs and the over-sized front doors. The inside of the hotel looked like a different hotel. The rustic, adobe look that marked the exterior's architecture was now gone. Instead the inside sparkled with a chandelier, a phone booth from the 1920's and a sign to 'Ye Ole' Pub'. They turned down the hall to their right as they stepped back in time to a classic English pub. A tasteful mix of modern and classic, the decor was inviting. Sebastian and William stopped at the entrance to stare in awe at the space. Before them, the bar ran along the length of the wall. The bar top was copper, whose color tones were echoed throughout. Just as a pub's walls must have been hundreds of years ago, the walls and the floor were earth-tones, blending reds, light tan and burnt brick colors. The bar's chairs were made of wood and leather, thick, wide straps of leather woven on the seat and back, giving the bar the feel of quality. The wall to their right was one long booth-bench with individual tables and chairs before it. The striped fabric on the booth echoed the bar's colors, in darker tones. The middle of the room had many sets of intimate tables and chairs. Along the far wall were windows, providing a view of the street and a fountain across the way. All around the walls, the ledges and on the tables, candles tied the classic pub feel to the modern, elegant mix. They also provided an intimate ambiance.

After taking in the sights, William held out his hand, pointing, "Where would you like to sit?" Later there would be few tables available, but right now they could choose the best the pub had to offer. Sebastian looked around.

"How about there?" he pointed to the far corner of the booth. "You can have the booth side, if you like. Go ahead, I'll get us started. What are you having?"

"Hmm." This was one of William favorite questions. "I'm buying, so I'll come with," he said, stepping toward the bartender. "Hello," he greeted. The bartender wore the black top and white apron uniform, his hair slicked back. "This is fun," he said turning to show Sebastian how excited he was. He held out his hand, inviting Sebastian to order.

"Three shots of tequila. What do you have?"

William did a double-take. He had expected Sebastian to order a glass of wine or maybe a shot, not three. He also noticed how calmly Sebastian had ordered the three shots! 'This man is planning to drink!' he told the bartender.

"Patrón, Milagro, Don Julio-"

"Patrón, please." Sebastian looked at William, reading his surprise. "Why don't I treat? I plan on having a few."

"Gold, silver or añejo?"

Sebastian looked at the bartender, pleased. "Oh, you have options for me! Uh," he thought, "I'll have to try the añejo another time. Silver, please."

"Hon," William put his hand on Sebastian's arm. "I'm celebrating. You know, my script. I haven't had a chance to celebrate, so I'm paying." William handed the bartender his credit card. "Tab please." He took a breath, thinking. "I was going to have what he's having, but… I'll have a Rusty Nail. We'll be at the corner."

They went to the table they'd chosen, relishing having found this special bar. What a great place to escape to.

"Ahh." William sat, pleased.

Sebastian's wood and leather seat was great, but he guessed that William's side, the booth-bench, was even more comfortable. He smiled. "So, you haven't celebrated? What did you do on this trip to LA that you are celebrating?"

"Began negotiations for the sequel! I'm so thrilled, Sebastian! I've worked for this for so long. It's finally happening."

"William, that's wonderful, amazing. I love the idea of going to the movies and telling people around me that I know the screenplay writer."

"Oh, stop! You'll make me blush!"

The bartender delivered their drinks and a small bowl of pretzels. He placed a beautifully designed 8 oz glass before William and three shot glass before Sebastian.

"Oh," William squeaked, reaching for his drink, "We haven't had dinner. Do you have a bar menu?"

"Yes, I'll bring it right over. Water too?" They guessed that the young bartender was probably in his late 20's— and wasn't gay. This made him a lot less fun and a lot less exciting to William.

"Yes, please." Sebastian answered, seeing that William's fun just lost some luster. Clearly William had hoped for a bartender to flirt with when food or drinks were brought to the table.

"So, we haven't talked, hon. Are we good?" William was cautious, since Sebastian had kicked him out the last time they were alone.

Sebastian shot the tequila down. Three shots- gone! He turned to face the bartender and raised his glass for another. "Yeah," he said, turning back to William. "We're good. Sorry, uh," he hesitated, running his hand through his hair nervously. "My dad, he, uh," he took a breath, "he slept with anyone he could and he let my mum know it. It was hurtful to her; it was weird and hard on me. My dad was gone or drunk almost all of the time. She would tell me that she just fell in love and married too young, but I could see how bad it was for her. She did everything for me." He paused as the next round of three shots arrived. William chose not to interrupt him, so he just watched the a shot glass disappear quickly. "I promised myself that I wouldn't be like my dad. I guess you could say he used sex as a weapon."

They both laughed at the reference to the song.

"Then when I was in my twenties, I saw a lot of people doing this, using sex to make themselves feel better, to manipulate other people- not so many that used it as a way to express love. I guess I had enough games growing up, William. I promised myself that sex would be meaningful in my life. I wish you'd told me before. Telling me afterwards just brought dishonesty into it for me."

"Sebastian, you are amazing, but I can't believe you! In some ways you are a man of such values, so open to life. But I don't know what world you're living in because you see things so differently." William looked for the bartender raising his glass, asking for another. He saw that people were beginning to trickle into the bar. "I don't want to overstep, man, but Katriana said that you are still saying you're gay. From what I understand, after Sam-" William cut his sentence off. He decided he better see how Sebastian was taking things before he called him a *hypocrite*.

Sebastian put his third shot glass down, empty. He stared at the three glasses. He welcomed the effect the tequila was starting to take.

"I'm gay, I always have been!"

"Hon, stop me if I'm saying too much, because I don't want to piss you off again."

"I can't talk with Cindy, so," he saw the bartender walking by. "This time, uh,- what should I get Will?" A new name being bestowed, establishing their friendship.

Will's eyes lit up, *Good, guess I'm not pissing him off. Maybe we'll be friends after all*, he thought. He looked to the bartender, "Bring him what I'm having."

"Rusty nail." The bartender repeated the order. *They better be big tippers!* The bartender was accustomed to being looked over, but in this bar, all of the staff were professional. They were polite and they were told not to engage the customers personally. He smiled cordially.

"Oh, and wings. Hon, are you hungry?" Will answered his own question. He raised his hand indicating that no response was needed. "You better eat. Uh, bruschetta or something on bread, please?"

"Bruschetta and wings, comin' up."

"Thanks." *Half the fun at a bar is about the wait staff's cute asses*, thought William. He could also get into a nice rack, but a straight guy? No fun, no fun at all.

"Look, I get it," Sebastian said, loosening up. "I'm a hypocrite. But you? How would Katriana feel about you looking for bartenders to flirt with?"

"Hon, she's the one who recommended the asses in this bar. I can look, I can even touch," he said, swinging in his seat like a kid getting what he wants. "She's married. She told me she doesn't expect anything from me." Will looked like he felt like hot shit. "She even told me I could bring someone home for a three-some."

"Really? Oh, that will go well!" Sebastian laughed. "What are you doing? Are you serious about her at all? Because when I see you looking at her, I think you're in love. You don't look like you're just out for a good time."

Will hesitated, measuring how much he should say, how much to confide in him. He would have asked for a couple of shots, to drink at Sebastian's pace, but it was clear who was going to be driving the Mercedes home. "No, you're right," his tone serious. "I'm trying to have fun because she's not as into me. I'm pretty into her. I do things I normally wouldn't just to keep her happy." Will smiled when he saw his wings coming. "And you, are in love with Sam; I think we are traveling the same seas, my friend."

Sebastian froze for a second, hearing Will's words. "Bullocks." He tried the bruschetta and then stood, waving to the bartender for another 2 Rusty Nails.

"Bullocks? You don't get excited, do you hon?"

"No point. I'm not one for drama."

"Are you sure you're gay?" Will joked.

"No. Not after Sam, I'm not sure of anything." Sebastian allowed himself to get even more comfortable because he needed someone to talk to, the tequila was easing him and Will was a great guy, after all. "I said I was gay last night and you should have seen her. I'm sure she's feeling so guilty about Kole-"

"Yeah, what a fox!"

"Not helping, hon." Sebastian drank his water. "I think I really hurt her. Worst thing I could have done when she's going to be seeing him!"

"Oh, sorry to hear that, hon." Will ate quietly, giving the conversation a little time. "Like I said, you're amazing, but an idiot too."

Sebastian sobered up for a split second, "Idiot, am I?"

"You're in love with her-"

"I am!" he interrupted.

"And instead of declaring your love, you said you're gay. You can be a bit stubborn, my friend."

"Bullock! Fuck!" He slammed his fist on the table. "You're right, you-" he bit his lip. His anger passed, "I don't want to lose her, Will."

"I know. Talk to your witches. Maybe they have a brew." Will suggested, raising an eyebrow.

"A brew?" Sebastian echoed, desperate for anything to fix things. At this point, he felt Sam slipping away and back to Kole.

"OK, look. For now, I'm going to change the subject because there's no point in being bummed. The idea is to enjoy this great bar and our friendship. So, hon, you were an *ass to me!*"

Sebastian laughed loudly. Tequila therapy had a way of taking some of the sting out of things, including being insulted. "Yeah," he tried to say. His laughter grew, providing some relief. It was contagious, they both laughed. Will was glad not to have angered Sebastian. "I was a wanker, man. I mean, you were too, but you're cute! Look, let's chalk it up to Iza. She stirred so many things in me!"

Again, they both laughed, agreeing to blame Iza. The bartender brought two more Rusty Nails over and they raised their glasses in a toast.

"To friendship!" Will said.

"To being friends, even after I've seen your wanker!" Rolling laughter followed.

Although Sebastian had been insulted a couple of times, he had to admit that Will was right. The tequila aiding his cause, he turned the resentment towards Will into gratitude. He was grateful that he had someone who understood being an ex-gay man, perhaps now being bisexual, being in love with a woman and, most of all, he was grateful to have his old friend to talk to again.

♥

After the tequila and the Rusty Nails, the next day Sebastian was most grateful that Will had driven them home and had pulled over in time so that the Mercedes' white leather seats stayed white.

He woke up with a headache. He walked out of his bedroom and saw Will, vaguely remembering that Will had asked if he could crash on the couch, Katriana had already gone to be by the time they'd gotten back.

"Oh, my head. I didn't drink enough water last night." Sebastian said, holding his head. "You want some tea?"

"Please." Will got up, walking to the kitchen. "Hon, sit. I'll make the tea. Hangovers get harder on me the wiser I get every year."

"Wiser?" Sebastian sat, letting Will make the tea. "Yeah, shite. Thirty-nine is knocking on my door."

"Oh! When's your birthday, hon?"

"Next week. Hey, last night,"

Will interrupted. "Listen, you let me talk with you honestly and I'm glad we're good again. The bar's called *Secreto*, I think we need some secrets between us." He offered the tea bag choices to Sebastian. "It was good to talk about Katriana and I'd like if you kept that between us."

"Yeah." Sebastian figured everyone knew how Will felt, so what was the secret. *Ah well, whatever.* Then Sebastian remembered something from last night, *Hey, wait!* "Will, did you call me an idiot last night?" Now Sebastian was remembering more of their conversation, "An ass?"

"Let it go, Sebastian. You anger too easily."

"Only with you, Will."

"Well, you should focus on Sam and asking the witches for a spell or a cure. I'm your friend, remember?"

"Yeah, alright. Ya wanker."

34

Roller Coaster Consulting

Sam went though the next several days in Boston in a haze. Fortunately, Cindy had met her at the airport, helping her get her suitcase. She had insisted Sam stay with her and Arthur. Cindy had, of course, talked with Iza the last night Sam had been in Santa Fe. So, Cindy knew that Sam and Sebastian had been spending all their time together until the last night's blowup. Cindy could see that a disaster was coming Sam's way in the relationship department. Either Sam was going to lose her friendship with Sebastian or destroy Nick. Either way, it was going to be heavy-hearted and painful.

Sam focused on updating her license the first few days she was in Boston while Sebastian was going to Chimayó, where his phone didn't work all that well. Just as well because she needed time to herself, time to figure out what she wanted. Of course, Nick didn't know she was spending time thinking about things, so he wasn't giving her that time; he was calling more now and told her that he was coming to see her in a few days.

Tonight Cindy wanted to spend some time with Sam so she took her to dinner. Cindy, who didn't cook, had several favorite restaurants; she took Sam to Italian. On their way home Cindy picked up a couple of bottles of wine and tequila. They hadn't talked about any of what was going on with Sam yet, so she figured drinks at home would help.

Sam and Cindy entered the apartment. "Arthur's not home, we'll have some time to ourselves, to chat." She set the bag with the bottles on the kitchen counter. "Funny, he's been working late a lot as of late."

It was obvious to Sam that Arthur had been living in a small bachelor pad and that Cindy had given it a woman's touch when she moved in. The apartment was much smaller than anything she knew Cindy would have chosen. Two small bedrooms and one bathroom might have worked for a single man, but not a married couple. Had the rooms been larger or had there been another room, Cindy would have had a home office. The front door went right by the kitchen which had an open wall facing the rest of the apartment. The counter top here also served as a breakfast area with barstools on the other side of the counter. Sam could see that the Formica counters and old cabinets needed upgrading. Next was a small, round table, the dining space, followed by a new leather couch, two matching living room chairs and a classical looking coffee table.

"Cindy, it looks like you've been upgrading the apartment."

Unaccustomed to spaces being so unkept, Cindy was uneasy. "Yes, we got new furniture, but I'd like to have the floors and the kitchen redone. For starters." Sam looked down at the old, faded tan carpeting. She smiled, knowing better, she said nothing.

"Sit, dear. You haven't told me how Santa Fe was." Cindy took a couple of wine glasses and shot glasses over to the coffee table along with the bottles.

"Sorry, Cindy. We were just-"

"Yes? I thought you'd forgotten about me entirely." Cindy teased.

"I know, sorry. I got your messages, we've just been so wrapped up."

"In each other, I heard. Don't worry, dear, I understand. Tell me, what's it been like to be pleasured by that tight little butt of his?"

Sam blushed, "Cindy!"

"Come on, dear!"

"It's fabulous! We have been doing it all of the time!"

"Oh to have the energy and to be young!"

"He's fantastic, he makes me feel like a princess - and then he just looks into my eyes."

"How romantic! I'm going to tell him to give Arthur notes."

"One thing though, I worry a bit. I mean," Sam's words began to pick up some speed. A sure sign things weren't OK in her world. "We're like broke between the two of us. He's only working part-time and I have my student loans."

"Well, no, Sam. Sebastian is making good money with the magazine right now and he has a nest egg from the previous work he did with the magazine."

"Oh?"

"You didn't know?"

"Well, I- uh, the magazine project is ending."

"Yes, next week, but he made good money considering that his expenses at Iza's aren't that high."

"Oh." Sam was surprised. "Well, I knew he paid cash when he bought his Mercedes, but I didn't know he had a nest egg. That's great," she drank from her wine glass. "But now he's looking to take cooking classes. That sounds so impractical, don't you think, Cindy?" She drank again, emptying the glass. Cindy refilled it. "There can't be any money in that. I'm just wondering, Nick's being trained for a great position. What kind of future could I have with a *gay* cook? He keeps saying he's gay, Cindy. Is he telling me it's just a fling?"

Cindy laughed, "I think you need to speak with your gay lover, dear. Iza told me that the specialty dinner is all sold out. Let me see," she paused, recalling. "Oh, yes, she said that he estimated $1,000 of profit."

"For the night?" Sam's eyes came into focus, reading Cindy's face. "Are you sure?"

"Yes." She lifted her glass, "I believe so, dear." Cindy smiled. Whatever was between Sebastian and Sam, it sure blinded Sam.

"That invite-only dinner? I thought Eric only invited a few friends." Sam was still trying to figure it all out.

"No. Sam dear, I think you need to *talk* with your lover *some* of the time. His little dinner has attracted quite a bit of attention. Apparently some big whigs in Santa Fe have reserved most of the night."

"Really?" Sam then realized that there was just one thing more surprising than all this information about Sebastian, "How do you know all this?"

"Sebastian, dear. We talk."

"When?" Sam couldn't figure when Sebastian had possibly talked with Cindy. It seemed like they had been together all of the time.

"I don't know, dear. Let's see-"

"Forget it. I don't know if I want to *talk* with him anyway."

"I see." Cindy could see that there were deeper issues at play here. How much money Sebastian made or whether he was in cooking classes were small issues compared to something deeper. "Dear, do you think he's gay?"

"Not if- Well, what does it matter? As long as he thinks so." Sam drank, biting back the tears.

Cindy saw this and changed the subject. "And Nick, dear. Did you say he's going to come visit?

Now Sam looked uncomfortable instead of angry. "Yeah, tomorrow."

"How are things with Nick? How are you feeling about him?"

Sam emptied her glass again.

"I see," Cindy's concern for Sam was growing. "Would you prefer a shot, dear?"

Sam's eyes said 'yes'. "What did Sebastian call it? Anesthesia?"

Cindy placed a shot glass and the tequila bottle before Sam. Sam poured herself a shot, drinking it down. "I feel so guilty, Cindy. I love them both." She poured another shot. "In different ways, but I guess I'd be stupid to think that I have a future with a gay man."

"I'm sorry, dear." Cindy sighed. Cindy was carrying her own burdens. She wasn't sure how many of Sam's she could share right now. "For what it's worth," she said, getting up and walking into the kitchen for two glasses of water. "I do believe he loves you. Has he said so?"

"Yes, but he's always said so." The alcohol was starting to alleviate her worries. It was also giving her the courage to speak what was on her mind more so. "The first time he went down on me, afterwards he told me he was gay!"

"He gave you oral sex?" Cindy almost dropped the glasses of water she was bringing over.

"Yeah, it was good too. He didn't behave like a novice." Sam's voice revealed her memory of the experience.

"He researched how, but I didn't think he actually *would!*"

"He what?"

"On the internet!" Cindy was on a wild ride now. She was raising her voice, starting to laugh hysterically and waving her arms in the air. "He didn't know what to do, so he looked it up!"

Sam's jaw hung open, "Oh, well, he found an informative site!" Sam joined Cindy on the wild ride of laughter. Then she saw that she was hitting highs and lows. "Shit! Cindy, every time I feel good about Sebastian, I think about him saying he's gay. I feel *rejected!*" Her mannerisms had dropped, but Cindy couldn't hold her laughter back, causing them both to laugh again. "I can't laugh - I can't! I feel guilty! Nick's so hot! So attentive!"

Cindy did all she could to contain her laughter for a few minutes. "Sam," she started, swallowing the funny thoughts in her mind, "I understand. You feel rejected and, your subconscious is turning your happiness into guilt. I'm sorry." Cindy now blinked repeatedly.

Sam looked at her as though Cindy were breaking; Sam was growing concerned. "Cindy, what the hell is wrong?"

Tears were forming in Cindy's eyes. "Dear, I want to know which one of them has the more pleasing rod - or mouth!" Again, fits of laughter possessed her. Through tears of laughter, she looked to see how Sam was taking her vulgar curiosity. "Sorry dear, in my day we didn't get to explore being young, attractive vixens. I'm trying to make up for it now!" This caused her to laugh at herself too.

Sam had taken a moment to process her words, because Cindy's blinking had looked like the start of a seizure. Realizing that Cindy was perfectly fine, just letting her wild, nasty side out, Sam suddenly laughed. Like a popped balloon, she blurted sounds and buckled over, her stomach starting to hurt from all the great-feelings. With wine and several shots of tequila in her, comparing her two lovers was fantastic!

"I don't know, Cindy. I should go another round and compare!"

"Take notes for me!" Cindy stopped, looking at Sam, shocked. "Sam, I think Arthur is having an affair. That's why I'm thinking about your love life. I'm not getting any love at home."

"Oh, Cin, I'm so sorry-" Sam tried to be compassionate, but the wine and tequila brought on more laughter and silliness. "I've got two horny guys, one's just gay. I could share!"

"Yum!," Cindy said. Seeing that the wine bottle was empty, she now gave herself some tequila. "I missed you, Sam. It's great to have someone to be able to cut lose with," she paused, staring at nothing. "It's also great to have someone to be able to talk to about these things. I had such a fascinating time at Iza's but life here has been so dry." She thought about her sex life with Arthur, "So dry!"

"What's going on with Arthur, Cin?"

Cindy took a deep breath and another shot. "I don't want to talk about it. I think we both need to laugh some more. We can talk about it in Bali. You are still going, right dear?"

"Yeah. I wouldn't miss it. I think I just need to figure out where I stand with my gay, reject-me lover before I get there. Why would I want that when I have my Nick-hunk who wants me?"

"Then let's go back to being dirty and light-hearted. Oh! I heard a sex joke the other day. Let's see…"

Sam could see that Cindy wouldn't be able to tell a sex joke to save her life, so she pulled out her phone and read one. Laughter followed. Cindy took her phone out, reading a couple of sex jokes before creating her own.

Sam was no longer thinking about Nick, the man she felt held her future, or Sebastian, the man who held her heart, but hen rejected her. She was just thinking about the funny jokes Cindy was trying to tell, but kept messing up. Her backwards jokes were great, and far funnier than well-told jokes would have been.

♥

The next couple of days went quickly. Sam spent time with Nick and asked Cindy to let Sebastian know that she would not be flying back to New Mexico. She would go directly to Bali. Sam was glad to be with Cindy. The night they drank had allowed Sam to sort through some of her feelings, just by talking with Cindy. It was a chance to cut loose and be raw with her emotions, which she didn't get to do again. The next days were all about seeing Nick and feeling guilty.

35

Lavender Fields

With the seasons turning, Iza had said this was a great time of year to go to Chimayó. She also said that Albuquerque was hosting its annual Balloon Fiesta, a long weekend of people showing and flying in their hot air balloons. She'd told Sebastian that it was a sight to see, there would be hundreds of colorful balls in the sky and that he should go. As amazing as it sounded, especially since people came from all over the world for this event, he said he'd try to get down to Albuquerque, but that wasn't where his heart was now. He was more interested in going to Chimayó and asking Iza if she had any magic up her sleeve for him.

Katriana said she foresaw a great trip to Chimayó, which raised William's level of enthusiasm even higher. Given that he knew that Eric liked Iza and since he wanted to talk to Eric about their upcoming dinner-event, Sebastian asked Iza if Eric could come too. Eric was thrilled to join, evidenced by his raised eyebrows. Those gray haystacks looked like they belonged on a bear, which would be a fair description of Eric's character. He too groaned more often than not as his primary means of communication.

The plan was to drive up on Friday, the trip having been delayed yet another day, and have dinner at the famous ranch restaurant. For two nights they would stay at a B&B that belonged to someone that Iza knew. She described the B&B as a lavender farm with flowing rows of bushes. She'd said that at the bottom of the lavender fields, the owner Lucy Torres, had bees, so the B&B sold lavender honey at local farmer's markets too. This estate was one of the oldest in the area, which accounted for the land that would otherwise cost a large fortune. Iza promised to point out the old aqueduct system the Spaniards had put in the area and that ran through the property, providing water for many farms. Eric and Sebastian would be staying in one room, William and Katriana in the second. Iza had promised that Sebastian would appreciate the homey rooms, which were decorated with lace, antique-styled furniture and soft, delicate touches. She also said that she'd booked herself the room with a patio, but wasn't sure that the men's room had one. "Sorry, but if you are nice to me, you can come over with a bottle of something," she'd offered. She kindly promised not to be picky about what kind of bottle they brought.

Saturday they'd have breakfast at the B&B and then head over to Chimayó's sanctuary, an old church deemed one of the 'Lourdes of the Americas'. This holy church, she said, was said to be on sacred ground; people came from all over praying for a miracle. Spontaneous healings were quite common, as evidenced by the crutches and many rosaries left behind by those who had received their miracle.

Iza's descriptions had the men impatient to go, not that Eric was. Bears like Eric probably made their own miracles.

"Our miracles are calling us!" William cried.

"*Sea paciente,*" Katriana told him, rolling her eyes. (Se would be familiar)

Am I irritating her? he wondered.

"Will's just enthusiastic. We've never experienced such a thing." Sebastian looked skeptical now, "I'm not even sure I believe in miracles."

"Hon, you should." Will said, giving Sebastian a look. 'You wanted a miracle, remember?'

Eric drove his Escalade so that everyone could ride in comfort and style. He would accept not contributions for gas and said he was happy to be invited. Some of his words were growled, but the message was clear. Sebastian was looking forward to spending time with Eric. He was drawn toward mentors, father-figures he felt he could trust.

♥

The old restaurant was a riot. As the hostess walked them through the restaurant, Sebastian could see the different additions that the restaurant had undergone. It was clear that this had once been a house but that the ranch's little restaurant had grown and grown so that new rooms had been added to accommodate the growing demand by visitors. They were fortunate because they were seated out back in the garden. No doubt this premier seating was due to another of Iza's many connections. Or Eric's, Sebastian wasn't sure.

Sebastian felt this was no ordinary garden, as he looked around. It was sweetly decorated with wild flowers growing tall in the pots that lined the narrow paths up the hill that had been carved out in layers to make room for a few more small tables. He noticed the stones in the pathways; each carefully placed to create a subtle pattern that added to the ambiance. Hanging strings of garden lights added color and the feel of fireflies; but all of these touches weren't responsible for the special feeling he had here.

He realized what was unique: he'd felt like he'd gone back in time, maybe a hundred years, to a garden party at the local big-shot's farm. Yes, that was it! He'd gone back in time. He appreciated savoring a night of new adventures with his friends, though he missed Sam. *What is she thinking?* he wondered. Avoiding maddening questions about her that he didn't have answers to, he turned his attention back to the night. He especially loved the rustic feel of the restaurant.

Dinner was a celebration and everyone had a great time. As long as he focused on his life's motto, enjoying himself no matter what, he enjoyed the evening and his friends. After dinner they headed to their B&B in the dark, ready for the next day's adventures.

♥

The sun rose above the lavender fields early. It was cool outside, so Sebastian had worn a short-sleeve button-up, jeans and his new wool sweater. Perfect for sitting out on his porch, watching the light purple haze of painted lavender before him.

He sighed. *Will she come back to me? Do I want a woman as a lover?* He felt a sinking sensation in his heart. *Do I have options or is everything out of my hands?*

"Morning angel. You look great in your new sweater. Come, I'll show you the property."

"Morning." They walked the length of half a football field smelling the lavender blooming. Sebastian waited for them to walk to a quiet corner. "Iza, I think I need a small miracle today."

"Sam?"

He nodded.

"Angel, what is that all about?"

"What is what about?"

Iza waited for him to answer, ignoring his question. They had walked down past the bee's hives to a sitting area. The property was walled off on all sides by trees and vines, giving privacy to the neighbors and also creating a heavenly garden. The house was on the other end of the land, uphill. Iza had pointed out the aqueduct which was about a foot deep and wide. The aqueduct revealed it's age, looking hundreds of years old.

"I think I blew it, Iza."

"Angel, you're gay. Why do you care? I haven't heard you say that you are in love and no longer care about a gender-orientation label."

Sebastian nodded his head. "You're right. No, I haven't said it out loud. I tried to say it to her." He raised his head, looking around. "You'd said that I should be more intimate, so I tried to tell her how I feel."

"And how do you feel?"

"I don't feel like I have the luxury of knowing, Iza. If she goes back to Kole, it doesn't matter how I feel."

"Wrong. How you feel is always important. I can't help you if you can't be intimate enough with yourself to know how you feel, angel." She put her hand on his leg. "Here's what I can do. Prepare yourself for Chimayó. Here's what you want to try to do. You've never come to class, so I don't know that you can even begin to pull it off, so listen very carefully. Let's see if you can re-write your past. I don't think you are that advanced, but you've surprised me several times."

Iza's tone joked, accused gently and then instructed. She gave Sebastian very specific instructions and then stood up.

"Breakfast time, let's go up to the main house. Then wait for the right time before you start."

"Wait, how will I know what the right time is?"

"You'll know. Don't worry about that. Get in touch with your feelings - and follow my instructions carefully!"

36

Chimayó's Little Church

The drive from the B&B to the church was short. Eric followed Iza's directions around town, past the church, to a small, steep road where the parking was. They looked around and saw a haven here: even though most of Santa Fe was high desert and dry, Chimayó was thick with green. Green grass and horses behind gates welcomed them in the parking lot. Stepping out of the car, the steep road they came in was behind them; a row of trees and the sound of a creek was fifty feet in front of them. They saw a wide path leading by an outdoor theater or sermon space and then leading up to the church. The steep walk up the path revealed new sights as they came upon ancient flowering trees and then a hole-in-the-wall restaurant. They could now see the church's courtyard and the church. Trees and benches by these created plenty of space to wander. A sign pointed past this area to the entrance.

They walked past the church and across a small bridge to the official entrance. A small building was to the side of an arch and walkway into the church. Iza said everyone had to go in the gift shop first, the small building. She said that they would want to buy a container for the sacred dirt, sacred water and perhaps a rosary.

William looked at the arch and walkway that crossed the creek, heading to the church.

"That's the holy water. Walk across it with great intent," Iza instructed. "But first, the souvenir shop."

Sebastian pulled Will's shirt to get him to walk toward the shop. "OK, OK!"

"Why a rosary, Iza? I thought you weren't religious."

"I'm not angel. People leave the rosary behind in the alter room or down on the chain-link fence by the parking lot when they receive their miracle. So, you probably want one."

"Can I get two?" William asked.

"No!" Katriana scolded, as Iza nodded 'Yes.'

"Erg." Eric groused.

A few minutes later everyone had Iza's required items. They walked over the bridge, looking serious and not really knowing what Iza meant when she said to walk 'with great intent.' *Good enough,* William thought, *Finally walking into the church.* Truth was that William's intent had been absent or weak since he'd been with Katriana, unless he was writing.

Outside the church's doors under a covered entrance were two places to fill the holy water containers. These would just hold about 3 ounces of water. Once they had collected their holy water, they all stepped in the church. The church was much smaller than William had imagined.

"Wow!" he said in amazement. "I thought it would be so much nicer."

"Quiet down, Will. You'll probably be hung if someone hears you." Sebastian warned.

"What were you expecting, cowboy?" Eric asked. "The Taj Mahal?"

William looked at Eric, "Well, yeah. I mean, a place of miracles? This place look like the church Laura in 'Little House on the Prairie' must have attended. A church version of a shack."

"Get with it, Will." Sebastian warned, but it was too late.

"¡Guillermo!" Katriana called and pulled William outside.

Eric and Sebastian looked to Iza. "What was that?" Sebastian asked. Eric turned and walked down the isle and found a pew to sit in.

"Let it go, it's time. Go." Iza followed Eric and sat in the pew behind him. They both closed their eyes and sat. And sat. A little later, Katriana and William would follow suit, sitting in the pew across from them.

Sebastian walked to the front of the little church. He saw two large open windows on either side of the walls. These were at the top of the walls, letting cooing pigeons in to sit on - and poop on- the wide ledges. *Disgusting*, he thought. Before him the church was like something that Will had made up for one of his movies, it was so unrealistic. There wasn't a traditional altar, only a simple podium to the side, but there was a wooden bas relief of all sorts of angels, figures, a Jesus in the middle, and other such images going up the wall. It was crudely carved and painted. Was Sebastian on one of Will's sets? Or did this relic belong in a museum and it was on loan? The whole sanctuary couldn't have been more than a hundred feet long and forty wide, Sebastian guessed. *This is stranger than fiction.*

He looked around and sat in a pew in the front. *OK, Iza said to talk. She said to be intimate.*

He pursed his lips, stalling. *Intimate about how I feel.*

Shite! I love her. Why do I love her?

He sighed and looked around. Behind him Iza, Eric and Katriana looked like they were somewhere else, in some far off meditation-land, he guessed. *Maybe I should go to class, learn what the hell meditation is.* Will smiled and waved at him. He nodded in response then looked forward again.

Bullocks. A few moments passed. Staring straight ahead at the bas relief, he knew Will would write about this place. He took a deep breath, trying to focus. *Iza said "Time doesn't exist. You can alter the energy."* He nodded his head, agreeing to try.

OK, ol' boy. 'Alter energy,' she said this would "alter the past."

He closed his eyes, not knowing how to 'alter energy.' Determined, he sat. *How did she say to alter energy? Re-do it?*

He continued to sit with his eyes closed, feeling crappy about Sam. All he did was think about Eric calling him a 'cowboy' and his responding he was gay.

Absolutely *nothing* seemed to be happening.

Bullocks!

Sebastian got up and walked through a doorway to his immediate left with a sign reading 'exit.' Just one step outside the sanctuary, but still in the church, there was a room to his immediate right with a two foot hole in the ground. He noticed that this doorway was rather short, so he ducked as he walked into a small room that couldn't have fit ten people at a time. The circle in the cement floor revealed dirt, obviously the 'Holy Dirt.' He scooped some, wondering if he should drink the holy water and eat the dirt, although signs had warned not to drink the water. *What do you have to do to get a miracle around here?*

"You found the holy dirt!" Will said, joining him.

"Will." Sebastian had come to one decision when sitting at the pew: he would try to stop sounding gay. No more 'hon.'

"I don't get what Iza, Katriana and Eric are doing in there, but they look like the real thing." Will kneeled down and scooped dirt into his container.

"Yeah, I know." Sebastian had just finished scooping up his dirt. He put the top on the plastic petri-dish looking container. It too couldn't have held more than a few ounces of dirt. "I bet you're going to write a movie about this place. It already looks like a set."

"You read my mind, hon! That's all I've been thinking about." Will placed the top on his container. "I don't know whether to bathe in this or eat it to get my miracle."

"You want a miracle? What do you want?" Figuring Will had it all with his writing career, he couldn't figure what Will wanted.

"Katriana."

"Oh, yeah. Right." *Poor Will, Katriana: the one thing he can't have. A married woman.*

They ducked their heads and came out of the dirt room. This last room was a sight. Just when Sebastian didn't think that anything could top the sanctuary, he was dumbfounded by this little prayer room. A pew on the left against the wall served as a place to sit and pray. This room was narrow, so there were no other places to sit. There were a couple of collection boxes in here, the one thing that the church had in every space, and a glass encasement with a small religious figure inside. They couldn't see the figure because people had left their crutches, casts, pictures and rosaries all over the glass case. They had also hung these items on a railing, that looked like it might be here for hanging crutches, and on a small altar. There were numerous crutches, triple the rosaries and quadruple the letters. This was a humbling site.

Both men froze, taking in the numerous proof of miracles left behind.

They took a couple steps over to the pew and sat, almost at the same time. They sat quietly for several minutes.

Sebastian finally broke the silence, "Keeping you quiet for so long might have been a miracle," he laughed. He raised his hand in the air, giving himself a point on his invisible scoreboard.

"You! Watch it, Katriana might scold you too."

"No, she won't."

"How do you know?" Will looked at Sebastian, questioning why he wouldn't have the same reprimand.

"Because I'm not sleeping with her."

"Oh, right."

37

Good Choices, No Choices

"Hey, did you get your miracle?" Will asked Sebastian as they sat in Chimayó's church, awaiting his miracle.

"Yeah," Sebastian soured his face. "I think I don't know how to pull it off though."

"Pull it off?" Will echoed.

"I guess it's like cooking, she gave me the recipe, but- shite if I know what the ingredients are or how to put them together!" He smirked, "Changing time! She's probably testing me, pulling my leg."

"Witches, eh?" Will nodded. Sebastian raised his head, pointing up with his eyes. Katriana had just walked into the prayer room they were in. She raised her finger to her mouth, indicating for them to be quiet. She sat by Will and began whispering in his ear.

Iza came and sat next to Sebastian, staring straight ahead.

"I heard the sweetest thing once: a friend isn't someone who makes you feel good, it is someone who makes you feel better about yourself." Iza turned to look at him. "Sweet, but untrue." Sebastian looked at her curiously. "See, angel, no one can make you feel or see yourself differently than how you perceive yourself. Than your self image."

"Self image?"

"Class. You should have come to class." She turned to Katriana. "Do you want yours to come hear about self image."

Katriana nodded.

"Class is in session, common angel." They all stood. Eric was to the side, waiting and watching. "Oh, take out your wallets. Leave a donation."

All three guys took their wallets out and followed orders.

"And bless the bills before you put them in," Iza directed as she walked out the exit.

Katriana watched as William opened his wallet, "*No, ése.*" He pulled out the $20 and looked to see if she approved. "*Sí.*" Sebastian and Eric followed William's example, not wanting to be scolded.

They walked out into the bright sunlight. Iza waited for them before she headed to the outdoor theater. They walked through the courtyard and stopped before the tiny restaurant. "Honey," she said to no one in particular, "get me a soda, please. Oh, and one for Katriana."

Eric walked into the restaurant. It was a small little dive. A couple of cheap plastic chairs and tables sat on one side, an ordering counter on the other. He walked to the window to order. He turned to see Sebastian and William.

"What do they like to drink?"

"Lemonade. I'll get them, Eric," Sebastian offered.

"No. What'll you fellas have?" No one was going to rob Eric of an opportunity to be a gentleman.

Ten minutes later they were all sitting on the ornate, but uncomfortable cement benches down near the stream of water drinking lemonade. The open theater, or sermon area, was created with detail. The cement benches had inlaid hand-placed mosaic tiles, as did the floor. One far corner had the name of those who had donated, carved into bricks. The area was covered with a roof, no walls. It was a beautiful, fall day. The sound of the running water, the tall trees swaying in the breeze and the many sticks placed in the shape of a cross on the chain link fence, or any other place a cross would stay put, gave everyone something to watch while Iza taught.

"Self image." She began in her deep, dramatic tone.

"Everyone perceives themselves a certain way and this is their self image. It has nothing to do with reality and, most of the time, the way people see themselves is inaccurate. People see themselves through the eyes they acquired growing up and through the eyes of their karma. For now, that simply means that a gorgeous woman, like Samantha, can look in the mirror and think that she's not all that attractive and that she needs to be successful in life to attract men.

"Your self-image is like a camera angle. It blinds you to one perspective of yourself. If your camera stood immobile in one corner of a house, never moving, then you would never see or experience the things that go on from the opposite side. If you were facing away from a window, you might miss the people and opportunities walking by behind you. You may never see the flowers growing in the window or the sun rising and setting.

"All three of you tend to have a good self image. You feel as though the world is your friend, aiding you to experience what you prefer. That is wonderful, but be careful. You want to always increase the flexibility of your self image. You want to remember that you are more than just a physical being so that you can continue to expand your perception, seeing a bigger version of yourself that goes beyond your body and your life."

She watched their brains taking in this information, digesting it as their stomachs would digest food.

"Now, most importantly. Sebastian, how do you perceive yourself? Are you a man? Are you a gay man? Are you a man in love? In love with a woman? Is your self-image so stuck in identifying yourself as a gay man that you hold tighter to that self image than you would to love?"

Ouch. Sebastian felt a jolt of pain in himself. "You're right-" Iza interrupted him, holding her hand up.

"Alright, give me some time with him. Eric, angel, I'll come find you afterwards to see how you are doing."

"Hmf," he snorted. "I'm fine. Never been here before, the energy is amazing." He turned and waked closer to the running water.

"Vamos," Katriana said, leading William back up the hill to the church's courtyard.

Iza moved so that she could watch the trees, the river and the crosses that had been behind her. She was next to Sebastian now.

"I think I've blown it, Iza."

She said nothing.

"You're right, I keep identifying in being gay, but," he searched himself. An uncomfortable feeling began to rise in him.

"There it is, that feeling. What's that?"

He realized that she seemed to know what he was feeling, but he let this go, focusing on what she asked him to focus on. "Uh, I'm getting uncomfortable, Iza. Like I said, I don't want to know how I feel in case Sam cuts me off."

"Cut's you off'? I thought you weren't dramatic, angel."

"I mean that she liked me as much as I liked her at first. I think she was just as in love with me when we first kissed." His heart ached. Frustration was falling upon him too. "Maybe it's like you'd said, we played it out and maybe now she's realizing that she made a mistake." He sighed, "Or it feels that way."

"Hm. Eric, would you call Katriana over?" she called, waving at him. Sebastian was confused, but trusted Iza, so he said nothing. They sat quietly until Katriana came over. To Sebastian's surprise, Will didn't follow.

"*¿Si?*"

"Angel, I want your read of the energy. My gay friend here thinks that Sam was heavily into him but has changed her mind and now thinks it was a mistake."

Katriana nodded. "*Sebastián,*" she placed her hand on his shoulder, ran it down over his heart and then back onto his shoulder. "I afraid you are reading it well. She was so connected to your energy, but why you say you are gay over and over?"

Sebastian looked surprised, *How would Katriana know that? Most of the time it was just Sam and I. Maybe Sam told the witches-*

"You right. It is unknown right now what she will do. She is undecided. She love you but she love him too. In different ways."

"Thanks angel." Katriana returned to William.

"I would say the same." Iza smiled compassionately at Sebastian. "You weren't able to rewrite your past."

"No," he looked surprised. "How do you know?"

"The energy hasn't changed, angel." She pat his knee, "Look, I'll give you a few tips." She raised her index finger. "Number one: you need to focus on your self image first. If you want to roll around around with a woman, then at least call yourself bi, angel. It's just a word, just a label. Number two: you *must know* who you are. You *must,* or the universe will never be yours. Sam will never be yours. Are you *in love* or not?"

"I am, I love her Iza. I don't-" he looked a bit panicked now, "I think I'll go crazy if I lose her."

"OK, I have more, you interrupted me, but I'm glad you're getting deeper into your feelings. Angel, you can't lose her, she was never yours."

Sebastian dropped his head in pain. She was right.

"I'm not being harsh, I'm being fair, honest. Now, if you want her to love you, you've got to work some magic."

"I tried."

"Angel, you're not advanced, but you amaze me because you do well. In Bali we'll go deeper into rewriting time and several other things, energy permitting. Right now, tell her how you feel."

"I can't. She asked for time alone - and - she's with him." His eyes were watering.

"So what? Don't bother with *what's happening,* angel. Focus on the energy. You have a chan-" she stopped abruptly. "Katriana!" Iza jumped out of her seat and went up to where Katriana was. She pulled her aside, rushed. A couple minutes later she returned. She looked different.

"What is it, Iza?"

"Nothing." She remained standing.

He gave her a look, he knew better. "Iza, I trust you. Don't lie to me."

"I saw something, energetically."

"What? Something about me?"

"No," she gladly answered without lying. "It will affect you, but I do not talk about others without permission."

She sat again, switching her tone to a warmer one. "Angel, what do you want? Who are you?- Ah, don't answer yet!"

Now she stood and looked all around. She looked to the trees before them across the water. She suddenly looked left, as if someone were whispering in her ear. Then she looked like she was pondering a secret. Finally she raised her head, no longer watching and listening. She stood.

"Angel, Bali is right around the corner. I don't have time to teach you how to re-write your past. Instead, I've been told-"

"Been told? By Katriana?"

"No, Silent Knowledge, angel." She looked up, recalling what she'd been saying. "Ah, yes, I've been told you are coming up to a crossroads."

"A what?"

"Crossroads. Listen angel. I'm offering you the chance to stay at the ranch and help me run my business. With your help the money could be great and I'll train you to run workshops. Eric has his eye on you. He's talked with you about the restaurant business. On a personal level, you are making some life choices: where to call home, who to love. William is still an option - I'm sure he hasn't said so, but I sense it. He is still attracted to you." Iza had still been standing and looking all around.

She sat by him. "You are fortunate, Sebastian. You have many upcoming choices. We only have choices in life when we are in the flow, doing well; when he have limited or no choices, it is because we are out of the flow. We don't know ourselves and life is forcing us in a given direction so that we will experience ourselves."

Sebastian glazed over, realizing the depth of her words. In his life he had choices when he was true to himself, but few choices when he'd lost his way. That was another reason why he was so adamant about his lovers. He knew that honoring himself meant choosing lovers who loved him, not dramatic, immature or wild lovers who were more interested in flirting and shagging to add another notch on their bedpost. Still...

"Iza," he gathered his courage. "I'm afraid I won't have a choice with Sam. I'm deadly afraid of saying I'm bisexual and then losing her; losing both my worlds."

"You can't lose yourself; you can only lose what you misperceived yourself to be." She paused. "Angel, that's how you feel, whether you admit it to yourself or not. Silent Knowledge knows how you feel, Sebastian. You can hide it from yourself, but not from Silent Knowledge." She laughed, "That's what makes denying how you feel so pointless. You aren't fooling anyone. We know how you feel about Sam." Now she looked at him, seriously, "But you can risk it all by denying who you really are and how you really feel."

He thought about this for a minute. "Admit that I'm scared to be in love with an engaged woman-" He sighed, looking down, heavy-hearted. Tears began to fall down his cheeks. He was broken, Sam had broken him. "I want to spend my life with her." Feeling so dependent felt terrible; admitting the depth of his feelings felt freeing.

She stood. "Angel, you are going to have to choose who you are very soon. That's how you want to choose your path. If you don't change your mind and rejoice about your love for Sam, then you will have lost, whether she loves you or not." Iza let these words sink in. "Is she seeing him?"

"Yes."

"Alright, work on *who you are* after lunch." Changing the mood, she stood. "Speaking of loss, if you don't take me to lunch now, you'll lose my friendship because I'll turn into an ugly, hungry ogre. I'm starving."

He laughed, "We can't let that happen. Thanks, Iza.

38

A Short Call

"*Sebastián*, are you looking forward to Bali?" Katriana asked, as they sat for lunch, back at the same ranch restaurant due to a lack of choices and they'd all enjoyed it last night.

"Of course," he looked at the time. "I'm on edge about seeing Sam though. Actually, if you'll all excuse me, I'll call her."

"What can we get you to drink?"

"Iced-tea, thanks Will." Sebastian got up to go outside to call Sam. His phone rang. It was the magazine. He'd call later. Mr. Howell had emailed something about extending his contract. Iza had been right, as she always was, he had choices before him. His phone's ringer played John Newman's song, "Can You Love Me Again."

His phone sang, "I need to know now, know now- can you love me again?" He sang along, walking outside to see the beautiful courtyard. He sat on a bench, closing his eyes.

Who are you, ol' boy? Find you before you call her. He remembered having heard Iza say to breathe slowly when you want to connect more deeply. He concentrated on breathing slowly. *Breathe.*

Breathe... I am all about love. I'm in love, it's OK. I'm happy no matter what. I'm in love no matter what.

He texted Sam, "I love you. You are my family."

He took another breath, getting ready to call her.

♥

Back in the restaurant Eric discreetly handed the waitress his credit card. "Thanks, sugar."

"I'll put everything on your card." The cute, young waitress said, giving away his secret. "So, margaritas all around, coming right up." She walked away obliviously.

"OK, now I need to talk with both of you," Iza said, looking at both men. "Angel, he's calling you '*Will*,' is he? You must have made up." Iza's look caught William's eye. Her question drew Katriana's attention. Katriana suddenly stared at William, though when he looked at her, he realized that she was staring at the space right next to him, which made him feel even more uncomfortable.

"Yeah, the night we went shopping and out for a drink." William felt like Iza was talking about one thing but really meaning something else. He wanted to ask about it, but didn't know *what* to ask.

"Uh-huh," she hummed, knowingly. She'd really been reading his energy to see if he was, in fact, still interested in Sebastian, as she'd told Sebastian. She was right, Sebastian still had a relationship with William available. He had many choices. She looked to Katriana, wondering how she felt about this. Katriana nodded knowingly.

Now Iza and Katriana turned their attention to Eric.

"Slipping the waitress your credit card. So, cowboy, you have money to burn? I would be happy to help you burn it, you know." Iza's question was meant to be a challenge. She looked to Katriana, their eyes agreeing to tease Eric for trying to pay for everything.

Eric looked up, "Oh?"

"They have the sweetest jewelry in the gift shop here." She called his bluff, "Something I've had my eye on for the longest time."

Eric stood. "You think I won't burn some money on it? Well, let's go see what it looks like, sugar. Let's see if it's worth spending my money or if you're just seeing how far I'll go."

"Oh!" Iza said, enjoying Eric standing up to her challenge. They stood.

"After you, sugar." They walked off toward the gift shop.

"Happy shopping!" William called behind them. Once they were out of hearing range, he turned to Katriana. "Did something just happen, Katriana?"

"What you mean?" she asked, avoiding him by looking at her drink.

"The question Iza asked, it was strange. It was like she was asking one thing but really another." He shook his head, "That doesn't make sense."

"*No, tienes razón.*" Now she looked straight at him, "She was reading your energy to see if you are still attracted to *Sebastián.*"

William was super-uncomfortable now. Was he turning red?

"Is OK. *Te dije,* it no matter." Katriana, of course, meant that it didn't matter if he was still attracted to Sebastian because she expected nothing.

Now William flipped from embarrassed to annoyed. "Maybe it should matter!" He began to lose it. "Katriana, I really like you."

"*Yo también.* You young, I married. William, I not getting divorced. We have no future."

"Why? Just because you are afraid to be in a real relationship?" He paused, waiting for a reaction that didn't come.

Do I dare? he asked himself.

"How long are you going to avoid *love,* Katriana?" He almost squinted, avoiding the backlash of his brash question.

Yeap, crossed that line, he thought as he saw her stand up, throw her napkin down and walk away.

Just then the waitress came by to look at an empty table, a question on her face.

"Yeah, come back later," William told her, acknowledging that he'd cleared the table.

I couldn't have written a better scene. Crap!

Iza was glowing as she and Eric came back and sat down. "Eric, it's too expensive a gift!" She looked from him to the sparkling necklace with a large peridot pendant hanging around her neck.

"It's nothing. To answer your earlier question, yes, I have money, Iza." He smiled because she was glowing like a princess with a new crown. "And I'm paying for lunch. I'm a gentleman, after all. I take care of people I care about. I insist."

"I'm flattered, angel," she said, feeling something new inside her. She was always attracted to men, but this was a different feeling. His words seemed to have struck her. Then she noticed that Katriana and Sebastian were gone. "Angel, you're here alone?"

"Oh, I might have pissed Katriana off."

"I'm sure she's fine. Very little throws her."

"Yeah," William spoke slowly, "I asked how long she was going to avoid love, since she won't let anyone get close." He twisted his lips to the side, saying "So, I blew it!"

Iza's eyes revealed surprise. "You went *there?*"

♥

It was an ideal, fall day. Sebastian sat in front of a window on a wooden bench. A large half-barrel with potted flowers bloomed next to him. His eyes now open, he saw people walking into the restaurant. A young woman in her late twenties with long, dark hair stopped, letting her girlfriends enter without her.

She smiled, "Hello."

Sebastian smiled back, "I'm flattered, but I'm about to call the love of my life."

"That's too bad. I'll be inside if the call doesn't work out for you." She blew him a kiss and walked in.

It always felt good to have someone hit on him. The part of him that was getting older and softer didn't care whether they were male or female.

He took another deep breath, *Calling the love of my life. Please let her love me back,* he prayed. He had never prayed before.

He swiped, dialing. She answered right away.

"Sebastian, I'm glad you called." He could hear no emotion in her words.

"Sam, I miss you. I need to talk to you."

She spoke quickly, "I only have a minute, Sebastian. Nick should be here any second. He's driving Cindy and me to the airport."

"To the airport?"

"We're leaving for Bali early. We both needed some time to ourselves. Time to think."

Now Sebastian could hear stirred emotions in Sam's voice. He heard Cindy in the background opening the apartment door.

"Sam-"

"I have to hang up. Let's talk in Bali. Sebastian," she was whispering now, "I'm pregnant."

That was all he heard because she'd hung up. Obviously, Nick had just gotten there.

"*Pregnant?*" He asked no one. Should he be elated or was she lost to Nick? She hung up because Nick had gotten there. Nick was taking them to the airport. *Pregnant?* She'd been with both of them in last month. Sebastian's head swam a bit, his life melting.

Am I going to be a father, or is Nick?

He took a few minutes to try to follow Iza's advice and know who he was, but it was hard to do. He felt like he had to tell his heart to keep beating because it, and life itself, seemed to have stopped. As though he'd been struck by lightning, everything around him was connected with a volt of electricity. Something was flashing before him but he had no idea what.

Iza walked out, obviously looking for him. "Angel, everything OK?"

"She's pregnant and on her way to the airport. Couldn't talk, didn't tell me." He was able to speak, but his eyes were still frozen, staring at the invisible headlights to the car that was simultaneously running him over.

"Didn't tell you who the father is." She said, completing his thought. She spoke softly, "She doesn't know, angel."

Iza's words did away with the invisible car, freeing him up. He looked dead at her. "How do you know?"

"I don't, angel. I sense it." Her voice returned to it's normal, wise and commanding self. "Alright, let's get ready to journey to Bali. This retreat just became a life-determining event for you."

Panic was setting in as he looked around. "Oh God," he looked at Iza. "I know who I am." The world had stopped. "I want to be a father," he said, gasping for a breath.

♥

Author's Note
& Bonus Materials

Connect with me, submit a message on my site! You'll also enjoy the bonus materials I'll post and email, like bonus chapters!

www.KBRaphael.com

Book 2 in my *Cake Life Series*, was very different, right? Sebastian's book, as my editor and I call *Desert Cupcake*, had a different style and invited in a lot more magic.

My husband and I were at one of our favorite restaurants in Delray (in South Florida) talking with our waiter. He asked if there was magic in my books, and I answered *Yes and no*. I told him that, as much as I love magic, I believe in magic that you and I can engage in, which science is becoming aware of:

"The 'reading' of the environment's signals (in the womb and after birth) enables the body's cells and their genes to make appropriate biological adjustments to support and sustain life. Since the environmental signals are read and interpreted by the mind's "perceptions," the mind becomes the primary force that ultimately shapes an individual's life and health."

- Dr. Bruce Lipton

https://www.brucelipton.com/resource/interview/interview-bruce-planeta-magazine-part-2

Through the study of quantum physics, science is finding that *how we perceive ourselves,* or our Self-Image, impacts our health, our state of mind, our happiness and our experience. Of course, spirituality has known this for some time.

"The physical world, including our bodies, is a response of the observer. We create our bodies as we create the experience of our world."
-Deepak Chopra

So, yes, my book has magic in it, but it is magic that you can use; it is magic that we've seen before in classes, journeys (or retreats) and in our every day lives. No wand needed! I encourage you to find that magic, happiness, purpose and meaning in your life— because they are there for you.

Similar to *Cake By The Ocean,* I love Sebastian and Sam's adventures and I hope that you do as well. When they came forward and told me (my characters unfold before me, I transcribe what I see and hear) that they were karmically bound and connected, I thought that was cool — and that it made perfect sense, since Sam they have each been a main character. I also see some of that 'bind' that they are and will work out together, which will continue to unfold in Book 3.

♥

About
Kopi Berries In Ancient Lands,
Book 3:

I'm not as far into writing Book 3 because I've side tracked with another project, "Manifesting: Creating Using All of You"

What I can tell you, without spoiling too much, is that trouble is brewing! A few new characters will be introduced, including a vixen who just wants to stir thing up. I'll also tell you that I know some about that major karmatic issue coming forward, to which my editor said "Oh, no!"

My husband described my books as being "realistic," because a lot of what happens to my fictional characters is like life. Shit happens. I like this because, as a reader, I like to take vicarious adventures and those adventures are best when they make me rethink my life, problems and the wonderful and positive things in my life.

Hope you feel the same!

For an excerpt of Book 3, visit www.KBRaphael.com

Again, I'm grateful for Sam, Sebastian and all my characters. I hope you have enjoyed them-

I have been a teacher of spirituality and self-help for over 15 years. I've taken people on sacred retreats all over the world on cruises, to pyramids and – one of my favorites- to Bali. In the past I've written non-fiction books on manifesting, Shamanic Egg Cleansings, and such, but I've also had a long, hungry romance with novel writing. In the winter of 2009 I started to feed this hunger when we went to live in the European-like, cobble-stone paved town of San Miguel de Allende in Mexico. The town is fun and magical. We rented a beautiful house in the middle of a terribly poor neighborhood – weird – where people's horses lived in their living rooms (our house had beautiful picturesque windows, no hay)! Anyway, something clicked because I'd awake in the middle of the night writing short stories.

Then this year, 2016, in the summer I continued Sam's adventure, which switched to Sebastian's— he's gone to Santa Fe, where I lived for ten years. It's the perfect place for him to find his meaning and purpose because Santa Fe has that kind of magic.

The Spiritual Side

What fascinates me about my writing process is two-fold: first, that my work in energy and spirituality have taught me to tap into the world of imagination and creativity, where my characters are born.

Second, since I am, first and foremost, a teacher of spirituality, I can't help but have ingredients of spirituality (which has a lot to do with self-help) into the mix. How that all comes together is like magic; some would say that I actually channel most of my books.

As such, (for those of you interested in spirituality/self-help) Sebastian's seeking of meaning can be magical for you: one of my students said she's looking for meaning in her life. I told her to watch Sebastian looking for his because, like his, it's not one thing. It's not obvious and it's something deeper in you. It's something that helps you define who you want to be and what you value.

Poor Sebastian, in Book 3 he will take his search for meaning even deeper! After all, that's the way life is, constantly evolving. Just when you think you have it figured out, it changes. Just when you think you know what's meaningful to you, you find that you don't. The more you know…

This book is even further imbued some spirituality. Someone told me that they liked 'learning' those spiritual lessons through the example of my characters because it made more sense.

May that be true for you too.

If you are a fan of my self-help meets novella-style of novel and spirituality, then please visit my site (below). With time I'll blog about myself, the books; I'll add classes I've created in the past, put a link into my YouTube channel and, of course, give you updates about my Cake Life Series and whatever follows that…

Again, if you are enjoying my books, reach out! I look forward to receiving fan mail.

❤ Florida Waves of Love to You,
Kalyn R Bastion
Kalyn@KBRaphael.com
www.KBRaphael.com
www.KBRaphael.com/cakelife